There Ain't No Money In It

Running Guns In The Mexican Revolution

Delbert Gilbow

Outskirts Press, Inc.
Denver, Colorado

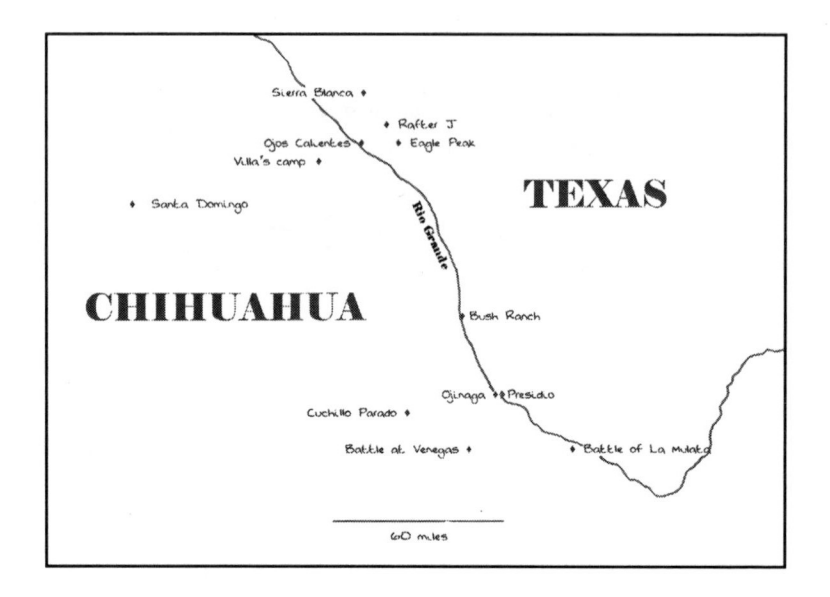

"...it is a sore travail that God hath given to the sons of men to be exercised therewith."

Prologue – 1910

Halley's Comet appears. Mexico is held in a strangle hold of absolute power. Elections are rigged, political opposition quashed by violence. Agriculture, mining, railroads and banks are owned by a small group of large landowners, called hacendados. Peons are forced from their traditional lands. Control is maintained by rurales, a murderous collection of thugs, and ex-bandits.

This is a work of fiction. The events and characters described herein are imaginary and are not intended to refer to specific places or living persons. The opinions expressed in this manuscript are solely the opinions of the author and do not represent the opinions or thoughts of the publisher. The author has represented and warranted full ownership and/or legal right to publish all the materials in this book.

There Ain't No Money In It
All Rights Reserved.
Copyright © 2009 Delbert Gilbow
v5.0

Cover Design by Delbert Gilbow

This book may not be reproduced, transmitted, or stored in whole or in part by any means, including graphic, electronic, or mechanical without the express written consent of the publisher except in the case of brief quotations embodied in critical articles and reviews.

Outskirts Press, Inc.
http://www.outskirtspress.com

ISBN: 978-1-4327-3645-3

Outskirts Press and the "OP" logo are trademarks belonging to Outskirts Press, Inc.

PRINTED IN THE UNITED STATES OF AMERICA

To Kathleen Gennaro

Special thanks to Jess McKenzie and Joan Worley whose help made it happen. And to John M. Koelsch of The Mexican Revolution Research Group who graciously translated Mexican Army reports of the Skirmish at Venegas Rancho and Battle of El Mulato.

Chapter One

The rising Arizona sun was barely visible when John Wesley Padget pulled the diamond hitch tight on the blue roan gelding. He snubbed the loose end of the line to the cinch ring and walked back to the bunkhouse. He looked around one last time at the accumulation of gear: pieces of harness, lariats, and the skin of a stock killing cougar tacked over one wall. He knew he would never see the place again. Wes was tall and rangy with a body tanned from working in the sun. He wore a faded plaid shirt tucked into a pair of canvas charro britches and over these a pair of knee length chinks. He buckled spurs over a pair of scuffed, unadorned boots that reached to mid-calf. He pulled on a fleece-lined coat and picked up his rifle. Very little blue was left on the action and the stock was scratched from hard use. His hands, strong from the roping he had done over the years, worked the lever action. He pulled a handful of cartridges from his coat pocket, and one by one stuffed them into the magazine. When it was full he jacked a cartridge into the chamber. Holding the hammer with his thumb he let it down to half cock. Shifting the Winchester to his left hand, he lifted a pair of saddlebags from a peg on the wall. He turned to leave and almost ran into the lanky form of Charlie Cramer.

Charlie Cramer, the owner of the Three C's, had a look on his face that would curdle milk. "Your leaving kind of puts me in a bind, Wes."

Inside, Wes winced. "Can't help it, Charley. I've ridden all the colts, most of them two or three times. Shorty can finish them up with one eye closed."

Charlie Cramer leaned his shoulder against the doorframe. "That letter was written three weeks ago and it's a long way back to Texas, Wes. You most likely won't make it back before she dies; you probably won't even make it there in time for the funeral."

Wes clamped his jaw down tight to keep from saying something he would regret. "I sure as hell won't if I don't get on the road, Charlie." Damned, he hated leaving this way.

"Here's your wages," Cramer said. "I wouldn't have hired you on if I'd known you were going to quit in the middle of the job."

Wes grimaced. Not counting the bills, he put them in his shirt pocket and buttoned the flap. He turned away and strode out of the bunkhouse to a tall dun gelding standing ground hitched alongside of the blue roan.

It was early fall on the Mogollon Rim, the morning cool and crisp with the smell of autumn in the air. It was the time for hunting bighorn sheep among the broken peaks, and mule deer along the canyon rim, the time to get ready for winter. Instead he was about to make a five hundred mile ride to West Texas.

Standing in front of the log bunkhouse, he looked over the ranch yard. Spruce and Ponderosa Pine shaded the house and the two-story barn. Wes ran his thumb and forefinger over his moustache and listened to the jays call back and forth to each other. He let his mind roll over the past eleven months at the Three C's. Charlie Cramer had always treated him right and gave him good horses to ride. He shook his head to clear the memories and shoved his Winchester into the saddle scabbard. Throwing the saddlebags over the dun's rump he tied them down with latigo strings. He pulled on his gloves, picked up the reins, put his boot in the stirrup and mounted. He tugged down on the brim of a weathered, sweat stained Stetson and looked down, studying the lines on Cramer's face. Finally he removed his right glove, bent over in the saddle and held out his hand. "I'm sorry, boss. I just don't have a choice."

The frown on Cramer's face softened. "If you get back this way, stop by, maybe I'll have a job for you."

The front door opened and Charlie's wife stepped out onto the front porch, drying her hands on her apron. She pushed a strand of gray hair back from her forehead and smiled. "Wes, don't pay any mind to Charlie you hear. Just do whatever you have to do and don't let any of those pretty Mexican girls get their hooks into you."

Wes took off his hat, revealing a head of dark unruly hair. "Adios, Mrs. Cramer—Charlie." He picked up the blue roan's lead rope, reined the dun around and started out of the yard. He paused at the gate and whistled. "Bandit," he called.

A multicolored dog jumped up from the shade of the bunkhouse and dashed across the yard nipping at the heels of the blue roan as he passed. The

THERE AIN'T NO MONEY IN IT

roan stepped sideways and arched his neck to look at the dog. Wes spurred the dun into a canter and rode out of the ranch yard.[1]

John Wesley Padget hadn't seen his aunt in fifteen years. Fourteen when he hired out to drive a wagon from Texas to Arizona for the Aztec Land and Cattle Company, he stayed and worked for them until he went to Cuba with Colonel Roosevelt and the Rough Riders. Now the need to reach his aunt before she died kept him riding through the night.

Trying to make up for lost time he rode at a trot and changed horses every four hours. He traveled southeast, and on the third day reached the southern foothills of the Mogollons. Here the country opened up, pine trees and clumps of sagebrush grew along the rocky slopes. Two days later he crossed into New Mexico and reined the dun into a dry wash, out of the cold wind blowing from the mountains. He dismounted and tightened his cinch. Gathering up a handful of mesquite limbs he built a fire and made coffee. Holding his cup,

---

[1] October 1, 1909

he hunkered down in the sand and looked at the darkening sky. A nagging fear that his aunt was already dead kept him from resting. He finished his coffee and tossed the dregs onto the fire. Before remounting he checked the shoes on his horses and with a sinking heart rode on.

Chapter Two

The Stockman Saloon in Silver City, New Mexico was empty except for the bartender and five men seated around a card table near the bar.[2] A slow moving ceiling fan stirred stale smoke that hung in a haze over the table. The smoke gave an oily taste to the cheap whiskey and deposited a grimy coating on the windows. Leaning back in his chair, Juan David Hamilton-Ochoa watched the loudmouth drunk sitting across the table. Dave was a slim, dark headed cowboy. He was wearing a leather vest over a blue cotton shirt. The vest concealed a shoulder holster under his left arm that carried a .45 Colt. A rawhide hatband circled the Stetson pushed back on his head. The five-card stud-game had been going on all day. Dave, stone sober, played with skill and by mid-

---

2 October 5, 1909

afternoon most of the money lay in front of him. Loudmouth had a pair of aces showing, but he was out of chips.

"I'll call that and raise a hundred," loudmouth said.

Dave inclined his head. "If you raise, you have to put some money on the table."

"I'm good for it; just ask Charlie," the man said, motioning toward the bartender.

"Sorry, friend, put up or shut up. I don't play against promises." He reached to rake in the money in the center of the table.

"Wait," the man said. "I've got eight broke horses out here in the street, Fort Bliss remounts. They're worth more than any hundred dollars. I'll put them up against the raise." The man pulled a notebook from his pocket and wrote out an IOU and tossed it into the pile of money.

"That's right, cowboy," the bartender said. "He brought them in this morning."

Dave picked up the IOU and read it. "All right," he said, and counted out one hundred dollars. "I call."

The man across the table turned his hole card showing a third ace.

Dave turned his hole card. "King high straight.

Go back to breaking horses, hombre, you sure ain't no poker player."

"Son of a bitch—nobody's that lucky," loudmouth said. He pushed his chair back from the table and reached for his gun, only to find himself looking into the bore of Dave's Colt. The ratcheting sound made as Dave thumbed back the hammer brought a sudden halt to the man's movement.

"Easy, friend, you ain't no gun hand either." Dave stood, and keeping his Colt aimed at the center of the man's chest, he motioned to the bartender. "Just step away from the bar and don't try for that shotgun. Keep your hands in sight." He motioned to the other players. "You! All of you! Get over there by the bartender. What's in there?" he said, pointing to a door in the rear of the saloon.

"A storeroom," the bartender said.

"All right, in you go," Dave said. He herded the men into the storeroom and shut the door. Dragging a chair from the card table he tilted and wedged it under the doorknob. "I'll shoot the first man that tries to get out," Dave said, loud enough so that he knew they heard him. Walking back to the poker table he gathered up the money and shoved it into his shirtfront. He picked up the IOU, folded it, and placed it inside the sweatband of his hat. He looked through the front window, and then stepped out of the saloon onto the street.

Eight bay geldings were tied to the hitching rail in front of the saloon. Dave mounted a strip-faced sorrel, and looked the bays over. Not bad for a hundred dollars. He snubbed the horses to a chunky steeldust mare wearing a pack and picked up her lead rope. Dave touched his spurs to the sorrel and rode out of town, leading the horses.

Dave urged the sorrel behind a granite boulder and studied his back trail through the scattered mesquites, searching for the posse he knew would be on his trail as soon as they found a way out of the back room.

When no one appeared by sundown he rode off the trail and into an arroyo. He hobbled the horses and spent a sleepless night without a fire, lying awake in the brush fifty yards out in the chaparral. He broke camp before dawn and continued southward still watching his back trail for any sign of pursuit. Sooner or later, he would have to fight for the horses, sooner or later.

Chapter Three

The need to reach his aunt before she died kept Padget riding through the night. He changed horses every four hours, keeping them at a trot. Occasionally, Bandit would jump up behind his saddle, ride for a time, then jump down again. Padget reached the southern foothills of the Gila Mountains just after sunrise the second day. The pines trees were stunted and sparse, sagebrush was larger and more closely spaced. He crossed the southern end of the continental divide at noon and reined the dun into a dry wash out of the wind where he got down and tightened his cinch. Gathering up a handful of mesquite limbs he built a fire and made coffee. Holding his cup Padget hunkered down in the sand and looked at the darkening sky. Worried he would not make it to the ranch in time; he finished his coffee and tossed the dregs onto the fire. Before remounting he checked the shoes on his horses. He rode on. By mid-afternoon he reached the chaparral flats that stretched all the way to El Paso.

Padget took a swig from his canteen and shook it, there was enough in the canteen to last him for two days, but with the last water forty miles behind him, his horses needed to drink. As the afternoon wore on he dismounted to walk the kinks out of his legs.

A cold wind blew down from the mountains behind him and moved the long green and red beans hanging like Christmas ornaments on the mesquite trees. Their movement added to the gnawing feeling of hunger in the pit of his stomach. He turned up the collar of his coat, hunched his back against the icy blast and remounted his horse. The morning sun was hidden behind a low hanging cloud layer and provided little warmth. He picked up the clear sharp smell of winter in the air.

Padget disliked pushing his horses, they were tired from the long ride, but the urgency of his mission overrode his concern. He spurred the dun into a short lope. He didn't know whether or not he would make it back in time, but it wouldn't be for a lack of trying. The Eagle Mountains in Texas remained a long way off and time to get there was short. Desperate to make time he kept the big dun moving. He refused to stop long enough to get a fire going. He felt guilty every time he stopped to rest the horses, shame stung like a quirt lash. If he got there too late he would never forgive himself. He should have written more often; that would have given his uncle time to let him know his aunt was sick. He closed his eyes in a silent prayer. I've never asked you much, Lord, but if you'll just do this for me I promise I'll….

With hunger gnawing at his insides he pulled his belt in another notch, wiped his moustache with the back of his finger and rode for the better part of the morning. Despite his anxiety and to his disgust, he couldn't stop his childhood memories of the Rafter J ranch; of the warm cook shack and the mouth-watering food there. He felt his throat tighten as recollections of hot biscuits and gravy, the sizzle of steaks in a cast-iron frying pan, and mounds of golden fried potatoes crowded into his mind. He'd better stop that. Claire was dying and all he could think about was food. The rumble in Padget's stomach almost covered the sound of Bandit's low growl.

The sound disturbed a red tailed hawk that rose from a mesquite tree, squawking as she flew off to the south. A coyote bitch, holding a jack rabbit in her jaws, watched him from the shade of a mesquite tree just off the trail. Suspicious of the dog and the rider carrying a rifle, she remained motionless and poised for flight. Padget glanced at Bandit whose attention was directed toward the red tail; he seemed not to notice the coyote at all. Padget looked back at the coyote and watched her for a moment from under the brim of his hat. He nodded toward the coyote. "Easy, pardner, we're just traveling through." His quiet voice apparently did not reassure the coyote and caution overcame curiosity. With one last look over her shoulder the coyote faded into the cat claw.

He kneed the dun forward and then reined him in, looking down at the tracks in front of him. He dropped the roan's lead rope and spurred the dun around in a tight circle as he studied the rolling terrain. Seeing no sign of immediate threat he climbed down from his horse. He knelt on one knee to take a closer look at the tracks. It appeared that ten horses, two shod, eight barefoot had recently traveled east along the trail. He pulled off his glove and felt the tracks; they were about two hours old. Most likely the tracks were made by a couple of cowboys bringing in loose stock, but, then again they could have been left by bandits, Mexico wasn't too far off.

He stood, hitched up his chaps and looked around. This time he searched the terrain out to the horizon. His eyes caught a brief movement, and then nothing. He squinted, staring hard. Finally he picked up the faint tell-tale wisp of dust between him and a windmill that stuck up above the low line of brush. Padget put his glove back on and stepped into the saddle. He unbuckled the flap on his right saddlebag and pulled out his field glasses. Looking toward the windmill he adjusted the focus.

Ten horses and a single rider suddenly jumped into view. They were moving at a walk toward the windmill. One of the horses carried a pack. That accounted for the second set of deep tracks. He watched them until they disappeared behind a screen of mesquite trees.

It sure looked like the rider he followed was

headed to the only water within a hundred miles. A gust of cold wind blew down his neck and he hunched his back. Padget tried to recall the layout of the land he was riding through. He pursed his lips and looked once more at the dust trail, weighing the risk. His horses needed water and he would fight for it if he had to. Without thinking, Padget pulled the rifle from the scabbard and placed it across his knees. He twisted in the saddle and studied his back trail, looking for any movement. Seeing none, he touched the dun with his spurs and turned off the trail. The blue heeler sniffed the tracks, followed them for about ten feet, stopped and looked back at him.

"Yeah, that's the way they went all right. Good boy, Bandit! Come on, son, we're going this way." He continued into the chaparral without stopping. The roan followed close behind, stepping around a clump of pear cactus.

Padget had almost nine months' pay in his jeans along with the money he had made from selling four spare horses. He felt pretty well to do for a twenty-nine year old cowhand that didn't weigh more than one hundred and seventy pounds. He'd worked his butt off for that stake and was tired of scrimping and saving. He wasn't about to lose his money to some damned outlaw, but he needed to be careful. This country seemed flat, but he knew that any one of a dozen arroyos could hide a hundred men.

Chapter Four

Late in the afternoon Ochoa noticed a wispy dust trail behind him. Well, here it comes, he thought. He pulled a Krag carbine from his saddle scabbard and placed it across his thighs. Watching through his field glasses he could make out one man and two horses. At least he didn't bring his friends, he thought. I sure as hell hate to shoot a man over a card game, but damn it, a bet's a bet. If a man couldn't stand to lose he shouldn't play cards. Ochoa rode on a short distance, reaching a grove of cottonwood trees surrounding a dirt stock tank and next to the tank stood a windmill. He put nose bags on the sorrel he rode and his steel dust pack mare. He tethered them to one end of a picket line stretched between two cottonwoods. At the opposite end he tied the other eight horses. "Sorry I don't have oats for you boys, but when

I started out I didn't plan on company." He tied a tarpaulin between two more cottonwoods near the windmill tower as a shield against the wind. He stacked his saddle and pack saddle on a second tarpaulin spread out as a ground sheet. He checked his Krag carbine and placed it against his saddle. He laid a second rifle, a Winchester carbine, within easy reach. He started a fire and waited. If he was going to have to fight, he would have a better chance in daylight.

Padget, not wanting to bite off more than he could chew if it came to a fight, made a wide circle to the south cutting for sign of anyone who might be meeting the rider up ahead. Satisfied that the man at the windmill had not been joined by anyone, he circled and approached from the west. It was almost sundown and Padget figured he could handle any trouble from the man he could see squatting by the small campfire. Nevertheless, he kept his eyes open as he rode into camp.

Ten horses were tied to a picket line strung between a pair of cottonwood trees. The man appeared to be cooking supper. He took note of the single action Colt on the rider's hip and the strap across his chest suggested a second pistol concealed under his leather vest. Most cowhands, if they went armed at all, carried only one pistol.

This man seemed to be prepared for trouble.

Ochoa watched the rider coming into camp from under the brim of his hat. The man was riding a tall leggy dun and leading a blue roan pack horse. He shoved the thumb of his right hand in his belt just in front of his Colt. A jolt of adrenaline shot through him. Sure as hell, he thought, I've seen that hombre before.

Ochoa watched the rider stop about 50 yards out. The icy wind turned the windmill fan that moved the sucker rod slowly up and down. The soft sound of water spilling into the wooden trough broke the silence.

"Hello the camp—my horses need water. I've got some fresh coffee and a slab of bacon to share if you can stand the company," the rider yelled. The roan pack horse, eager to drink, blew through his nose and stepped alongside the rider, stamping his left forefoot at being kept from the water.

Ochoa stood up and with his left hand motioned the rider down from his horse. It wasn't the man who lost the remounts. He looked closely at the dog trailing behind and gave the horses a swift glance. He noted the rifle carried across the pommel and the rattlesnake skin wrapped around the low crowned hat pinched in front. Thick black whiskers covered most of the rider's face below the eyes. His chinks were damned near worn out and the bronc busting spurs he wore showed hard use.

He looked again at the dog approaching him, "Bandit?" The dog wagged its tail. Ochoa moved his hand away from his revolver. "Well, I might have known... you been making so much dust I thought maybe you was drunk. Now I can see that it's just because you got kicked in the head by a bronc. Get down, Padget and rest your saddle."

The rider stared. "Ochoa? David Ochoa? Is that you behind all that hair or has a grizzly bear done et you?"

Ochoa watched him let the hammer down on his Winchester and jam the rifle back in the scabbard.

"Damn, my butts tired, I'm getting too old for this," Padget said. He walked over and shook Ochoa's hand. "I ain't seen no posse. What in the world are you doing in this part of the country?"

"Same as you, Padget, on my way to the Rafter J."

"What in the world takes you there?"

"Your uncle's got a little problem with a cat killing his livestock, and horse thieves stealing it.

He wired me last week, hired me to come down."

"How do you know that's where I'm headed?"

"Well for one thing you're on the right trail, and another is that Walt told me you might be on your way back. Heard about your aunt; I'm sorry."

"Let me give my horses some water, Pard," Padget said as he slipped the bridle off the dun and led his two horses over to the tank.

The dun stretched his neck over the rim of the trough and nudged the water, blew the dust out of his nostrils, sniffed. Only then did he drink. The roan wasn't quite so delicate, Ochoa noticed. He just shoved his nose under the water and sucked it in. When he had his fill he jerked his head up to look at the strange horses on the picket line, the action threw water on Padget standing close to the dun's head.

Padget wiped his face with his sleeve and pulled the saddle off the dun and the pack from the roan. Ochoa watched him as he staked the roan on a long rope and turned the dun loose to graze. Padget rummaged through his pack and turned around with a bottle of bourbon.

"Frost on the pumpkin tonight," Padget said. He half filled his cup with coffee, and then topped it off with a large splash of whiskey. He tossed the bottle to Ochoa. "Damn, it's sure good to see you. How long has it been now, two, three years?"

"More like five since you left the Open A M Bar," Ochoa said as he caught the bottle. "Where did you go after you left? Three of the four saloons went bust and all of the looloo girls took off for Denver."

"Yeah," Padget said. Holding the cup in both hands he took a sip. Ochoa noted that Padget didn't take off his gloves. "That's all in the past; I gave up them fancy women and expensive liquor."

"Seriously, where did you get off to?" Ochoa said.

"Oh, just seeing the country, I was up in Canada for a while, made it up to Alaska Territory and back. How about you, Dave, stay with Huston all this time? Are you and the old man's daughter raising a family?"

"No, that didn't last," Ochoa said.

"Don't pull my leg, when I left you were flat out headed for the altar," Padget said.

"I was, the old man wanted us to get married, and Mary Ann had her mind pretty much set on it too."

"So, what made her change her mind?"

"Oh, it wasn't her. She's a fine woman. I just got

to thinking of all the country I'd never seen and the trails I hadn't rode. I left about three months after you did."

"What did she say when you told her goodbye?"

"I left her a note. I'm a coward, I knew she'd break down and cry if I told her I was leaving. I rode up to Trapper's Lake and spent the winter at Sizemore's running a trap line."

"Can't say I blame you much," Padget said. "Marriage ties a man down."

"When the snow melted I drifted on down to Pagosa Springs; I've been there ever since."

"Are you still trapping?"

"That and a few head of cows. Got lucky in a card game and won three sections, a cabin, and a barn."

"Well there might be some chance of turning you into a Christian yet," Padget said. He sloshed another shot of whiskey into his coffee and tossed the bottle to Ochoa.

Ochoa caught it, took a slug, then set the bottle down. Ochoa looked into his pack, took out a pair of plucked sage hens, and ran a wooden spit through them. "Shot these this morning," he said, as he fixed the spit into the dirt. He mixed up flour, baking powder, salt and water, and made biscuits. He could hear the grumble in Padget's stomach. The aroma of cooking biscuits wafted on the air around the campfire.

"Good looking string of horses, Mano," Padget said, nodding his head toward the picket line.

"I'm taking them to Fort Bliss. I hear they're paying good money for remounts there."

"You take to raising horses?"

"No, but you might say that I got a good deal on these," he said, and laughed.

Padget raised one eyebrow.

"I stopped off in Silver City night before last and got into a little game at the Stockman's."

"You win those ponies in a poker game?"

"Sure as hell. One rancher had too much faith in three aces."

Padget laughed. "Hell, I'm in the wrong line of business, I ought to take up cards."

Padget picked up his Winchester and jacked the cartridges out on to the tarpaulin. He searched his saddlebags and pulled out a piece of cloth and began wiping the dust from the rifle's action. Bandit lay down on the edge of the tarp looking out into the darkness. Ochoa picked up a bottle and his rifle, and sat down beside Bandit. He worked the cork loose from the bottle, took a long swig, and tossed it to Padget.

"You ever miss the Army?" Ochoa asked.

"What brought that up?"

"I don't know, just remembering I guess," Ochoa said.

"About like I'd miss a broken leg."

Later, they stacked the clean rifles against the pack saddles and passed the bottle back and forth as they sat drinking and talking about places they had seen, line shacks they had lived in during winter, barbed wire, outlaw broncs, San Juan Hill, dysentery, Teddy Roosevelt, hunting Stone Sheep in the Alaska Territory, lion and bear in Grand Canyon, rustlers and bad-men.

The soft gray dawn came as a surprise.

Chapter Five

Padget opened one eye to a faint streak of red in the eastern sky. He spat the dark brown taste out of his mouth and sat up. The cool fresh air smelled good. Ochoa lay on his back with one arm flung over his eyes, the other arm still held a bottle. Padget struggled to his feet staggered away from his bedroll and urinated into the sagebrush. Buttoning his jeans he nudged Ochoa with his boot. "Come on, you're burning daylight."

Stiff-legged and bleary eyed they made a quick breakfast of bacon, coffee and left over biscuits, packed up and headed east. Anxious to be on the road Padget lined the horses out on the trail. Ochoa rode lead and Bandit nipped at the heels of the horses.

Three days later Ochoa sold the horses at Fort Bliss and pushed on. Leaving Fort Bliss, they picked up the old Butterfield Stage road just outside of town and headed east.

Monday they passed through Sierra Blanca and crossed the railroad tracks at Eagle Flat and turned south climbing the foothills toward the Eagle Mountains.

The density and variety of cactus increased as they climbed higher along the wagon trail through a narrow boulder strewn canyon. It was sundown when they rode past the holding corral into the yard of the Rafter J. A lump rose in Padget's throat, nothing much had changed.

The adobe ranch buildings spread out across a grassy shelf that overlooked the valley below. The two story house, shaded by huge elm trees, had new shutters and there was a small circular space of grass and flowers in the center of the yard that had not been there before. The verandah that ran across the entire length of the house now had a porch swing at one end.

Across the dirt yard the long bunk house,

flanked by a pole corral, looked like it did when he left. The foreman's quarters and the barn, which formed the southern boundary of the headquarters place, had a new coat of paint. The clean smell of fresh water came from beyond the bunkhouse where the springs emerged from the ground to form three very large pools. He glanced at the cedar covered slopes that rose steeply upward and ended in bare rock three hundred feet above the flat. Tired and dusty, Padget and Ochoa turned their horses into the corral and unsaddled.

Chapter Six

The house appeared empty. Padget climbed the stairs and quietly opened the door to his aunt's bedroom. He stepped softly into a large room filled with the distinctive odor of rubbing alcohol. Claire lay in a four poster bed positioned between two arched windows on the east wall. A black leather doctor's bag sat open on the cedar chest at the foot of the bed.

Padget crossed the room and looked down at the woman who lay sleeping. He remembered her kindness when his father got killed by an outlaw bronc and how a year later she had hugged him and wiped away his tears when his mother died of scarlet fever. She looked deathly pale lying under a patchwork quilt up to her chin and wearing a blue flannel nightgown. One hand lay outside the quilt clutching a handkerchief, her eyes were closed. Padget looked at the blue veins on the back of her hands. Just like one of her porcelain cups on the mantle downstairs, he thought. Her eyes opened with a flash of blue, then widened. She raised her hand to her throat. "Sonny!"

Ma used to call me that too. "All the way from Arizona just to see you," Padget said.

She patted the bed. "Come over here and let me look at you."

Padget removed his hat and dropped it on the floor. He pulled a chair close to the bed and dropped down in it. He leaned forward and took her hand and brought it up, rubbing it softly on the stubble on his jaw and kissed it gently. She grasped his hand tightly between hers and held on as tears rolled down her cheeks. Lord but she's lost a lot of weight. He looked closely at her face for any sign of pain. "How are you feeling, Darlin'?" he asked.

She gripped his hand harder. "Fine, now that you're here."

"I've been gone way too long, Claire. I came as soon as Walt's letter caught up with me."

Behind him Padget heard the click of the door opening. "Ah, you must be Wes." He turned. A stranger was standing in the doorway. He was dressed in black, wearing a coat that partially hid the stethoscope hanging around his neck. It did not hide the revolver on his right hip. The stranger walked quietly to the foot of the bed and closed the doctor's bag.

"I'm glad you're here. She has talked of nothing else for a week now." He stuck out his hand. I'm Ira Bush; give me few more minutes with her. Later you can talk to her for a while."

Padget shook his hand. He leaned over and kissed his aunt again. She was smiling when he left.

Padget carried his gear into the Rafter J bunkhouse. The smell of socks, harness leather, and tobacco filled the air. He touched the cool clay bricks; it was good to be home again. He looked around the room. Eight bunks were arranged along the walls around a small round pot bellied stove that glowed dull red in the middle of the floor. Someone had tacked a red serape over the back wall, and rifles, scabbards, lariats and other personal gear hung from pegs near each bed.

Ochoa sat on a cot near the door unpacking

his saddlebags. "This is a far cry from some bunkhouses I've been in, hell it even has windows."

Padget unrolled his bedroll on an empty bunk and pulled a towel from his pack and held it up. "As I remember, Maria is strong on the social graces, so you might want to wash up before supper." He walked though the door. Ochoa picked up a towel and followed him to a large spring fed pool.

"Eagle Springs," Padget said, stopping at the edge of a large pool. "They are what give the ranch its name. It used to be a stage stop before the railroad and a water hole for the Apaches before that. Nobody knows why the water is so cold; it stays that way all year long."

Hair brushed and dressed in clean clothes Padget and Ochoa sat down for supper. Eleven men sat around the table. Walt, at the head of the table, gestured toward the one Mexican male. "Wes, you remember Miguel." He swept his hand around the table introducing the cowboys. "That's Shorty Davidson, Billy Shakleford, Mac Stots, Ken Hays, John Hickey, Luke Smith, my nephew, Wes Padget." He inclined his head toward Ochoa. "And this is David Ochoa; he's here to track down the lion."

Doctor Bush walked in and quietly sat down at

the table. "I am happy to announce that Claire is over the worst part, and with a few days rest she should be on her feet again."

"Wes, this is Doctor Ira Jefferson Bush; from El Paso," Walt said and pointed with his coffee cup to Padget. "This is my nephew, John Wesley Padget."

Padget stood and shook hands with Bush. "We met in Aunt Claire's room. I'm in your debt, Doctor. Thanks."

Walt indicated a smallish man sitting on his left. "This is Harvey Phillips. He's from New York."

A long curved scar stretched from the outside edge of Phillip's right eye to the corner of his thin lipped mouth. Dark piercing eyes, hooded by long bushy eyebrows, stared back at Padget. He looked more like a vulture waiting for something to die.

"Phillips," Padget said. Catching the attention of the doctor, Padget leaned slightly forward and said. "How sick is my aunt, Doc?"

"She is still not out of the woods, the nitroglycerin will help, but she needs rest. Your aunt has a heart condition that depletes her strength and the condition is serious. But, if she will follow my directions and stop wearing herself out, she'll be around for a good many years," Bush said. "This happens to a lot of Texas women who work as hard as your aunt."

"Walt said that you came all the way from El Paso; that means a lot to me. If there is ever anything I can ever do for you all you have to do is ask."

At that point Maria, Rafter J's cook, served the food. Padget filled his plate three times before Walt pushed his chair back from the table and announced that there was brandy and cigars in the study. Shoveling in a last mouth full of peach cobbler Padget stood up. "I want to look in on Claire. I'll join you all in a few minutes."

Padget walked quietly up the stairs to his aunt's room knocked on the door softly and entered. She was sitting up in bed with an open Bible in her lap. She smiled, her blue eyes sparkled.

"Doctor Bush said you would be up and around tomorrow, how do you feel?"

"You know, I thought I'd never see you again, Sonny."

"Claire, its O.K. I'm home now."

"You're the only child I have—when you didn't come after the war and didn't write..."

He wiped the tears from her cheeks with his forefinger. "Hush! I'm here."

"Walt's getting old"—Padget put the tip of his finger to her lips shutting off her words

"I'm home," he said.

She turned her head. "I want grandchildren around, Sonny, my own."

"Whoa, slow down..."

"Oh, I don't mean right away, but before I get too old to enjoy them."

He rubbed the back of his hand along her face. "Claire, we'll talk about this later. We will. I promise. Right now you're tired and need to rest."

"I am tired. Promise me you will be here in the morning, Sonny."

He stood. "I promise. Now get some rest. And don't worry, I'll be here tomorrow." He would be here tomorrow, next week, next year, for as long as she needed him.

Chapter Seven

Padget tip toed down the stairs and eased quietly into the study. Midst shelves filled with books from the floor to the ceiling, Walt, Bush, Phillips, and Ochoa sat drinking brandy and talking softly. A fire crackled in a stone fireplace bravely driving back the cold autumn night. An ancient desk, polished to a high sheen with bees wax, stood in front of a large bay window that jutted onto the porch.

A warm flush of contentment coursed through him as he thought about the many hours spent here with his uncle. Running his fingertips over the copy of *The History of the Decline and Fall of the Roman Empire,* that lay open on the library table he breathed in the pleasant odor of pipe tobacco, leather, and furniture polish. He smiled, recognizing a worn copy of *Oliver Twist*.

Bush unlimbered his long legs stood and pointed to a tintype. "Is this you, Walt, with General Kearny?"

Walt nodded. "It is." He held a box of cigars. He opened the lid and extended the box to Bush. The faint odor of fine tobacco reached Padget.

Phillips moved across the room to stand beside Bush. "Union, I see."

Padget looked at the brass-framed photograph that showed his uncle, standing alongside of a one armed general.

Walt's brown eyes narrowed. "Do you find something improper with that?"

Phillips turned and clicked his heels. "Not at all." The scar on his face was vivid in the lamplight. "I served too, Second Battalion, Seventh Cavalry."

A smile appeared on Walt's face. He extended the box of panatelas. "Cigar?" He filled a snifter of brandy and handed it to Wes. Refilling his guests' glasses he raised his snifter in salute. "To fallen comrades."

Padget raised his snifter drained it and let his mind range back to the day he helped bury four companions in a lonely rock strewn canyon in northern Arizona. He had been sixteen years old, riding for the Hash knife Outfit; he and six other riders followed a band of rustlers into a blind canyon and got caught in an ambush by a man using a buffalo gun. Unable to reach the rustlers with their carbines, four cowboys and three horses were killed before they retreated out of range. The clink of Walt refilling the glasses brought him back to the present.

Walt rolled a cigar around in his fingertips and sniffed it. He bit off the end and spat it out. He stuck the cigar in his mouth, wiped a match across his thumbnail and lit it. He rotated the match until he had the cigar going, then he waved the match out and dropped it into an ashtray. The pleasing aroma of expensive cigar smoke filled the room. He took a long deep drag on his cigar and slowly blew out a cloud of blue smoke and watched as it rose toward the ceiling.

He turned to Ochoa. "When I wired you I thought we had a mountain lion working the area." Peering at Ochoa over his cigar, he asked, "Do you know anything about jaguars?"

"Only a little. What I do know I learned down near Hachita, New Mexico," Ochoa said. "What makes you think it's a jaguar?"

"Something about the way those horses were

killed. Tell me about your Hachita lion," Walt said.

Ochoa shrugged. "Sure, it's not much of a story really. I was hired out to the Pitchfork spread just west of Hachita. They had a jaguar running loose and creating havoc. I tried traps, dogs, bait and poison. Nothing worked. Finally one night he came right up to the line shack where I was staying."

Phillips drained his glass and set it down. "That was foolhardy, even for a jaguar."

"He was on top of the feed shed next to the horse corral," Ochoa went on. "The moon was low and full and I could see him clear. He crouched there looking right at me, his tail switching back and forth." Ochoa snapped his fingers. "Just like that he was on me, damned near before I could get my rifle up. When I dropped him, I could reach out and touch him." Ochoa finished his cognac in one swallow and put his glass on the table. "Mountain lions and jaguars are different though."

"Different, in what way?" Walt asked.

"They're just different; the way they hunt, the way they lay up, you might find them on the same range, but they avoid one another."

Walt leaned back in his chair. "We'll take a ride out to Horse Canyon tomorrow and I'll show you the last place this lion was, that I know of."

There was a pause in the conversation. Phillips made a steeple of his fingers and put them against his lips. "Speaking of trouble, I heard about a shooting near McNary a while back."

"That'd most likely be Bill Matson's barulla with a rurale," Walt said.

Phillips narrowed his eyes. "Do you know what was it all about?"

"Only what I've been told. According to Bill he stopped in across the river for a drink and some rurale took exception to him wearing his six gun," Walt said.

"Was Bill hurt?" Padget asked.

"It's been my experience that anytime you get shot it hurts. They traded lead; Bill took one in the leg and walked away. The rurale didn't."

Padget glanced over at Ochoa who had his arms folded across his chest and stood with his back to Walt's array of books on the far side of the room. He had his head cocked to one side, listening to the conversation.

"The rangers have been pretty busy lately," Walt said. "There's some gun running between here and Ysleta. It might have had something to do with that."

"You don't mean to tell me that this Matson was running guns?" Phillips asked.

Padget shook his head. "Bill wouldn't run guns."

Walt puffed his cigar. "No, Bill wasn't, but the rurale may have thought so."

Bush stretched his legs out in front of him, crossing them at the ankles. "There is a lot of talk in El Paso about running guns for the revolution."

"There has always been talk of a revolution; as far back as I can remember," Walt said. "It's all talk."

"I wouldn't exactly call the attack on Las Vacas, and Palomas talk," Bush said.

Walt shrugged. "What did that get them? They were ran off and arrested. Some of them were shot up pretty bad."

Bush glanced at Phillips and back to Walt. "I think we may well see more of that as time goes on."

"It's more likely we will see more arrests like the ones last June when the rurales came across the river into El Paso and rounded up some of the rebels and took them back to Mexico," Walt said.

Bush shrugged. "The relations between Mexico and Texas have always been pretty volatile."

"The problem isn't between the Mexicans and us. It's between the haves and the have nots." Padget motioned to the west. "I was at Cananea during the strike there. That was one of the bloodiest put downs I ever heard of. Those miners were getting about twenty five cents a day. Hell, a swamper in a saloon makes more than that."

Walt waved his cigar. "Three years ago Flores Magón and his bunch thought they could take over the country. They even took the town of Jiminez for a short time and tried it again in El Paso and in Columbus, but where are they now?"

Bush waved his hand in dismissal. "Magón is a wild eyed anarchist. However, Diaz and his cronies are worse; they are stealing the communal property away from the small landholders; from the men who fought the Indians, men who paid for the land with their blood."

"Well, if it comes to a showdown the smart money is on Diaz," Walt said. "Look what he's done for Mexico."

Padget ran the back of his forefinger over his moustache. "It's pretty clear that Diaz does a lot for the rich, but the peons have been pretty much left out of the deal. We used to get a steady stream of peons coming by the Three Cs—most of them so hungry they could hardly walk."

The sound of the grandfather's clock chiming mid-night echoed throughout the house.

Walt stood. "We've all got a long day ahead of us tomorrow. So if you gentlemen will excuse me, I'll just look in on my wife and go to bed. Help yourself to the brandy. Wes, did you boys get settled in all right?"

Sitting on his bunk Padget pulled off his boots and dropped them on the floor. He removed his shirt and laid it on top of his Levi's. He placed his hat on top of the pile. "Mano, what did you think of Phillips and Bush?"

"Phillips doesn't say much, but you can see with one eye that he's one smart hombre. Bush, now there's a river that runs pretty deep, and not everything's floating on the surface where you can see it."

Padget turned the blankets down on his bunk, preparing to climb in. "Somehow I got the feeling that Bush is pretty sure there's going to be a fight down there, and he ain't on Diaz' side either."

"Claro," Ochoa said. "I've got a hunch those

two hombres are involved in the revolution up to their butts one way or another. Phillips was a little too interested in the fight between Matson and that rurale to suit me."

Padget blew out the lamp. "You noticed that did you?"

Chapter Eight

Still sleepy Padget pulled his coat on over one arm. He shifted his rifle to his left hand and worked his other arm through the sleeve. He stepped from the bunkhouse and buttoned his coat as he walked across the yard. He peered at the horses inside the corral; they stood shoulder to rump, tails clamped down tight, and their breath visible in the cold morning air. The odor of hay and horse manure filled his nostrils.

Walt stood by the porch holding the reins of a big sorrel gelding, talking to Bush and Phillips who sat in a buggy. Bush nodded at something Walt said and slapped the reins. The buggy pulled out of the yard.

Catching up to Padget half way across the ranch yard, Ochoa asked, "Why do I get the feeling we over slept?"

Padget pulled his hat down on his head and walked into the corral. Walt mounted his horse rode over and pointed to a horse in the center of the remuda. "Wes, try that big bay with the strip face, his name's Jack."

Leaning his rifle against the gate Padget unlaced a lariat from his saddle and with a quick underhanded toss sent the rope across the horses and dropped it over the head of the bay. He pulled up the slack and the horse walked quietly to him. He spoke to the horse in a low calm voice as he eased the blanket and saddle over his withers and pulled the cinch tight. He shoved his Winchester into the saddle boot. Buckling his chaps around his waist he hooked the leggings, reached into the chaps pocket and pulled out a pair of buckskin gloves.

Walt laughed. "Grandma's slow too, but she's old. Dave, why don't you try Jug, that big chestnut with his head up over there?"

Padget pulled on his gloves and turned the collar up on his coat against the morning chill. He swung into the saddle just as the first gray light of dawn showed over Eagle Peak. He leaned forward in the saddle and rubbed the neck of the bay feeling the strength of the horse under him.

They climbed steadily in single file through the sagebrush that covered the mountainside. With Walt in the lead, they worked up and around the face of the mountain and crossed a small dry wash. The trail grew steeper and more difficult and the wind forced Padget to squint as he looked down across Eagle Flat.

Far off in the distance he could see the buggy carrying Bush and Phillips moving along the Old Spanish Trail toward Sierra Blanca and beyond that he could see the east bound freight train; it was almost due north and passing Alamore Siding. The black smoke poured from the stack and swept back over the cars behind the engine. In the distance, Sierra Blanca, the mountain that gave the town its name, loomed against a dark sky.

Ochoa came up behind him. "You can look farther and see less in this country than anyplace I've ever been."

"You can from up here," Padget said.

The trail grew steeper through Goat Canyon. At the head of the canyon it turned south. They topped the ridge and a black tailed buck broke from the chaparral bouncing stiff legged through the brush. A swift moving shadow crossed in front of Padget. He looked up to see a red-tailed hawk

THERE AIN'T NO MONEY IN IT

high overhead, gliding southward. In the southwest the sky was filled with vultures; wings spread wide, sailing around and around on the wind. There was no question where they were headed. They rode down a side draw into Horse Canyon. Here the trail leveled out and they could see, scattered off to one side, what was left of five horses.

Vultures were everywhere, obscuring the remains of the dead horses with their black bodies. Walt pulled his pistol and shot twice into the air. "Get away from there..."

Stuffed with putrid horsemeat, too heavy to get off the ground, the vultures collided into each other as they staggered about in panic, attempting to fly. When the riders got closer the vultures began to expel the contents of their bowels and vomit. After a long run, one by one, they struggled into the air rising slowly in a black whirling mass.

Padget pulled his neck scarf up over his nose. "Whew! That'd gag a maggot."

Side by side Walt and Padget rode to the nearest carcass. Padget dismounted and looked for tracks left by the lion. Hundreds of vulture tracks obliterated any previous sign. Walt pointed at the carcasses. "There wasn't a bite gone when I first found them, just killed and let lay."

Five horses, three colts and two mares, were scattered over what Padget estimated to be about two and a half acres. How in Hell one cat managed to kill so damned many horses he didn't know; one—two maybe—but five? A jaguar was fast, but so was a stampeding bronc, and after the first fifty yards a horse could flat outrun a lion.

Silently the three riders spread out and started cutting for sign. Padget, about a hundred yards out to the southwest, found the hoof prints of fast running horses overlaid by far flung tracks of a large cat. He dismounted and stepped off the distance between paw prints. They were twenty feet apart. The cat had been running full out. He pulled the bandanna down and spread his hand over one of the lion tracks. It was a damned big cat. Leading his horse he walked back along the tracks. Whoa, what's this? A second set of cat tracks converged with the first. He measured one of the tracks with his hand. Bigger than and paralleling the first set of tracks for a ways, and then diverged off to the southeast. Padget felt a rush of excitement and looked up just in time to see Ochoa wave his arm.

Ochoa turned in the saddle pointing to the edge of the carnage. "Two sets of tracks right over there... you might want to look at them. Jaguars made them all right, tracks differ from a mountain lion, they're more rounded and don't show the three lobes on the pad."

Padget mounted Jack and slowly followed the tracks toward Ochoa. He could see where the bigger cat had spun to the north throwing dirt out of his tracks. A few feet farther on the tracks turned abruptly back to the southeast. The horses had tried to turn back, but the lion cut them off. Padget looked down at the ground. The sign was plain, there were definitely two cats.

They followed the tracks and found where the lions turned away from the trail, changing directions towards the river. "Looks like those two got the herd milling, then pulled down five horses before the rest got away," Ochoa said.

Walt pushed his hat back and scratched his head. "Looks like you boys will be earning you keep. Ochoa, you can't see it, but John Branson's ranch is right over there, you remember it son." He pointed to the south. "Jose Griegos's farm is about five miles on upriver. Between here and there, at the mouth of Frenchman's Canyon, is Jack Hightower's place. Just over the next ridge is Ed Layton's ranch. That's the layout; Wes can fill you in later."

Walt turned in his saddle and pointed to the north. "You boys use the old Macadoo place down in the flat yonder. That's Devil's Ridge behind it; that low-lying string of hills. No one lives there now, and it's a lot better place to hunt out of than the Rafter. Fenced yard for your dogs, Ochoa... barn is in pretty good shape. You can cut out four or five good horses apiece to take with you. The sooner you get started the better. Charge anything you need to me at Griegos's store."

"That ought to work," Ochoa said.

It was almost sundown when they got back to the Rafter J.

The Macadoo place consisted of a weather-beaten two-room shack standing gray inside a fenced yard with a tack shed slanted off to one side. Outside the fence the skeleton of a barn waited to fall down with the first strong wind that might come along, and beside it a corral stood empty in the morning light. They turned the horses into the corral and pumped the trough full of water, then carried their gear into the house.

"Bunks are still in good shape and the well

works," Ochoa said, as he pumped the handle and filled a cup with water. "I want to boil out the traps before we start."

They spent the evening getting their equipment ready for the trail. Next morning before sunup they packed Button with traps, cartridges and supplies to last for four days.

Chapter Nine

Excitement surged through Padget over the prospect of tracking the jaguars. He pulled his hat down tight and caught his blue roan Skeeter and saddled him. Holding the cheek strap in his left hand he pulled the roan's head around to keep him from bucking. He swung into the saddle with one deliberate motion. The horse danced sideways trying to pitch, but gave up when he couldn't get his head down. The cold morning wind brought with it the pungent odor of greasewood. Padget wrinkled his nose at the smell and turned up his collar against the wind.

Ochoa whistled. A strip-face sorrel walked up and stuck his head into the halter Ochoa held. Scratching the sorrel's ears he gave him a lump of sugar. He whistled again and called, "Belle."

THERE AIN'T NO MONEY IN IT

A black and tan hound came trotting out from the barn.

An hour after sunup, half way up Horse Canyon, they came across the trail of the lions. Over a week old, the tracks were barely visible, but the dogs had no trouble following them. Belle ran along the trail with her nose close to the ground. Bandit trailed along behind with his head up putting his nose down only when the tracks changed directions. The sun was high overhead when they reached the base of Panther Peak. Lion tracks showed plainly around a small seep spring.

Ochoa bent over the tracks. "It looks like they spent some time here."

From the spring, the trail continued southeast across a sharp ridge and into a steep rocky canyon. Padget winced as sand particles struck his face. He tightened the stampede strings on his hat. "Wind's picking up." He pointed to the northwest. "Those clouds over Sierra Blanca Peak yonder don't bode well."

Ochoa studied the huge iron colored thunderheads. "I don't know anything about Texas, but in New Mexico that would spell storm. We're liable to get our butts wet before this day's out."

Padget dismounted, pulled his bandanna from

his neck and tied it around a sotol stalk near the trail. "That's a gully washer heading our way sure enough. It's going to wipe out these tracks. If I have to I want to be able to find this place again." Wisps of sand now scudded across the ground and the bandanna stood straight out. Padget remounted and pointed to the west. "There's a line shack over that ridge about two miles, a place called Frenchman's well, I don't want to be caught out when that storm hits."

The trail grew steeper as it curved around the canyon rim and led down to the line camp. They rounded a bend where they should have been able to see the camp. Blowing sand obscured it from Padget's view; he could barely make out the corrals and the line cabin. Bandit growled and Padget turned to Ochoa. "There's something wrong about the whole layout."

Struggling against the wind, they finally reached the clearing where a one-room shack with a rusted tin roof stood on the west side and faced a windmill across the yard. A corral stood alongside the windmill derrick. The windmill fan shrieked in the high wind and the stream of water it pumped out showed clear and smooth where it ran into the arroyo behind the camp. The raw smell of death permeated the air.

Padget and Ochoa sat their saddles, looking at the mangled carcasses of two dead horses scattered across the corral. Bandit, the scruff hair raised on his neck, walked stiff legged around the dead horses toward something lying on the ground near the line shack. The black and tan hound followed, her tail stiff and straight. Ochoa whistled and she ambled back to him. Padget rode over to where Bandit was sniffing at a pile of rags and he almost gagged.

He stared at the man who lay face down in the center of a large brown stain near door of the cabin. All that was left of a red plaid shirt hung in shreds about the torso of the dead man. A gaping hole in his left side exposed an expanse of ribs, a rope of purple intestines clawed out and strewn off to one side; lay in the dust beside the corral. Ragged nails of two toes stuck through a hole in the sock of a bootless foot. A bloody stump was all that remained of the cowboy's left leg. His head had been torn from the spinal column and a Smith and Wesson .44 Russian, the hammer back at full cock, was clutched in his outstretched left hand. The right arm was bitten off below the elbow. The area reeked of lion piss.

Padget looked up at Ochoa. "Looks like he came out of the cabin to see what was stirring up the horses, and got pulled down from behind." He shook his head. "He hasn't been dead long; the buzzards haven't got to him yet. The poor son of a bitch didn't have a chance."

Lion tracks crisscrossed the yard. Padget pulled his Winchester from the saddle scabbard jacked a cartridge into the chamber and let the hammer down to half cock. He held the rifle with his fingers through the lever and his thumb on the hammer. Careful not to step on the tracks he studied the dead cowboy for a moment, then reached down and rolled him over. He fought the gorge rising in his throat. The game had changed radically and it was too late to do anything about it. It was a race to find the lions before they killed anyone else.

Ochoa came over and knelt down beside Padget. "They always seem to do that," he said.

"What are you talking about?"

"Go for the groin area. I've watched Mountain lions with deer and they always start at the groin."

"I hope he was dead," Padget said. "I'd sure hate to be eaten that way." He pried the dead fingers from around the revolver, uncocked it, and broke open the cylinder. "Not a shot fired."

"Que mala suerte," Ochoa said. "I've heard that once they've eaten human flesh they won't stop...man killers... nobody's safe as long as they're on the loose." He made the sign of a cross over his chest, apprehension plain on his face.

The wind's intensity and low moaning sounds came from the corral as it blew through the cedar rails spinning the windmill fan and furiously shaking the derrick. Padget crossed the yard and pulled the brake handle down until the fan stopped. He tied it in place with a piece of bailing wire. He picked up a bucket, filled it with water, and walked back to the dead cowboy. He washed the blood off as best as he could he stuffed the entrails back into the body.

Entering the shack he spied the cowboy's bedroll and pulled the tarp from around it. Folding the tarp and a threadbare wool blanket over his arm he returned to the body and spread the tarp and blanket on the ground next to it. "Give me a hand rolling him in this will you, Mano?"

Wrapping the body in the blanket they placed it on the tarpaulin, folded the ends, lapped the sides over and tied them together with a lariat. They carried the tarp wrapped cowboy inside to a corner of the room and laid him on the bunk. Ochoa wiped his forehead with his sleeve. "We better take care of the horses."

A gust of wind blew Padget's hat off, but was stopped from blowing away by the stampede straps. He let it hang on his back while he made a picket line with his lariat. Leading the horses to the leeward side of the shack he tied them to the picket line. There wouldn't be any sense trying to put them in the corral with all that blood.

Ochoa walked up and put his hand on Padget's shoulder. "Jaguars return to a kill, my bet is that those cats are still around, maybe close."

Padget glanced around the landscape. "Bandit would raise hell if those lions were anywhere within a long rifle shot."

Both dogs were quiet. Bandit stood still, staring off into the mesquite. Belle, with her nose down on the ground explored the yard.

Padget, rifle in hand, circled the clearing. He felt the hair on the back of his neck rise and had the feeling of being watched. He glanced at the iron sky and sniffed; even the air carried the smell of evil. Dark heavy storm clouds hung low over the entire western horizon, and sheets of lightning lit up the storm front that rapidly moved toward them. Off in the distance, thunder rumbled along the Quitman Mountains, echoing through the canyons like distant cannon fire.

Chapter Ten

The feeble gleam of the coal oil lantern pushed back at the darkness inside the line shack and cast a pale light over packs and saddles stacked on the floor. Dimly outlined by the lantern light, the canvas wrapped body of the dead cowboy lay against the back wall. Ochoa shrugged away the uneasy feeling of being cooped up with a half eaten dead man, sometimes he hated his job.

From a stack of newspapers beside the stove he picked up an old copy of the El Paso Times. He tore a page from the newspaper, wadded it into a loose ball and lifted the lid on the cook stove. He put the paper wad into the firebox and from a Hercules Dynamite crate selected several sticks of kindling and arranged them in a row across the paper. He whipped a match across his jeans and the odor of sulfur filled the room. Letting the flare die down he lit the paper and felt the sudden rush of heat against his face. Watching the flame until he was sure it had caught on he replaced the lid. Filling the coffeepot with water he rummaged around the cupboard, found a can of Arbuckle's coffee, dumped in a handful, and set the pot on top of the stove. He stood there, eyes unfocused. What would have been a short chase and a sure kill now was one big question. The lions could be miles away by the time they found the tracks again. And until they found the tracks again, the game would be Blind Man's Bluff.

The sound of the coffee pot boiling over broke into his thoughts, and odor of burned coffee filled the cabin. He lifted the pot from the stove and poured two cups of coffee and sat down across from Padget who was staring through the window at the storm that raced across the chaparral toward them.

He was halfway through his coffee when the storm plowed into the line camp like a freight train. The wind shook the cabin like a terrier shaking a rat and Ochoa almost dropped his cup. The storm rattled the clapboard siding so loudly that he couldn't hear what Padget said — something about the horses. Lightning cracked; flashing an eerie blue light through the windows, lighting up the line shack in brief erupting bursts. The smell of ozone filled the air and between lighting flashes the cabin seemed darker. Thunder followed immediately and sounded to Ochoa like dynamite charges going off in a mine tunnel.

Increasing in velocity, the wind rattled the walls and almost ripped the shack off its foundation. Sheet after sheet of rain slammed down against the tin roof unchecked as the storm hurled itself up the canyon.

Ochoa opened his mouth to relieve the pressure on his ears and noticed a leak in the roof. He jerked his Krag from under the leak, wiped it dry and laid it across the table. He would need his rifle when he caught up with the jaguars and didn't want it rusty. He leaned over and looked out the window. "It's been raining like a cow pissing on a flat rock for the last two hours, now it's turned to sleet."

"A west Texas storm," Padget said. "Peculiar for this time of year, but it should let up pretty soon, at least I hope so because I don't believe there's enough wood in Texas to build an ark."

Ochoa clumped down in a chair across the

table. "Mano, except for a few scraggly pines up in Horse Canyon and a cottonwood or two I haven't seen enough wood around here to build a two hole outhouse." He nodded toward the body in the corner. "He gives me the spooks. We ought to bury him pretty deep when the storm lets up."

"We better take him down to Hightower's place," Padget said. "It's only a couple of miles and Jack will want to write a letter to his family."

The center of the storm passed over the line shack and enveloped the Eagle Mountains. Thunder echoed off the peaks and into the canyons below; rain and sleet continued. Ochoa sat next to the stove where the heat made him sleepy. He straightened his head and looked out the window and sniffed at the fresh smell of rain as it cleared away the smell of death. All they needed now was for this to turn into snow. He stood up and crossed the room to where his gear lay. He unbuckled the flap of one saddlebag, reached into it and pulled out a bottle. Pulling the cork he took a swallow and offered it to Padget. "That ought-six you carry, I haven't seen many of them around.

Padget took the bottle and poured his cup half-full of whiskey and handed the bottle back. "I bought this one after I lost a shootout with a buffalo gun. I see you're still carrying that cannon you stole from the Army."

Ochoa nodded. "I put it away for a while when I started trapping. It kicks like a mule and the time I really needed it I didn't have it with me." Holding the bottle in one hand and the cork in the other he shrugged his left shoulder.

Padget slapped his hand down on the table. "I don't like it at all."

"What's that, compa."

"The way those cats did this puncher, killing him is one thing, eating him is another."

"Did you ever run into a grizzly, Wes?"

"I saw a few in Alaska. I can't actually say I ever ran into one. Why?"

"I don't know which is meaner, a jaguar or a grizzly."

"Meaner? In what way?"

"Chew you up and eat you meaner."

Padget leaned back in his chair. "I know a bear will kill you if you get careless, but I never heard of one eating anybody."

"They will eat you. There was one that ate a sheepherder. That bear didn't leave much but the ribcage and part of the backbone, and to top that off the same grizzly damned near made bear shit out of me." He poured more whiskey into his cup. "After that, I started packing the Krag again."

"Where did all this take place?"

"Southwestern Colorado. That bear was a sheep killer too."

"You used not to have anything to do with sheep," Padget said.

Ochoa held out a sack of Mail Pouch. "Here, want some?" Padget shook his head. Ochoa stuffed a wad into his mouth tasting the sweet acrid chewing tobacco. He licked a stray strand from his lip and closed the pouch, putting it in his coat pocket.

Padget raised his voice to be heard over the sound of the rain slamming into the shack. "Go on with your story, there's got to be more to it than that."

"I was following his tracks down this steep canyon, hoping to get a shot at him when he came boiling out of the timber on my left side. I got one shot off before my horse dumped me. That shot must have confused him some because it didn't seem like he could make up his mind. He looked at me, and then back at the horse. While he was thinking that over I shot him four more times. Then he was on me, he bit my left shoulder and shook me like a rat."

"Break you up much?"

Ochoa shook his head. "It must've put me out for awhile when I hit the ground because the next thing I remember was me laying there on my back and not hearing anything." He glanced over at the dead cowboy in the corner of the line shack and a shudder ran through him.

"I tied up my shoulder with what was left of my shirt and lit out for the ranch to get my Krag and another horse. Next morning I caught up with him. He was still on his feet, but the first shot out of my Krag hit him hard and knocked him down. I put the second shot through his chest as he turned towards me. That one cut the top off his heart and kept on going—all the way through him—stopped in his right ham.

Padget walked across the floor and looked at the dead cowboy. "We've got to find those lions and fast."

Chapter Eleven

With a few distant thunder claps the storm ended. Padget and Ochoa walked out into the late afternoon sun. Quiet and orderly the chaparral stretched out for miles, the chemise and sagebrush glistening from the rain. Glad to be outside Padget pulled his hat down low over his eyes and looked around the clearing. The ground around the shack was washed clean and except for the horse carcasses in the corral it appeared that nothing out of the ordinary had ever happened. The air smelled clean and crisp. He turned to Ochoa. "I guess God didn't like the mess around here and wiped the slate clean."

"Or maybe the devil is just taking care of his own," Ochoa said.

"I damned sure don't like that idea very much," Padget said.

They wiped down the horses and put the pack on Button. They carried the dead cowboy from the line shack and laid him down on the ground. Padget put a blindfold on Button and they lifted the dead cowboy across the pack and tied him face down. Even with the blindfold, Button didn't like the load and danced sideways. Padget pulled the rope through the cinch rings and snubbed it.

The trail to the Hightower ranch was steep, rock strewn, and narrow. Padget and Ochoa rode in silence all the way to the ranch. Jack Hightower came out onto the porch as they rode up. "I heard you were back, Wes. What's that you have slung over your pack horse?"

"I don't know who he is. We found him up at your line camp at Frenchman's Well. He's pretty much used up." Mrs. Hightower wiped her hands on her apron as she walked out on the porch. "I wouldn't let the women folks look at him."

The next morning after breakfast Padget and Ochoa stood in the bright morning sun outside the Hightower cook shack gazing at the vast expanse of land spread out before them. Padget picked up a stick and knelt in the dust. Using the stick he scratched a map on the ground.

"We can cover more ground and have a better chance of finding those lions if we split up here and cut for sign. I'll go east along the Eagles. You go west and we'll meet up at Ojos Calientes."

With the stick Padget pointed to the west. "Those are the Quitman Mountains right over there. You can see the road to Sierra Blanca and on the other side of the road is Red Light Draw. North about seven or eight miles you will run across the Old Spanish Trail. It crosses the road and the draw; you won't have any trouble finding it. When you get to it follow it toward the Quitmans for another seven miles and you'll come to a wagon road... about here." He scratched another line on the ground. "The old Henshaw place is about a mile up the road here." He pointed to a spot on the dirt map. "You can spend the night there. Nobody lives there or at least it was vacant when I left for Arizona, there used to be an old house with the roof falling in and a stock tank, it's the only place you can get water.

The road goes through the canyon and on down to the river. When you get to the river, Ojos Calientes is downstream about fifteen miles, you can't miss it. There's a big hotel and the out buildings are all painted white."

Still holding the stick he turned and pointed toward the east, then swept it to the south. "I'll cut sign along the foothills of the Eagles down to the Branson place. Then, I'll ride upriver and meet you at the Ojos Calientes. It shouldn't take you more than two days, three at the most. If you get there first just hang around. I'll do the same. There used to be a cantina in the hotel, maybe you can get a drink if you have to wait too long."

Ochoa nodded toward Button. "Are you going to take the pack horse?"

"Why don't you take him? Padget said. "I'll stop over at Dick Layton's place or maybe Branson's. You won't run into much over that way."

Ochoa put his foot in the stirrup and swung into the saddle. Padget handed him the lead rope. "Watch your top knot."

Ochoa grinned and touched the brim of his hat. "Watch your'n."

There would be a good deer crop this year. Padget had never seen so many deer tracks. He walked his horse through the chaparral along the

THERE AIN'T NO MONEY IN IT

foot of the Eagles looking for any indication the lions had come this way. He watched a skinny old brindle colored cow with a crooked horn trailing a scrawny late born calf eyeing him between the sotol plants.

He spent the night with Dick Layton and rode into the Branson ranch just before noon the next day. Branson met him on the front steps. "Get down and rest your saddle."

Padget told him about the two jaguars. "I thought maybe there were two sets of tracks when my bull got killed. You didn't cut any fresh sign down this way did you? I've got my riders carrying saddle guns as it is."

"No sir, not this time, nothing I could find," Padget said.

Branson spat a stream of tobacco juice off the front porch and hit a dirt dauber in mid-flight. Squinting against the sun's glare he turned back to Padget. "When you get back to town you might want to tell the sheriff that two nights ago seven or eight Mexicans came across the river down by the spring. They rode up to the house loaded for bear. All of them had rifles; two of them packing those bolt action Mausers and every damn one of them wearing enough ammunition to start a war. The leader was a big cold-eyed son of a bitch who said his name was Urbina. I've run across some hard cases in my life, but this bunch is sure enough looking for a fight. I had the coosie give them something to eat and they rode on up river."

"Say they were headed?"

"Didn't say and I didn't ask. Have you eaten yet? Dinner will be ready pretty soon."

"I had a bite with Dick Layton and I need to get on with my rat killing, but thanks just the same."

Padget left Branson sitting in a rocking chair on the front porch and walked to his horse. He mounted and rode west along the north bank of the river looking for tracks along the dusty wagon road and soon ran across the sign of eight horses coming up from the river. The tracks reached the road and turned west toward the Griego farm. That's the bunch John was telling me about sure as hell. They're back on this side. If it's not one thing it's six. We've got enough trouble without a bunch of damned Mexican bandits all over the place.

He dismounted and studied the tracks. When satisfied he could remember the details he tightened the cinch, stepped back into the saddle and

THERE AIN'T NO MONEY IN IT

rode on. A mile from the Griego farm the tracks turned south and crossed back into Mexico. Padget arrived at the farm just as the sun went down behind the Quitman Mountains. He hoped that Ochoa was having better luck.

Chapter Twelve

"Bandits, border trash, peons with guns." Don Jose Griego slammed down his glass, spilling wine on the table. Immediately, a servant appeared to remove the glass and mop up the wine with a linen towel. A second servant replaced the glass and poured more wine.

Seated across the immense mahogany table from Griego, Padget watched the blood flush his face. The spicy aroma of Mexican food permeated the room.

Griego took a sip of his wine and placed the glass gently down on the table and wiped his lips with a napkin. "Forgive me. They were here, but they stayed on the other side of the river. My segundo Raul said they left night before last. They grow in number each year. They are nothing but border scum made bold by this wild talk of revolution."

Padget looked at his host over the top of his wine glass. "You don't think there will be a revolution?"

Griego paused with the fork halfway to his mouth. He peered at Padget. "Never!" he said. "President Diaz will never permit it. Francisco Madero, to his shame, is responsible for all this wild talk. He, himself, is a hacendado; his family owns most of Coahuila. We even attended Berkeley together." He shook his head and put the fork down.

"Madero is my friend, but it is incomprehensible that he wrote that...that irresponsible book. He is impossible. Do you know he had the absolute temerity to send a copy of the book to Diaz? What a fool! Because of his book everyone from Ojinaga to Juarez is talking of nothing but revolution."

Padget placed his hand over his wine glass to prevent the servant from filling it. "The men who came by night before last; are they revolutionaries?"

Griego leaned forward over the table. "Vaya revolutionaries! They are bandits; thieves who take advantage of unrest to rob and plunder." Griego sat back in his chair and took a deep breath. "Because of Madero and his book, contrabandistas are now beginning to smuggle arms into Mexico. It can only cause more robbing, more killing."

Padget leaned back in his chair. "Is there a lot of smuggling going on?"

Griego rubbed the bridge of his nose. "The increase in smuggling is so great that President Diaz ordered the border completely sealed. I received a letter last week from an old friend, Colonel Emilio Kosterlitzky, about this matter." Jose looked closely at Padget. "Small ranchers on both sides of the river are bringing guns into Mexico." He picked up his wine glass. "The rurales know about this and will catch them. It will take time; the border is long and the police cannot be everywhere at once." He sipped his wine.

Padget crossed his arms over his chest. "I ran into a Colonel Kosterlitzky a few years back. We were sent to Sonora; a place called the Cananea Mine where strikers were holding some Americans hostages, he is the head of the policia rurales in Sonora, if I remember right."

Griego smiled. "All of northern Mexico I wish. May his tribe increase! I see you are already acquainted with my friend."

"Just a nodding acquaintance." Padget thought

he was one of the meanest sons-of-bitches he had ever met. He hanged the poor bastards at the mine.

Griego spread his hands. "Forgive me, Wes. How are Walt and Claire? Señora Griego tells me that Señora Johnson is quite ill. May God in his mercy restore her health."

Padget smiled. "Fine, they're both well. Walt is still able to sit the hurricane deck of a cow pony and Aunt Claire is up and about, almost good as new." A doctor from El Paso is looking after her." Padget uncrossed his arms. "By the way, I haven't seen Leo, Hector, or Robert since I got back. How are they?"

"Hector is in Mexico. Leo is in town looking after the store and Robert is attending Sul Ross. He graduates this spring and gets married the next week."

"Robert's getting married?"

Griego nodded. "Now that you are back, perhaps you too will find a good woman and settle down. I hear from Señora Griego that Señora Johnson would like to have grand children."

Padget pushed his chair back from the table. "I think not, I'm an old bachelor that no decent woman would look at twice. No girl in her right mind would want to marry a forty a month cowhand?"

"Ah, but you are Walt's heir. You won't be a cowboy all your life," Griego said.

"I don't think Walt's ready to be buried just yet. Anyway, there's still plenty of time to find some gal that's long in the tooth and get married." He had made it this far without some female messing up his life and he wasn't about to start now.

Chapter Thirteen

The sun against his shoulders made Ochoa drowsy. He wrapped the reins around his saddle horn and pulled his feet from the stirrups letting them hang loose Indian style. He closed his eyes and mulled over in his mind the fact that the lions had become man-killers. They could be anywhere, headed in any direction. There wasn't a snowball's chance in hell he would find them before they made another kill. He opened one eye and looked around just in time to see the shadow of a Red Tailed Hawk skitter across Bear's withers and move across the landscape. He opened both eyes and looked up and watched the hawk soar westward toward the mountains on the skyline. The lions could well be across the river and back into Mexico. Then again, they could have circled back to the Eagles and be wreaking havoc on

Walt's livestock while he and Wes were out on a wild goose chase. He was going to have to put some traps out soon.

He came to a caliche packed wagon road that showed white against the dark green of the chaparral. He nudged Bear with his spurs coaxing him down the steep bank onto the sandy bottom of the arroyo west of the road and turned north. The arroyo, a corridor much-used by the animals living in the chaparral was stitched with tracks. Every critter, but the ones we're looking for, he thought. The sun was directly overhead when he arrived at the junction of the Old Spanish Trail. Again he touched his horse with his spurs and leaned forward as Bear lunged. The effort crumbled the bank down into the arroyo as he climbed out. The sun was going down behind the Quitman Mountains when he arrived at a wagon road. To the west the road was lined with sotol and cactus and led downhill toward a pass through the mountains.

The creaking of the windmill reached him in the dusk. Ochoa stepped down and loosened the girth. Removing his saddle he dropped it in the dust. He unlashed the pack and led both horses to the water trough. The house, a wind blown one-room shack, stood alone in a fenced yard. Weeds chocked the flowerbeds that ran along the length of the house on one side. Except for a single rose bush, that somehow survived, the weeds had taken over. He scratched Belle's ears. "Well girl this is a hard scrabble place sure enough, but good enough to spend the night I guess." He led the horses inside the fenced yard and put his saddle and packs under the single scraggily Chinaberry tree. There were more trees on his place back in Colorado than he had seen in the whole State of Texas and a damn sight more water.

Ochoa gathered up a handful of twigs and started a fire. He fed it small sticks until it was going well. Watching closely for rattlesnakes, he gathered wood. He dragged a dead mesquite tree close to the fence and stomped on it. Over the noise of the breaking limbs he heard Belle emit a soft growl and dropped his hand to her neck. The coarse hair of Belle's hackles stood straight up under his hand. The hound was looking east, following whatever was out there beyond the firelight and she didn't like it one bit. He pulled his Krag from the scabbard and chambered a round. "Easy girl, what is it you hear?" At the sound of his voice she gave her tail a single wag and sat down on her haunches, but kept looking eastward. Ochoa fed more wood on the fire. Belle remained where she was, he watched her while he cooked supper. He was drinking his second cup of coffee, staring into the darkness when Belle stood up, hackles no longer raised, she walked to his side and lay down. "Whatever was out there's gone, huh?" he said.

Ochoa woke to every sound during the night, he dreamed about the lion in Hachita. Finally giving up on sleep he stirred the ashes of the campfire and got a blaze going. By the time he finished breakfast it was light enough to see. He emptied the coffeepot onto the smoking campfire, saddled Bear and rode along the wagon trail down into Quitman Canyon.

Indian paintings on the vertical face of the sandstone caught his eye. He traced the outline of the red ochre stick figures painted on the rock with his finger. Apache, he thought. He nudged Bear into a walk and continued down the trail. Two black tail deer, antlers silhouetted against the skyline, watched him from high up on the slope to his left. As he looked, something startled the deer and they left the hill in a dead run. Deer didn't usually move that fast.

A flock of crows erupted from across the canyon to his right, noisily protesting whatever scared them up. Ochoa felt the hair on the back of his neck rise and a cold chill ran over his shoulders. He reined in Bear and searched the canyon walls for any sign of what might have jumped the deer and scared the crows; nothing that might offer a clue was visible in the landscape.

He glanced down at Bell trotting alongside Bear. She seemed unconcerned, but the wind was blowing in the wrong direction for her to smell whatever might be out there.

Ochoa decided that he didn't like Texas very much. There wasn't enough water to take a bath in, nothing tall enough to break the wind, everything seemed to have thorns. Compared to his place in Colorado it didn't even make the first cut. He should quit running, and go back and try to make it up with Mary Ann. Guilt pushed down heavy in his stomach as he thought about the way he left her without saying goodbye. He ought to go back and marry her. He knew better than that! It wouldn't be six months before he took off again. Fishing in his saddlebags he produced a sack of Mail Pouch, opened it and took out three fingers of tobacco. The sweet aroma made him hungry. He wadded the tobacco and shoved it into his mouth. The sweet taste made his mouth water. Wiping his lips with the back of his hand he folded the top of the sack and stuffed it back into the saddlebag. With his tongue he worked the wad around his mouth until it was just right, and then spat out a stray strand that refused to stay put. He'd made his bed; he'd sleep in it.

The canyon opened up into a wide greasewood and cactus choked valley as he neared the river. He stopped at a windmill to water his horses. Loosening the saddle, he tied the horses to the derrick, pulled the brake to stop the fan and tied it back. He climbed the ladder to the top and crawled out on the platform. Hooking one arm around a leg of the derrick he adjusted his field glasses. A few cattle were scattered over the valley; downriver a trail of dust rose in the air. Somebody was moving cows back from the river. Turning around he looked for a long time through his field glasses studying the canyon he had just ridden through. He scanned the hillsides for movement.

He climbed down, mounted his horse and continued toward the river. The sun was high when he arrived at the trail running along the Rio Grande. He turned east cutting for sign in the loose dust that lay like a blanket over the road. A mile east, he found fresh tracks of several shod horses coming up from the river headed north. The tracks probably accounted for the dust he had seen earlier. Farther along he met a Mexican vaquero who rode for the Diamond A. The cowboy told him that he had seen the tracks before, but had never seen any riders. Ochoa asked him if he thought they were rustlers. The cowboy said he didn't know and he didn't know if anyone was missing stock. Other than those that had been killed by the lions the Diamond A was in good shape.

Chapter Fourteen

It was called Indian Hot Springs or Ojos Calientes. Pilar Martinez would always think of it as her second home. Newly whitewashed, the Rudd Ranch headquarters lay sprawled under an immense grove of cottonwood trees on the U.S. side of the river. Blindingly white in the afternoon sun the two-story hotel brooded over a palisade of out buildings. A rock wall held in check the invading chaparral and a hard packed caliche yard surrounded the main building like a moat. The white of the caliche reflected the sun's rays back into the sky.

Pilar rode the half a day's ride south of Sierra Blanca three times a week to teach the children from the poor families across the river. The inhabitants were all Mexican and the strongest cultural ties lay south of the border. That is, all were Mexican

THERE AIN'T NO MONEY IN IT

except Jewel Rudd, who might have been Mexican, so far as anyone could tell.

Pilar sat in the shade of a copse of cottonwood trees that shaded the hotel and read aloud from *Oliver Twist*.[3] She read in English — *"he was badged and ticketed, and fell into his place at once — a parish child — the orphan of a workhouse — the humble, half-starved drudge — to be cuffed and buffeted through the world — despised by all, and pitied by none."* She read to a group of children who ringed her in rapt attention like so many blackbirds perched on a fence. The scene reminded her of the one room school at Sierra Blanca she attended as a girl.

Disturbed in her reading by the sound of a horseman, she looked at the tall rider who rode up to the hotel on a blue roan and dismounted. His back was turned as he tied his horse to the rail in front of the hotel, but there was something strangely familiar about him. For some reason she could not tear her eyes away from this cowboy and watched him pull a carbine from the saddle scabbard and unstring his saddlebags.

He threw his saddlebags over his shoulder, turned and looked straight at her. He touched the brim of his hat in greeting. She felt the warm rush

---

[3] Wednesday October 20, 1909

of blood in her face and dropped her head, looking back to the book she held. She should be able to cope with the greeting from a strange man; she often clerked in Griego's store and was seldom bothered by flirting cowboys. A simple greeting shouldn't cause her feel awkward. The children giggled.

She straightened, lifted her head and translated the passage into Spanish. When she finished she saw the cowboy had entered the hotel. "That is all for today," she said. The children scattered like a covey of quail. She rose to her feet, placed the book on the bench, and turned toward the hotel lobby. She glanced up at the second story of the hotel and saw Jewel Rudd sitting in her rocking chair. She seemed interested in the cowboy's every move too.

Pilar entered the hotel behind the cowboy. His carbine leaned against the desk and his saddlebags were thrown over his left arm as he signed the hotel guest book. He needed a haircut. She walked behind the desk and looked at the register as the cowboy wrote. Reading his name she smiled, the awkwardness vanished and she felt a thrill course through her body. Fifteen years ago when he rode away, she thought she would never see him again.

Chapter Fifteen

Padget picked up the pen and began to write his name in the register when the girl entered the hotel and moved around him. Carrying a book, she stooped under the barrier. Padget saw her face at an angle and at the same time saw the firm set of her chin.

She smiled and said, "Hola, cowboy."

"Buenos dias," Padget said, and was careful not to stare and not to look away.

She set the book down on the counter and he noticed her handsome brown hands. Now she looked him full in the face and smiled.

Her teeth were white in her brown face and her skin and her eyes were the same tawny brown. She had wide cheekbones, laughing eyes, and a straight mouth with full lips. Her hair was the dark brown of a mink's coat just washed in a cold mountain stream.

She smiled in Padget's face and put her hand up and ran it over her hair pushing it back behind her neck.

He could see the shape of her small up-tilted breasts under the white blouse. Every time he looked at her Padget could feel a thickness in his throat. He looked down at the pen in his hand and signed the register.

The voice coming from somewhere above his head had the same quality as a well-honed skinning knife. "Are you a new hand at Eagle Springs or did you steal that horse?"

Padget turned. Standing above him an old woman with eyes the same faded blue as her sunbonnet stared down at him. Gray hair that long ago might have been blonde framed a lined and sunburned face.

The girl behind the desk answered for him. "It's Wes Padget, Jewell; he is Walt Johnson's nephew. He doesn't look much like the boy I went to school with though, he's grown some." She laughed.

Her soft voice sent a strange sensation through him. Padget stared at the younger woman. "Pilar Martinez?"

She smiled and nodded. "You've been gone a long time, Wes, some of us, including your aunt, thought you would stay away forever."

He looked into soft brown eyes that were watching him and his throat tightened again and he felt an idiotic grin start to build. *That skinny little girl Bill and Dorothy took in all those years ago has turned into the prettiest woman I've ever seen.* Words would not come. He felt his ears turn red.

"How is Claire?" Pilar asked.

The older woman descended the stairs and stepped closer. She wrinkled her nose and stepped back. "You need a bath."

"I hope to take care of that as soon as I get a room," Padget said. "Claire is doing fine, Pilar. The doctor gave her some medicine that seems to be doing the trick."

Jewel Rudd tilted her head back and looked at him with narrowed eyes, "It's about time you got back. Somebody's going to have to look after the ranch pretty soon. How long are you going to stay this time? This country is hard enough to live in without you men folk running off all over creation."

He didn't know what to say to her. His business

was his own and certainly not this old crone's. He was saved from answering her by the sound of horses outside. Padget strode to the door and looked out to see Ochoa ride up to the front of the hotel and look around.

Using the arrival of Ochoa as an excuse to get away from the two women, Padget retreated from the hotel onto the porch. "Hola, Mano," Padget said, and walked out to where Ochoa was sitting on his horse.

Ochoa smiled when he saw Padget. "Como le va?" He swung down from the saddle and the small bells on his spurs jingled faintly. He looped the reins over the hitch rack and loosened the cinch. Belle lay down in the shade of the cottonwood trees. "That was a long ride you sent me on, pardner."

"Come on, I'll buy you a beer and you can tell me about it. Hell, I'll do more than that I'll buy you supper," Padget said.

Ochoa stopped. "Momento, mano, I'll get my rifle."

They walked from the hot bright sunlight into the cool dimly lighted cantina. Choosing a table against the far wall, Padget pulled a chair from a table and sat down. Bandit lay down at his feet.

Ochoa put his rifle and the bandoleer on the

floor, and then sat down on Padget's left. As he did he pulled a 32-20 Smith and Wesson from his shoulder holster and shoved it in his belt in front of his right hip, the grip to his left. Padget noted that both pistols were in close proximity and easily reached.

Chapter Sixteen

Padget leaned back in the chair and looked around the room. The cantina, set off to one side and separated from the rest of the hotel by a pair of intricately carved swinging doors, remained cool in the afternoon's heat. A highly polished bar ran the entire length of one wall. Placed around the room against the perimeter there were a number of tables covered with red and white tablecloths. The middle of the floor was left open for dancing and a broad passageway at one end of the bar revealed a woman in the kitchen beyond, rolling out tortillas near an immense adobe oven. The odor of beer, green chiles, and tortillas cooking in the oven made him smile. He was hungry.

Still feeling the pleasant impact of his encounter with Pilar, he relaxed. There was no doubt that a girl as good looking as Pilar would have at least one boy friend, he thought. Probably several. Still, there was a thing called luck and a cowboy could hope. "Could we get a couple of beers?" he called out. "And something to eat?"

The bartender quit polishing the mirror, put down the towel and filled two mugs and started around the bar. He stopped short, almost running into Pilar who walked into the cantina from the hotel lobby.

She took the tray from the bartender and motioned for one more beer and stood leaning against the bar looking directly at Padget. There was a hint of a smile on her lips.

He hadn't noticed before, but she was dressed for riding. She wore silver spurs on black boots that showed beneath a dark brown divided skirt. Her legs slanted long and clean against the cloth of the skirt. Gold earrings flashed in the afternoon sunlight. Every time Padget looked at her he could feel the thickness in his throat.

With deft movements the bartender set out the third beer. Pilar picked up the tray and walked across the room the sway in her hips slightly exaggerated. Padget pushed back his chair took off his hat and scrambled to his feet.

She stopped close to him, much too close; he

could smell her clean and fragrant hair. Her nearness unbalanced his senses. She brushed against Padget slightly and the warmth of her body mingled with his as she set the tray on the table. Raw adrenaline shot through Padget when they touched. Her laughter reminded him of the sound of small silver bells.

"Buenos dias. Soy Pilar," she said to Ochoa.

Ochoa stood, bowed and took off his hat. "David Ochoa. It's my pleasure, Pilar."

Pilar looked back at Ochoa, one eyebrow slightly arched. "No habla español?"

"Si, señorita. Hablo español; only I speak English better."

That's pure unadulterated bullcrap, thought Padget.

Pilar smiled and set the beer down on the table. "Mind if I join you two?" Without waiting for an answer she pulled a chair out and sat down, taking a sack of Bull Durham and papers from her vest pocket. She opened the sack and holding the paper in her left hand dumped tobacco into it. Catching the string in her teeth she pulled the sack closed and laid it on the table. Taking the filled paper in both hands she twirled and smoothed it into a slim cigarette.

Padget glanced over at Ochoa who watched

her as if he had never seen anyone roll a cigarette.

She put the paper against her mouth and with a pink flick of her tongue licked the edge; sealing it. She looked a question at her audience. There was a flurry of action as Padget and Ochoa searched their shirts.

Ochoa was the quicker of the two. He pulled a wooden match from his shirt pocket and flicked the head of the match with his thumb so hard that a piece of burning phosphorous lodged under his nail. He jerked back his hand, shook out the match and stuck his thumb in his mouth. "Umm, that hurts."

Padget laughed and dragged a match across the leg of his jeans. It burst into flames and he held it for Pilar.

Smiling, she cupped his hand, pulling it closer and lit her cigarette. Still holding his hand she took a deep breath and exhaled the smoke, blowing out the match. "Hey cowboy, do you know that I had a crush on you all through the third grade?" she said, releasing his hand.

He felt a hot flush rush up his neck and he cleared his throat. Before he could answer Jewell Rudd came into the cantina. Padget watched her over Pilar's shoulder.

Jewel Rudd paused, and then walked over to the table.

Ochoa stood up as Pilar looked around. "Mrs. Rudd. This is David Ochoa, Padget's friend," she said.

Ochoa pulled a chair from the table for her and bowed. "Will you join us?"

"No, I've got things to do. You're the one Walt sent for; the lion hunter? Are you any good at what you do?"

Ochoa smiled politely.

"Dave is the best hunter and trapper that I know of. He's very good and that's fortunate because we've got two jaguars working hereabouts," Padget said. "They killed one of Hightower's hands over in Frenchman's Canyon."

"If there are two man killing jaguars working over this country, what are you two doing sitting here on your butts, drinking beer in the middle of the afternoon? You ought to be out there after them."

"The storm night before last wiped out the tracks and we haven't been able to cut their sign. Dave made the loop through Quitman Canyon and I worked the foothills down to Branson's."

Jewell said. "Well, I hope you're as good as the

money we are paying you." She walked away from the table leaving them alone in the bar.

Ochoa shrugged. "That woman could scald the hide off a bull elk with her tongue."

Chapter Seventeen

Tomás Urbina sat on the ground, leaning against his saddle drinking mescal. Lying around him in various positions of repose six men watched closely as Urbina contemplated the man standing in front of him. A seventh man was cooking over an open fire.

He tilted his head back and drank deeply from the bottle of mescal. He considered what to do about the man standing in front of him. The man was a fool and had disclosed the location of their home base to Griego's foreman. And that meant that the federales would soon have the information and would be waiting for them to return. They could no longer go home. Why did God allow such stupid men to exist?

A trickle of liquid ran down Urbina's chin. He

drank deeply again from the bottle, then wiped his lips with the back of his hand and looked at the man who cowered before him. "So, tell me again, Rafael, what you told the Segundo of Griego's."

Rafael looked down at the ground and did not meet his captain's gaze. "It was nothing, Tomás. We were talking about home and I said only that I was from Parral."

Urbina chewed on a dirt-encrusted nail and spat. "Nothing? Are we not all from Parral? Is that not the place we will return to when we leave this God forsaken place?"

"Yes, clearly."

"Now, the hacendado knows where we go. He will inform the rurales."

"I'm sorry, jefe."

"Give me your pistol, Rafael."

"My pistol?"

"Si, your pistol."

"Por que?" a look of terror distorted the man's face as he handed him the pistol.

Urbina cocked the pistol and pointed it at Rafael's right eye. "Por que? Por que, I am going to shoot you with it."

"You joke?"

Urbina shot him in the head. The report

shattered the evening stillness. The man fell forward to the ground, blood from the wound soaked into the sand changing the color to a dark red. "No. I do not joke."

"Pablo," he said to the man standing by the cook fire, "fix me some food after you drag this dog turd away, I'm hungry." He tilted the bottle of mescal up and sucked the worm into his mouth. It crunched as he chewed. He tossed the empty bottle into the brush.

Urbina tried to remember how long he had been with Villa. They had killed, robbed, fought and whored together back even before Doroteo Arango became Pancho Villa. During that time he had become Villa's strong right hand. He was proud of his service to the bandit leader and he always carried out his duties, well…sometimes not exactly. This time, Villa sent him to find a safe route from Texas for a load of rifles and ammunition that would be brought into Mexico for the revolution. Three weeks of hard riding finally brought him to discover the obscure trail from Texas to Villa's camp. He was on his way back with the information now.

Stopping at the Griego farm had been a mistake, a costly mistake. Even though he did not cross the river, Griego was dangerous, a Diaz supporter. But his men had been hungry, and he allowed them to stop for food at the small settlement across the river from the Griego rancho. Alas, Griego's foreman lived there, a bootlicker and a spy. He would tell everything to Griego who would then inform the guarda fiscales and when he did, home would no longer be safe. They would be waiting for them when they returned to Parral. I should have killed that damned Segundo. Cagarse Rafael! Cacarse el segundo! Parral can no longer be our home. Urbina spat in distaste; he burned with hate, he hated hacendados, he hated the church more. He hated them both almost as much as he hated the fiscales and he hated fiscales almost as much as he hated gringos.

The sun reflected brightly from his crossed bandoleers as Urbina rode across the Rio Bravo. He glanced back at the far bank; he was in the United States now that he had crossed the river. It did not matter; he had crossed the border many times, sometimes peacefully, sometimes in a hail of bullets. He wasn't afraid.

He had not bathed for weeks. He smelled of dirt mixed with sweat and horses and blood. It did not matter what the woman in Ojos Calientes might think about the way he smelled. Today he was going to bed the woman called Pilar, one way or the other. There would be no more games for her to play.

Urbina noticed the horses as he rode into the yard. Two of the brands on the horses were unfamiliar, but one he recognized. A tall bay had the Rafter J brand burned on his left hip. A warning flashed through his head. The ranch of that brand was owned by a tough, hard man named Walter Johnson. The riders pulled up in front of the hotel in Ojos Calientes.

Urbina had questioned all of the peons along the river about army patrols and Texas Rangers and he gathered information about the ranchers on the Texas side. He knew all of the brands of the ranches within twenty miles of the river and knew how many riders each had. From experience he also knew that most Texans hated Mexicans. The feeling was mutual.

Perhaps they were Texas Rangers. He hated rinches[4] more than the fiscales. Swinging his right

---

4 What Mexicans call Texas Rangers

leg over the pommel he slipped from his gray gelding to the ground. He pushed back his hat so that it hung from the leather stampede straps and loosened his pistols in their holsters. He led his men toward the hotel.

He walked softly across the lobby, the huge rowels of his spurs muffled by the carpet. Carefully, he pushed open the swinging doors that separated the hotel from the cantina and stepped into the dark room. He paused to let his eyes grow accustomed to the dim light.

As water flows around a rock in the middle of a stream, his riders spread out to either side of the door as they entered. Urbina walked to the end of the bar and leaned against it. The rest of his gang peeled themselves off the wall and lined up along the bar. Their movement surrounded Pilar.

Chapter Eighteen

Padget, in the middle of telling a story about hunting mule deer in the Mogollons Mountains of Arizona, heard the noise of several riders approaching from the direction of the river. The sound of horses thundering into the yard echoed throughout the cantina. He glanced at Pilar who stood by the bar waiting for their glasses to be refilled.

Eight Mexicans filed into the cantina, nondescript except for bandoleers of ammunition that crossed their chests. It looked to Padget as if the revolution had already started. The tallest wore a charro jacket with silver buttons sewn on the sleeves and his pants were stuffed into knee high boots with large spurs that dragged the floor. His flat brimmed campaign hat hung down his back, suspended there by leather strings knotted with a silver band that glinted in the light from the window. He was dark and had large hands. His eyes were dead flat, and unrevealing. A pair of Russian .44 revolvers hung from a cartridge belt strapped around his waist.

A chill ran up Padget's back. This had to be the bunch John Branson told him about. What a hell of a time to have a woman around. If things went wrong she could be hurt or killed. He pushed his chair back from the table; if a fight started he didn't want anything getting in his way. He heard the sound of Ochoa shifting his weight, and out of the corner of his eye saw him drop his hands beneath the table.

One of the Mexicans, whose face was pockmarked with smallpox scars, quit the bar and moved over to lean his back against the wall. Pockface leaned against the wall and folded his hands over an ivory handled revolver shoved inside his belt.

The man with the campaign hat moved down next to Pilar and leaned on the bar. He said something Padget couldn't hear. A pang of jealousy hit Padget in the stomach; the man was altogether too familiar with Pilar.

Without being told, the bartender lined up shot

glasses in front of each bandit and poured tequila. The tall man tossed down the drink and spoke to Pilar.

She didn't reply and turned toward Padget. The bandit grabbed her arm.

Pilar jerked free, spilling beer and almost dropping the tray. "Let go of me."

Anger replaced jealousy in Padget, as Pilar dodged the outstretched hand and hurried across the floor. Still carrying the tray with the spilled beer, she reached the table and whispered, "Have care, that one is Tomas Urbina. Es un mal hombre."

Padget felt the hair on the back of his neck rise. Hell, a man with one eye could see that. "Sit down, Pilar, Ochoa is about to tell me how he put the quietus on a lion out near Hachita." If these hombres wanted to fight, he and Ochoa were in it up to their butts.

He looked at Pilar. Her eyes were wide and fearful and she kept glancing at the Mexicans along the bar.

His head inclined slightly to one side, the tall man scowled in their direction. He tilted his head toward the end of the bar and one of the bandits moved to the wall on the left and leaned against it, his feet spread apart. He looked straight at Padget, folded his arms across is chest and grinned.

Padget felt the tensing up of the muscles along his shoulders. "Get ready, Ochoa, things are about to go to hell in a hand basket." He spoke low, out of the side of his mouth.

Urbina quit the bar and walked toward their table. He smiled as he moved across the floor and his spurs made chinking sounds against the tile. Sweat shone bright through the black stubble on his face. A braided rawhide quirt hung from his right wrist. It swung back and forth with each step the bandit took.

With his hand close to his pistol, Padget watched the tall Mexican approach. He was aware that the bandits against the bar were smiling; waiting for whatever might happen. Out of the corner of his eye Padget glanced at the bandit leaning against the wall to his right.

The tall Mexican reached the table. Here it comes, Padget thought. With his left hand the bandit leader caught Pilar by the arm. "Querida, it's been a long ride. Come. Leave these gringos and drink with real men."

Anger coursed though Padget. Who in the hell did this Mexican think he was anyway. "Maybe that trashy behavior is acceptable where you come from, but this is Texas. The lady doesn't need you to tell her what to do and she sure as hell doesn't need you to pick her friends. Take your damned hands off her, I won't tell you again!"

Urbina's eyes widened, narrowed to slits, and a wild look of hate crossed his face. With the speed of a striking rattlesnake he lashed out with the quirt. After that everything happened at once.

The quirt never reached its destination. Padget caught it in his left hand and pulled, jerking with all his strength.

Pulled off balance, Urbina pulled back.

Using the motion to step forward, Padget put his weight into an overhand punch, hitting Urbina in the solar plexus.

The bandit doubled over in pain.

Padget released his hold on the quirt and shifted his weight. He hit Urbina at the base of the jaw with his left fist, slamming the Mexican headlong onto the floor.

As the bandit leader fell, Padget heard the elongated explosion two pistols make when they go off at the same time. He jerked his Colt and still crouched, pointed it at the five men at the bar. Two of the Mexicans were down on the floor, slumped under their sombreros. The man on the left was lying on his back with his right hand holding an unfired pistol. As Padget watched, the bandit's legs twitched in death.

He swung the muzzle from left to right and back again. "You all right, Pard?" he asked Ochoa.

"Gooder'n snuff," Ochoa said.

The Mexican on the right was sitting down with his legs stretched in a vee in front of him, and except for the blood seeping from his mouth looked like a drunk sleeping it off. A Colt, half drawn from its holster, dropped to the floor as the dying bandit fell over on his side.

The sound of the pistol hitting the floor provoked one of the bandits to grab for his pistol.

Padget and Ochoa fired at the same time. Two bullets slammed through the bandit and into the bar. The man toppled forward onto his face and the smell of gunpowder permeated the air.

"Manos arribas." Ochoa called out. The remaining four Mexicans stretched their arms over their heads. One knocked off his sombrero in his hurry to obey.

The bartender, who had dropped behind the bar when the fight started, stood up with his hands raised. After that, no one moved so much as an eyebrow.

Padget looked at Ochoa. Wisps of smoke floated out of the barrels of both of Ochoa's pistols and both were cocked. He turned to look at Pilar. She was standing at the table, one hand at her throat, the other clutching the back of a chair.

Padget walked over and looked at the man who lay against the right wall. Blood was seeping from a hole in the center of his chest. Making sure he didn't get between Ochoa and the four Mexicans at the bar he then walked over to the other man on the floor. This one had a hole in his chest about an inch to the right of center. The third man had two holes an inch apart over his heart.

It was plain to see that the remaining Mexicans had any interest in continuing the fight. With fearful eyes they watched Ochoa who was crouched like a tiger ready to spring.

Reaching down, Padget grabbed Urbina under the arms and jerked him to his feet. He pulled the .44 Russian pistols from the holsters and threw them behind the bar. He found a knife tucked in the back of Urbina's belt and pitched it onto the table. Motioning with his Colt, Padget told the four Mexicans to drop their gun belts.

THERE AIN'T NO MONEY IN IT

"Afuera. Llevan los muertos," Ochoa told them.

The Mexicans dragged the dead men from the cantina across the hotel lobby and into the yard where the horses were tied. Padget left the discarded guns on the floor and followed Ochoa into the yard. He went to the bandit's horses, removed the rifles from their saddles and dropped them in a pile on the ground. He found a pistol in one of the bandit's saddle bags and added it to the pile. Ochoa told the bandits to tie the dead men across their horses and mount up.

Urbina, still groggy from the punch, tried to mount his horse. He lost his balance and fell back to the ground. Padget holstered his pistol and pulled him to his feet. "Get on your horse, greaser, and go back to Mexico where you belong."

Urbina staggered, caught his balance and walked to a big gray gelding, grabbed the horn and dragged himself into the saddle. He clutched the reins in his left hand and looked straight at Padget. Without a trace of fear he said, "My name is Urbina, Tomas Urbina. Remember it, because I will remember this always."

With that, he swung his horse's head and jabbed spurs into the gelding's sides. The big gray squealed and took off at a run, jumped the fence and was into the river and out of sight before anyone could move. The four riders followed, leading the three horses with the dead men slung across the saddles.

Pilar, Ochoa, and Padget stood in the yard looking at each other. Pilar stood with her arms crossed over her breast, Ochoa held his carbine with the stock on his right hip, Padget rubbed the knuckles of his right hand. "Have you ever seen any of those hombres before, Pilar?"

She nodded. "Yes, Urbina, and two of the men you shot and perhaps one or two of the others, they're all insurrectos. They fight to free the poor people from the yoke of tyranny."

"Do they come here often?"

"They have been here several times. They usually come with their leader, a man named Francisco Villa."

"What are they doing around here?"

"The one called Villa has a cousin, Lupe Sanchez, on the other side of the river. He comes to visit her, usually to give her money."

"They look more like bandits than revolutionaries."

Her eyes flashed. "They are not bandits; they

are insurrectos, the only men in Mexico who will fight the hacendados and the rurales. And they are generous to the poor people on the other side of the river. Whether you like it or not, there will be a revolution, and those men are a big part of it. Diaz will soon be overthrown. It has taken a long time, but it will happen soon."

"You sound glad."

"I am glad. It is the only way the poor people of Mexico will ever escape slavery."

Ochoa broke in. "Maybe we ought to call the sheriff. Do you have a telephone here, Pilar?"

"There won't be any need to call the sheriff," Jewell Rudd rasped from behind them. "I would appreciate it if you boys would just ride out of here. You've done enough damage already and they may come back. I don't want you to turn my hotel into a battle ground."

Padget turned to look at her. "What if they do come back?"

"They've been here before. They don't give us any trouble," Jewell said. She picked up a shotgun leaning against the wall.

Bandit growled. Padget snapped his fingers lightly and the growling stopped. He motioned with his right index finger, and the blue heeler ran across the yard and jumped up behind the cantle of his saddle. Skeeter rolled his eyes and stepped to the side, then settled down.

Jewel Rudd nodded toward Padget's rifle and saddlebags lying on the hard packed ground beside her. "Pick up your traps and get away from here for awhile."

"Mrs. Rudd," Padget began...

Jewel Rudd motioned with the shotgun. "I don't need an argument from you, just get on your horses and ride on out of here. Do it before I get mad."

What the hell had gotten into her? Padget wasn't ready to leave. There were a lot of questions left unasked, and he didn't know when he would be able to see Pilar again. Not wanting to cause Jewell further distress he put his hands up in mock surrender.

He picked up his saddlebags and hefted them over his shoulder, and then careful not to anger her more, picked up his rifle. Holding it by the stock, he gently pushed it into the saddle scabbard. Ochoa was already mounted.

Padget put his left boot into the stirrup and swung into the saddle, lifting his leg and bending his right knee to miss his dog. Reining his horse around, he nodded to Pilar. "Hasta mas ver," he said, as he raised his hand to his hat brim. "Mrs. Rudd." He touched his horse with his spurs and moved away from the hotel.

Chapter Nineteen

The trail broke out of the chaparral choked canyon and onto the wide valley floor. Here and there a sotol plant thrust its single stalk above the chemise and sagebrush. Padget pushed his hat back and scratched is head. "That's a first for me."

"Getting run off?"

"Having a woman run me off with a shotgun."

"I guess she didn't much appreciate us shooting up her hotel," Ochoa said.

"God bless her heart, she's seen a lot of hard times in her life. An Apache war party staked her husband Clayton over an ant hill, and her oldest son got killed at Antietam. Indians, horse thieves, bandits, droughts have sure as hell been hard on her. I can't blame her for not trusting anybody. Hell, she had three daughters die of scarlet fever, all within a week of each other. And as far as I know, her youngest son Dixie's still running from the law. He jumped bail a few years back and is hiding out in Mexico from a federal warrant. She's got to be tougher than whang leather just to survive down here. No, I can't say I blame her."

Ochoa shoved a wad of chewing tobacco into his mouth. "Are you going to tell the sheriff?"

"The sheriff will want to know about those bandits being on this side of the river and I want to get our licks in before someone else gets to him."

They rode silently for a ways; finally Padget said. "That little exhibition back there... you share any of your trade secrets? First time I ever saw a man use two pistols at one time."

"That's why I carry two."

"A man usually packs two guns in case he shoots his pistol empty," Padget said.

Ochoa spat a stream of tobacco juice at the edge of the trail. "It wasn't all that much; I had both pistols out when that second hombre started moving. When that tall hombre made his move I was ready. The rest was just a little trick my uncle Lyle showed me when I was a kid."

"It was enough to save our butts back there," Padget said.

"That big ugly sucker thought he was the cock of the walk, didn't he. That is, until you put the quietus on him. That was one heck of a punch; out before he hit the floor. Tell you what, you show me how to throw a punch like that and I'll show you that little trick Uncle Lyle showed me."

Padget pulled his hat low over his forehead. Skirting the edge of a buffalo wallow, he noticed tracks of several horses. The grass was cropped down. Pulling up, he dismounted to look at the tracks.

Ochoa leaned on the pommel of his saddle and looked down at him. "Were you scared back there?"

Padget remounted. "Me? Scared? Up against a room full of Mexican bandits, all of them loaded for bear and itching for a fight? Damned right I was scared. But, that was before I found out I was running with a gun hand."

"Sure is a pretty woman back there," Ochoa said.

"You noticed that too did you?" Padget said.

"A man would have to be dead not to notice."

A covey of bob white quail ran from a clump

of cat claw to another, calling to each other as they ran. Right behind them a fox burst from the chaparral. Skeeter jumped sideways and started to buck. Jarred out of his thoughts, Padget pulled the roan's head up. The horse crow hopped a couple of times and quit.

Seeing the riders, the fox skidded to a halt and disappeared into the chaparral the way he came. Belle ran into the brush after him and Ochoa whistled her back. "Come on girl. Stay with me."

Padget spurred Skeeter into a lope. He wanted to get the talk with the sheriff over with and it wasn't going to be fun.

Chapter Twenty

Jewell Rudd was angry. She stood with her hands on her hips looking at three dark brown stains on the cantina's wooden floor. "Damn, damn, damn." She kicked the mop bucket, spilling soapy water across the floor.

Why the hell did those two Rafter J hands have to be around when Urbina showed up? It was enough to harelip the governor.

Picking up a brush she got down on her knees and began to scrub the floor. "Don't just stand there, Pilar, let's get this mess cleaned up." Her motions became more agitated. "We're living dangerous as dynamite." She wiped the water off the floor with a bar towel and stood up, pulled a chair out from the table and clumped down in it.

Pilar folded a bar towel and wiped the floor

dry. Wiping the perspiration from her cheek with the back of her hand she wrung out the towel and placed it across the lip of the bucket.

Jewell poured a stiff shot of whiskey into a glass and drank it in one swallow. She pointed to a chair across the table. "Sit down, girl." She motioned again to the chair across the table. Pilar sat down.

"What went on in the bar, Pilar?" She refilled her glass. "That damn fight's going to cause all hell to break loose, who started it anyway?"

Pilar grimaced. "Tomás."

"What set him off?"

"Nothing set him off, he was looking for trouble when he came stomping in ... he got angry...I was talking to Wes and Dave...you know how men are..."

Jewel looked at her. Pilar blushed. "Well, they are."

"Villa's not going to like this one damn bit," Jewell said, "and I sure as hell don't want the sheriff down here."

"Dixie?" Pilar said.

"Tell me this; what have you said to give Urbina a reason to start a fight over you?" She watched Pilar's face closely.

"I've talked with Tomás, but never... anything about...that would make him think..."

"Like you came on to Padget?"

"I didn't come on to Padget! Even if I did, no man owns me."

"No?"

"Just because I had a beer with an old friend..."

"Making eyes at him – you knew he was a ranger in Arizona."

"What do you mean by that?" Pilar asked.

"Lawmen usually don't change. We've got to get those guns into Mexico. If we don't, you can kiss the revolution adios. And if Padget gets wind of what we are doing, he's likely to bring the house down."

"You think...?"

"I don't know, but there's too much riding on this to let a silly flirtation between you and some ex-ranger, who doesn't give a damn for Mexicans anyway, ruin everything."

"I wasn't flirting."

"I wasn't flirting," Jewel mocked.

"There's more to it than that."

"Like what?" Jewell said.

"Wes was the first man, any man, who ever stood up for me."

"And shot my place up doing it," Jewel said.
"That part scares me."

"It should. Your two cowboys killed three men in there and did it without even breaking a sweat."

"Oh my God, I know. Tomás's men outnumbered them four to one. I didn't think they had a chance, yet they just shot their way out of it. It was over before you could count three. Proficient, ruthless even... When the action started, they didn't hesitate. I've never seen two men work so well together... it makes me go all queasy in the stomach."

"Just like he did back in school?"

Pilar's brown eyes flashed. "I've never seen a man killed before today. One minute they were standing there; the next they were dead. It was so sudden."

"Men get killed on this border, Pilar, and you had better get used to it. The revolution is on its way; a lot of men are going to get killed pretty soon." Men dying didn't bother her she had seen too much of it for that. If the rich bastards who owned everything got killed so much the better.

Chapter Twenty-one

The single room behind the court that housed the sheriff's office was cramped. A woman swept the stairs that lead up to the jail on the second floor. Padget waited for the sheriff to respond. Pete Moore sat in a swivel chair behind a desk shoved against one wall, getting fat from too much easy living since he quit cowboying. He leaned back in the swivel chair and swung his feet up on a desk that had burned by a hundred cigarettes and scarred by spur rowels. He scowled at the two cowboys standing in front of his desk. "Who did you say they were?"

"Mexicans. Bandits from the way they looked," Padget said. "They were all carrying rifles, pistols, enough ammunition to start a war." Pete most likely didn't give a damn about three Mexicans being shot, Padget thought. But having Mexican bandits running around in his part of El Paso County was a horse of different color.

The sheriff shouted through an open door. "Harve, come down here."

Boots clomped down the stairs and a tall man with a star pinned over his shirt pocket entered. He glanced at Padget and Ochoa, and then stood silently at the end of the sheriff's desk with his thumbs stuck in his belt.

Pete pulled a carbine from the rack behind his desk and tossed it to the deputy who caught it with one hand. "Ride over to the Ranger camp and tell them there's a bunch of Mexican bandits down around Indian Hot Springs. Tell them that two Rafter J hands shot a couple of them yesterday. Tell them to get word out to Doggie Wilson and Jack Hightower. They'll want to know."

The deputy turned to go.

"Before you leave town," the sheriff continued, "stop by and tell Ma I'll be a little late for supper." The sheriff stood up from his desk. "You boys come with me. I want to talk with Bill Matson. He's in town and still has his hand in with the Rangers."

A man and woman, both suntanned and gray, sat in a porch swing drinking coffee. The man was tall and heavy framed, the woman slender and graceful. "Hello, Pete."

Padget looked at Bill Matson, feeling the scrutiny of Bill's piercing look. Recognition spread across Bill's face. "I heard you were back," he said.

"Good afternoon, Bill." Padget shook Bill Matson's hand, and turned toward the woman. He removed his hat. "Mrs. Matson."

"Bill, these boys got into a fracas with some Mexican bandits down at Ojos yesterday," the sheriff said. "It is probably the same bunch that's been stealing horses."

Bill's eyes flashed. "The hell you say, who's that with you, Wes? I don't believe I've seen him before."

"This is David Ochoa, we go back a ways. He's the hunter Walt sent for. I didn't see anything to make me think they were rustlers though."

"Bandits, rustlers, the same breed of cat," the sheriff said.

"I don't know if they're rustlers or not, but the same bunch paid John Branson a visit four or five nights ago. He fed them and sent them on."

The sheriff shook his head. "John won't feed no rustlers."

"He won't turn a hungry man away either. He's got all his riders carrying saddle guns and that's because of his losing stock to the jaguars. If they were rustlers, by now he and Griego would be robbed blind."

Bill leaned forward in his chair. "You said jaguars. Do you mean there is more than one?"

"We're pretty sure there are two."

"No wonder we've been losing stock, what about that bunch of Mexicans Pete's talking about? Here, sit down. How about a cup of coffee?"

Padget dropped into the chair Bill indicated. "Branson and Griego both swear they're bandits rather than rustlers, Griego thinks they are running guns into Mexico. He believes somebody's getting ready for a fight down there."

"There might just be something to it this time, but I doubt it." Bill pointed toward a chair. "Have a seat, Dave, you take cream and sugar?"

The sheriff shook his head to the offer of a seat. "Something to what?"

"The stories we keep hearing about them being fed up with Diaz."

"Well, ain't been no shots have been fired yet.

All that talk about revolution is just an excuse for them to come across the river. John Hunnicut lost thirty head of rough stock last month. We trailed them through Red Bull Canyon as far as the river. They're moving stolen stock into Mexico. Harve's making the rounds right now about this bunch down at Ojos." He shuffled his feet. "I've got to get on home to supper. Say hello to Walt and Claire." The sheriff touched his hat to Dorothy.

Dorothy Massy watched him leave. "You boys stay for supper. You won't get to Eagle Springs in time to eat."

The late afternoon sun glinted on her eyeglasses as Dorothy refilled Padget's coffee cup. "How is Claire getting along, Wes?"

"She was up and around when we left," Padget said. Getting ready for Thanksgiving."

Bill shoved his plate back. "I heard that a doctor from El Paso was taking care of her."

Padget used a biscuit to wipe the last of the gravy from his plate and shoved it into his mouth. "The doctor wants her to slow down some, but you know Aunt Claire. He did say she had a few more years left in her though." A whiff of hot peaches and sugar reached his nostrils. He put his coffee cup down and took the bowl Dorothy handed him.

The first taste burned his mouth, and he jerked the spoon away. He blew on it to cool it off.

Ochoa picked up a spoon. "Walt told us that you had to punch a hole in some rurale down in McNary," he said around a mouthful of cobbler.

"You heard about that? Talk sure gets around," Bill said. "Actually, it was in Por Venir."

Padget took another bite of cobbler. "What happened that got you crosswise with a rurale, Bill?"

"Damned if I know. I'd been across the river before and never had a problem, even when the rurales was in town. Hell, I even talked to this Garza once or twice. He's never been overly friendly, but that day he was bent out of shape about something."

"What made him pick on you?" Padget said. He pushed his empty peach cobbler dish to the middle of the table, drained his coffee cup and set it alongside the cobbler dish.

"Not a thing that I could see. He said I couldn't carry a pistol in Mexico. Hell, I had it stuffed down in my waist where you could hardly see it. He said he was going to arrest me for bringing arms into Mexico."

"Running guns?" Ochoa said.

Bill looked around and picked up a well-used briar bulldog pipe from the table beside his chair and loaded it. He packed the tobacco with his thumb and pulled a wooden match from his vest pocket, scratched it underneath the table and held it over his pipe, twirling the flame. Shaking the match out, he flipped it into a coffee can on the porch. Bill blew out a great cloud of dense blue smoke that hung under the porch roof in a thick haze. "I don't know what was on his mind. He told me I was under arrest and that he wanted my gun. He must've thought he had me buffaloed. Well that's his mistake; he should have already had his gun out. I drew my Colt and got off four shots while he was getting off one. He hit me in my left leg though. I hung on to the bar and just kept shooting 'till my Colt was empty. Finally, he went down, and after a while stopped kicking. When I was pretty sure he couldn't shoot anymore, I made it out to my horse, climbed aboard and parted the river so fast I didn't even get wet."

Bill rubbed his leg and stretched it out in front. "My leg was hurting like hell so I tied my bandanna around it and rode on into McNary, and then I came on home." Bill took a sip of his coffee. "Dorothy swabbed it out. The bullet missed the bone; it's getting better every day."

Ochoa shook his head at a second helping of cobbler. "Diaz's bunch running scared, are they."

"Talk's cheap," Bill said, "they may want to fight, but so long as the pelados don't have guns I doubt there's much of anything's going to happen. Bandits and rurales run this part of Chihuahua, and if you ask me, the rurales are worse than the bandits. If they arrest you, it's a one way ticket to the graveyard. They work for the hacendados and keep the peons in line. That's just about all they do." He blew a smoke ring and watched it disappear, and then blew another.

"You don't think there is much chance for a revolution then?" Padget said.

"I don't know who's going to lead it, whoever he might be; he had better be pretty good? Say what you want to about Diaz, he has a good Army."

"I hear the name Madero mentioned," Padget said.

Bill relit his pipe. "That little sawed off runt? That's a laugh."

"You believe all the talk about revolution is just talk and you don't think that anyone's going to stand up to Diaz?" Ochoa said.

"There's one hombre, an outlaw named Villa.

He's got quite a following, or so I've been told. He keeps the rurales pretty busy between El Paso and Piedras Negras anyway. Funny guy for a bandit though, he don't drink or smoke, neither one. I've heard he has a cousin, a woman who lives across the river at Ojos Calientes. But can he stand up to the army? No, I don't think he or any other bandit can."

Padget held his hand over his cup when Mrs. Matson started to refill it. "Did you ever hear of a Mexican named Tomás Urbina? He was with that bunch Ochoa and I had the trouble with. He's rides for Villa I'm told. He and some other Mexicans have been hanging around Ojos Calientes."

"Urbina? No, I can't say that I have, but he would have to be with Villa or he wouldn't be in this part of country. Between El Paso and Ojinaga; Villa's top dog on the other side of the river."

Padget stood up and pushed his chair back "If we are going to get home tonight we better get going. Mrs. Matson thanks for supper, especially the cobbler."

Padget and Ochoa were saddling up when Dorothy Matson walked out into yard waving a package wrapped in paper and tied with a string. Padget jerked the cinch tight and turned toward her.

"Wes, I almost forgot, will you take this pattern catalog to Claire? It came in just last month and I know she'll want to see it."

The trail to the Rafter J passed the Macadoo ranch house and they stopped to water the horses. "Bill seems like he knows which end of a gun the bullet comes out, but he moves kind of slow for a pistolero," Ochoa said.

"Generally, Bill is pretty level headed, but he can be a mean son of a bitch when he's been drinking. It doesn't happen much anymore, since he married Dorothy. She's taken most of the kink out of his tail. Still, mixing it up with Bill is kind of like kicking a rock; you nearly always come away wishing you hadn't. And another thing, being old doesn't mean he's slow ... I saw Bill use a six gun once, he made greased lightening look like sorghum molasses in the winter. I doubt that he's slowed down much."

They gave the catalog to Claire and rode back to the Macadoo place. They had to quit fooling around and get after the lions; Walt would be all over them like the wrath of God if they didn't produce.

Chapter Twenty-two

Ochoa enjoyed preparing for a hunt. If the truth were to be known, he loved preparing for anything. He dug his traps out of a canvas bag, selected several number four and a half traps and inspected the drag chains. He replaced two broken, and seven damaged links that he thought might break if a jaguar put up a hard enough fight.

He hauled water from the well, filled a wash tub that he had set on top of the stove and dropped in the traps. Jaguars usually avoided human smell around a carcass and the only way to get rid of the smell was to boil the traps. Waiting for the water to heat, Ochoa pulled a jar out of his saddle bags. It was rolled in an old feed sack and tied with a piece of string. He untied the string, unrolled the feed sack and laid it aside. He looked at the pint Mason jar. It was about three quarters full of a thick, dark brown liquid. He picked it up and shook it, unscrewed the lid and held it out to Padget.

"This works on lions. It should work pretty well for jaguars. Take a whiff." The fetid odor of rotting flesh filled the room.

Padget jerked his head away from the jar. "Whew. Put the damned lid back on, Mano, that'd make a buzzard puke."

It was always that way when someone smelled it the first time. "Cats seem to like it," Ochoa said with a smile on his face.

"What's it made of?"

Ochoa replaced the lid. "Wildcat piss, rattlesnake, ripe prairie dog."

Padget stepped back from Ochoa. "Most God awful stuff I ever smelled. Hard to believe anything would even get close to it."

"Critters don't feel about smells the way humans do," Ochoa said. He wrapped the jar back in its cover and retied the string. "A dog will get down and roll in a carcass that's all melted down and stinking to high heaven."

"You have any idea where we might find those lions?"

Ochoa shook his head. "No more than you do.

We'll most likely have to wait until they make another kill."

"There are a hundred places between Eagle Peak and Quitman Canyon for those lions to lie up in," Padget said. "The Apaches used this area all the time, and the Army never did run down a renegade band of Mescalaros that pillaged this country for years."

"What I can't figure out, is why anyone would want to live in this country at all," Ochoa said.

"That's hard to say. It's always been tough place to live. Never was much grass and cows have to walk so damn far to get enough to eat, they use up whatever strength they get just going to water. If it weren't for the Army there wouldn't be anyone living here at all. It's a hard country, but the people here seem to love it. Walt tells me that Apaches ran through this country unchecked, right up to the time I was born," Padget said.

Ochoa coiled the drag chains around the traps and repacked them. "Sometimes trouble comes on two legs, sometimes four, and sometimes it snakes up on you a slithering along the ground." He tied the top of the sack. "If my hunch is right, finding those lions is going to take a lot of hard riding, and we'll probably be all over this country before we're done."

Padget nodded. "One blessing though, there aren't many places for them to get water; the river, a stock tank or two and that's about it," he said. "Where do you plan on starting?"

"Where they chewed up that cowboy."

They ran in the horses and spent the rest of the day trimming hooves and re-shoeing them for the hard trail ahead. It was dark when they quit working.

Clouds squeezed in between the Quitmans and Eagles forming a low ceiling over the valley. The horses were nervous and had to be lassoed. Padget and Ochoa saddled up and packed the equipment in the cold, quiet dawn. The wind was still, nothing moved and the birds were silent. Dark gloomy clouds crowded around the peaks of the Quitman Mountains, casting dark shadows against the sloping foothills. The Eagle Mountains looked like they were painted in chocolate. Bandit and Belle trotted in a wide circle at the edge of the hard packed yard, anxious to get on the trail. With traps, equipment, and food to last four days they rode out.

A premonition of danger suddenly gripped

Ochoa. Then, just as suddenly, it was gone. He shook off the feeling and whistled for Belle. He looked over the saddle at Padget. "I've got a sneaking hunch we'll hear from those lions pretty soon."

Chapter Twenty-three

Lost in thought, Padget looked down at the remains. She hadn't been much of a cow, even before the lions got to her. What they had left, a brindle hide and one crooked horn hadn't been that hard to find. The circle of buzzards swirling over Cottonwood Canyon signaled the kill site. He was surprised it was so close to where they had found the dead cowboy. Padget wondered what happened to her calf and he didn't know how in the world he missed those tracks the first time. It was pretty obvious the lions hadn't gone far after the storm. Could they still be close by? Padget felt the surge of excitement. The familiar pad prints showed plain in the soft ground. The tracks led away from the kill, southeast over arroyo-cut country toward Oxford Canyon.

They crossed two canyons south of where they

found the cow. The tracks turned up into the rim rock toward Eagle Peak and the trail became difficult to follow. Suddenly, Belle bayed and scrambled up the trail. Ochoa whistled and called out, "Get back here." The black and tan stopped and looked at Ochoa and back in the direction the trail. She started off again following the tracks.

Ochoa whistled once more and Belle slowly came back to his side. "Those lions will eat you up and spit you out in little pieces if you don't stay with me," he said. Leaning down over the saddle, watching the ground, Ochoa followed the trail.

Padget rode off to the side, looking for tracks and trying to remember what he knew of this part of the country. He had been here only one time, and that was before he went to Arizona.

The trail ran through an outcrop of shale and the tracks disappeared in the hard rock. Belle and Bandit scrambled over the loose shale with their noses close to the ground until they ran into a vertical rock wall. The dogs stopped and ran back and forth along the base, frustrated by the barrier.

Turning aside, the cowboys sidetracked until they found a break in the rim rock which led to the upper slopes. On top, they picked up the tracks; they were still headed into Oxford Canyon.

THERE AIN'T NO MONEY IN IT

A hundred yards into the canyon, the trail led into a pond surrounded by Madrone and Hackberry trees; coming out the other side, they continued up over a steep ridge.

Padget pushed his hat back on his head and studied the trail, still trying to remember the trip through this part of the Eagle Mountains with his uncle years before. Coming to a decision, he turned to Ochoa. "We'll have to turn around. If my memory's right, there's a trail a little way back that leads over to the next canyon. With any luck we ought to be able to pick up the tracks on the other side."

They turned around and rode back until they found a faint pathway through the chaparral. The trail got so steep that Padget had to use his spurs. The roan lunged upward, lost his footing on the steep slope, and slid downhill. Afraid Skeeter would fall, Padget stepped down and grabbed the horse's headstall and pulled. The effort helped the roan regain his balance and they made it to the top.

It took the better part of an hour to find the tracks and the horses were tiring. A short distance farther on the tracks disappeared on a granite outcrop. They dismounted, loosened the cinches, and left the horses to rest; they quartered the area on foot, cutting for sign. There was not a track, a scuff mark, or any indication that the lions had ever been there, the jaguars had simply vanished.

Ochoa turned to Padget and said, "I never thought it would be easy, but this is another matter entirely." He turned his horse. An hour later they were back to the carcass of the dead cow.

Stepping down off his horse, Ochoa pulled the sack of traps onto the ground and separated the chains. Curious, Padget watched him. "What makes you think this is going to work? Didn't you say that traps didn't any good with that lion down in Hachita?"

"We will have to check them in a couple of days and see."

"We're only a couple of hours away from Ojos Calientes," Padget said. "We can cut for sign along the river. Maybe the lions headed back to Mexico."

"Maybe, and maybe that good looking, long haired señorita is there too," Ochoa said. "Not that thought ever entered your mind."

Reaching the river between the Griego ranch and Ojos Calientes, Padget pulled up and pointed to the ground. "Seven or eight riders and they weren't in any particular hurry." In the thick dust of the road hoof prints of several horses showed up plainly. The tracks entered the road from the south and turned west.

"What do you make of this, Campo?" Padget nodded toward the tracks. "The same bunch we had that run in with?"

"If it is, they picked up some more men," Ochoa said.

The sun slipped down behind the mountains and a mist rose from the river. It spread out in a dense fog over the bank and crept across the land. An eerie quiet settled over the darkness. No a sound could be heard from the brush along the river. The fog grew thicker; even the chinking of the bit chains seemed muffled.

"It's darker than the inside of a coal mine," Ochoa said.

As the fog got thicker, Padget couldn't make out the trail. He got down from his horse and walked. "We ought to come to a fork in the trail that leads to Ojos pretty soon — here we go." He remounted and turned up hill, climbing slowly through the thick chaparral. Padget could not see the trail and he let the roan pick the way up and around the face of the hill.

The trail climbed several hundred feet, then

flattened out where it crossed a dry arroyo. Padget pulled his bandanna off and wiped the moisture from his face. He peered into the night looking for a familiar landmark. As he did, the lights of the cantina at Ojos Calientes appeared dimly through the fog. "There!" Padget said, pointing down hill toward the lights.

There were no other horses at the ranch when they rode into the hotel yard and stepped down. Flipping the reins over the rail, Padget pulled a slip-knot in them. He motioned for Ochoa to follow and walked through the hotel into the cantina where Pilar stood behind the bar polishing glasses. She turned when they walked in. Her eyes widened and her mouth bent into a smile when she saw him.

A voice from the rear of the room exploded the quiet of the cantina. "You boys are pushing your luck."

Padget turned around to look at the old woman. "Good evening, Mrs. Rudd," he said.

"I thought you boys would have stayed away from here. You must be gluttons for punishment," Jewel said.

"We were following the lions and the trail gave out not far from here," Padget said.

"You might as well stay for supper, it's about ready. You've got just about enough time to put your horses away and wash up," Jewel said.

Later, the four of them sat around the kitchen table eating enchiladas and chili rellenos. Padget pushed his plate back. "We saw tracks of seven or eight riders between here and Griego's place."

"That would probably be the tracks of a cavalry patrol out of Fort Hancock. They were by here this morning."

Pilar refilled their coffee cups and set the pot back on the stove. When she sat down her eyes rested on Padget's face for a long moment. She shook her head, and her black hair whirled around her face.

Padget felt his throat tighten, his voice sounded strange to him when he asked, "Anybody feel like playing cards?"

"You boys can stay up all night if you want to, but Pilar and I have work to do tomorrow. You probably want to talk to Ed Sherman, he lost a mare night before last, come on Pilar."

Padget and Ochoa saddled up and rode out of Ojos Calientes following the wagon road upriver and back over the route Ochoa had followed when they split up after the storm.

"There sure seems to be a lot of traffic crossing the Rio Grande. There were fresh tracks here the last time I was down this way," Ochoa said. Tracks of where ten shod horses came out of Mexico crossed the road and continued north into the Quitman Mountains showed plainly in the dust.

The Sherman ranch was tucked back in Red Bull Canyon near a seep spring. Ed Sherman was a bachelor and the place showed it; there wasn't anything on the ranch that wasn't absolutely necessary. Sherman's foreman guided them along a steep ridge through a low lying saddle that joined two jagged peaks and into Hackberry Canyon. He motioned with his right hand at the remains of a gray mare. "She was too old to ride; she came and went pretty much as she pleased. You could set your watch by her in the morning. She always showed up around daybreak, looking for a handout. When she didn't show up one morning, we went looking for her. Manuel found her, or what was left of her, night before last."

"We'll put some traps out, although I don't give it much chance, maybe they'll come back," Ochoa said. "It would be better if you keep your dogs home for awhile; they could lose a foot in one of these."

Two weeks later the cats had not returned, nor had anyone run across their tracks. Padget and Ochoa scouted the ridges, the arroyos, the canyons and the hills without success. October turned into November without a new kill. It seemed that the cats were gone.

Standing on a ridge overlooking Red Light Draw, Padget glassed the terrain with his field glasses and wiped his forehead with his sleeve. "Most likely they went back to Mexico."

Ochoa spat a stream of tobacco juice between his boots. "Maybe, maybe not."

Chapter Twenty-four

Early in November, Walt Johnson rode into Sierra Blanca to attend a stockman's meeting. The fall work at the ranch was nearly done and training had begun with a string of colts to be sold to the Army. By the end of the third week, the horses were gentle enough to sell for remounts.

Thanksgiving Day, Padget stood near the corral and watched two of the ranch hands sweep the yard. As far back as he could remember, Thanksgiving and Christmas were the only two holidays celebrated each year at the Rafter J.

Claire decorated the main house in fall colors. She covered the dining room table with a white linen tablecloth and placed a centerpiece of dried flowers; red, brown, and gold, in its center. Normally, Marie cooked whatever she chose, but on holidays Claire closely supervised the meal preparation. A wild turkey, brought in by Miguel was stuffed with piñon nuts and chocolate; cooking in the oven, it filled the house with the aroma of roasting turkey and could be smelled all the way to the bunkhouse.

Padget clapped Ochoa on the shoulder. "We've got plenty to be thankful for this year; Claire is up and healthy, the jaguar problem may not be completely solved, but we haven't had any trouble lately, and the horses are ready for market."

The Rafter J foreman Miguel and his wife Maria lived in a small house at one end of the ranch yard with their three children. Normally the family ate there alone, but on holidays everyone, including the ranch hands, was all expected to eat dinner in the main house. Consequently, the house was packed. Shrieking with laughter, children raced through the kitchen, chasing each other until Maria called them down.

Rosa, three years old and still sticky from hot chocolate, climbed into Walt's lap and gave him a kiss, smearing chocolate on this cheek. When she tried to wipe it off he stopped her. "It isn't often I get a kiss from such a pretty girl, I think I can stand a little bit of love in the form of hot chocolate, it may be the best kind anyway," he said.

Claire came over and sat on the arm of his chair. "You know I always wanted a daughter of my own," she said to Walt.

Walt patted her hand. "You're a little bit long in the tooth for that, Honey. Maybe you ought to talk to Wes. Its high time he settled down and quit running around."

Maria and Miguel's five year old, Thomas, followed Ochoa around imitating every move he made. Ochoa patted the top of his head and rubbed his stomach. Thomas mimicked every gesture. Soon everyone was laughing.

Twelve year old Manuel sat by Padget and asked him to tell stories about the Arizona Rangers and the outlaws he had known. With a very serious face, he announced to everyone that was going to be a ranger when he grew up.

Over the noise of Thanksgiving, Padget heard the sound of a fast running horse approaching. The noise broke through the holiday peace.

"Rider coming in fast," Walt said.

The men filed out of the house onto the porch just as Harvey Miller charged into the ranch yard, riding a lathered up, wall-eyed blue roan. He reined his horse to a stop.

"Get down, Harve," Walt said. "You're just in time for dessert."

"Don't have the time, Mr. Johnson. We're getting a posse up. Sheriff asked if you could spare a couple of hands to help out. We're forming up over at the Matson place. They run off about twenty head of Bill's horse stock. I need to get on back. Will you give us a hand?"

Walt nodded. "But hold on there, Harve, that roan is plumb run out, change mounts before you kill him. Shorty rope Banjo for him."

Harve swapped horses and rode off back the way he had come. When the deputy was out of the ranch yard Walt spoke. "Wes, you and Ochoa get your gear. Shorty, saddle up Blue and Dynamite for them. Miguel, have Maria put some grub together for these boys, enough for three or four days."

Billy Shackelford, the youngest cowboy that rode for the Rafter J, stood in front of Walt. "I'd sure like to go along Mr. Johnson."

"No, Billy. You don't have military experience. That's what the sheriff needs right now. Anyway we've got a lot of work to do. That new bunch of colts isn't even close to being ready."

Walt smiled. "And you're the best bronc rider we've got. I need you here."

Billy ran off to help Shorty Davidson catch the horses.

Chapter Twenty-five

Padget loosened the cinch on his horse and considered the five other riders already at the Matson ranch when he and Ochoa arrived. Each carried a rifle in his saddle boot; each wore a pistol. While he waited for the sheriff to appear, two more riders came in. One of the late arrivals read the brand on Padget's horse and rode over. "I wouldn't have recognized you, Wes."

Padget shook hands with the red headed cowboy and watched a smile appear on his face. "Well, if I was blind in one eye and couldn't see out of the other, I'd recognize you, Shorty McCorkle," Padget said.

Shorty was four or five years younger than Padget; somewhere in his mid-twenties.

"You've been gone a long time, Wes. Must be

ten or twelve years now."

"Try fifteen, Shorty," Padget said.

Before Shorty could answer, Bill Matson and the sheriff walked out of the house and onto the porch. They faced the riders and the sheriff held up his hand. He waited until everyone quieted down. "Pete Colmenaro got shot last night over in Binocular Canyon. He's alive—barely. He chanced onto a bunch of Mexican bandits running off some Diamond M horses and those murdering sons-of-bitches have a head start on us."

Bill Matson stepped down from the porch and took the reins of his horse from a rider. "Maybe we can catch them before they get too deep into Mexico. We're already a day behind." He stepped into the stirrup and swung on his horse. "Let's go."

He led the riders out of the ranch yard into the brush. The movement of the posse broke the stillness of the chaparral and a covey of quail whirred from the ground. Two of the horses tried to buck. The commotion startled a black tail doe with two fawns that disappeared into the sagebrush.

The posse picked up the trail of the stolen horses east of the Quitman Mountains and followed it through Binocular Canyon down to the Rio Grande. The tracks were less than two days old and easy to follow. They led across the river and turned southwest toward a small hamlet called Talón, located at a crossroads on the Mexican side.

The posse rode all day, reaching Hueso Spring before darkness overtook them. "There's water here. We'll make a cold camp. No fire. Don't know how far they are ahead," Bill Matson said. Guards were posted and Bill passed out cold biscuits and jerked beef. He put a piece of jerky in his mouth and looked around at the circle of cowboys. "They're traveling faster than we are. We'll be up early, so get some rest."

Padget sat on the ground, his back against his saddle, looking at the stars. He pulled a piece of jerky loose with his teeth, chewed it and took a bite of a cold biscuit that Maria had packed for them. "Mano, who watches your spread up in Colorado while you're down here chasing horse thieves?"

"I've got one hand, an old man who feeds the stock and makes sure the place doesn't catch fire," Ochoa said. "Why?"

"I don't know. I was thinking maybe I'd like to go elk hunting when we finish up here."

"We've got to catch those cats before we go anywhere."

"I said, after we finish."

"You're on, Compa. When we get those cats, we'll go visit Colorado for a spell. Maybe eat some tortillas and drink some tequila. Right now I'm going to catch some shut eye." Ochoa rolled over on his side and pulled a saddle blanket over his shoulders.

Padget could not go to sleep, and with a strange foreboding he watched a full moon climb in the sky. He stayed awake all night and the feeling was still there when he saddled his horse in the early morning.

Dawn was still four hours away when Bill got the riders up. There was barely light enough to track the stolen horses.

"Padget, you take the scout," Matson said. Padget spurred Dynamite and rode out in front. The rest of the posse followed him in single file. Shortly after sunup they reached the junction of Hueso and Armagosa Canyons. Stopping at the water hole located where the two canyons met, Padget studied the tracks. "They didn't make camp last night Bill," he said, "We're still a day and a half behind them." Bill spurred his horse into a lope, taking over the lead.

To make up for lost time the posse alternated

between a trot and a short lope. At mid-morning he pulled up and stepped down from his horse. "Okay, let's make a fire and have some coffee. We'll go on in half an hour. There's a little place called Talón on up ahead about seven or eight miles. Maybe they stopped there." Two hours later Bill led the posse into a group of weathered adobe huts clustered around a well.

Padget looked down on a white bearded old man. Wizened and gray with age, he squatted by the side of the well in the shade of the lone mesquite tree. His sombrero further shaded his face as he watched the riders. His eyes were sullen and hostile and opaque with cataracts. Just like an old wolf, Padget thought. He allowed his gaze to move over the scattered huts.

"Hola, Isidro," Bill Matson said. The old man squinted in the harsh mid-morning sun looking closely at Bill. Then recognition brought a smile that seemed to break his face. "Mi Capitan," he said.

Bill spoke to him again in Spanish. After a short time, people quietly began to appear from the adobe huts. Soon the street was filled with people staring at the posse. Unsmiling, and without apparent emotion, they watched the riders.

A pretty, young girl edged close to the old man who put his arm around her and smiled. "This is my niece, Juana. She will be fourteen tomorrow, Capitan."

Bill and the old man, with his arm still around his niece, continued to talk for awhile in Spanish. Finally, they stopped and Bill mounted his horse. He reached into his vest pocket and said, "Por tu Sabrina." He tossed a twenty dollar gold piece to the old man.

Turning to the posse, "They were here all right, but didn't stay; they picked up some grub and pushed on without resting. That was day before yesterday. The old man says the rurales are in the area too. Damn.... Come on." He reined his horse to the west and jabbed him with his spurs. The big gray leaped into a run.

Dust boiled up around them as the posse rode after him. Padget looked back and saw the pretty young girl standing with the old man, and though he didn't know why, he raised his hand in a farewell gesture.

The sun became hotter and the dust stirred up by the horses' hooves settled over the riders as they pursued the bandits into Mexico. Padget noticed that the vegetation began to thin out as they rode further into the desert. Chamise replaced mesquite as it grew drier, and salt bush soon replaced the chamise. The posse rode through the night and on into the early morning.

Abruptly, the tracks they were following scattered, going off in a dozen different directions. Padget rode to the crest of a small hill where he scanned the horizon with his field glasses. The flat desolate panorama offered nothing for his view. There was not even a wisp of dust to mark the riders they were following.

Bill rode up to him. "Not a sign, Bill, I'm sorry," Padget said.

Bill waved the posse around him. He sat his horse in the middle of the group, chewing a piece jerky. "Well, boys, that's it. We'll rest here tonight and start back tomorrow. Hell, we should've stayed home and enjoyed a good turkey dinner."

Matson pulled the saddle from his horse and dropped it on the ground. He slumped down against it and pulled a sack of Dukes Mixture from his vest. He rolled a cigarette and stuck it in his mouth. He struck a match on his chaps, lit it, sucked deeply and blew a smoke ring into the air. He took a deep breath and let it out slowly, reached into his saddle bags, took out a bottle, pulled the cork, and took a long swallow. Turning from the waist he handed the bottle to Padget.

    Disappointment was written all over Bill's face as Padget reached over his saddle to take the proffered bottle. Bill looks old, he thought. He drank and passed it to the next rider. "Cheer up, Bill, things will probably be better tomorrow."

Chapter Twenty-six

A strange apprehension filled Isidro. He shielded his eyes from the sun with his left hand as he looked at the dust cloud. He strained his eyes to see and suddenly, a line of riders appeared out of the brush. They wore high crown hats and short charro jackets. A chill ran up his back even though the morning was quite warm. He noted the sabers that were now visible in the hot morning sun. The sabers hung straight down from the saddles.

His apprehension changed to fear. Rurales! "Madre de Dios!" He turned to his niece. "Juana, go and tell the others to stay indoors."

The leader rode a big black horse to the well and reined his mount to a stop. Cold, merciless eyes stared down at Isidro. The other riders moved into a line that stretched across the narrow street.

"Buenos dias, señores," Isidro said.

The man on the big black looked down. "Buenos días, Viejo, how are you this day?"

Isidro felt a chill sweep over him again as he looked up at the unsmiling face. "I am well, and you, sir?"

"We are tired and our horses need water."

"Please! Water your horses."

The leader of the rurales did not move. "Tell me, Viejo; the riders that came through here yesterday, who were they?"

"Vaqueros."

"From which ranch?"

"I do not know. They didn't stop."

The rurale leader motioned at the well. "The only water within twenty miles and they didn't stop?"

"They watered their horses, but they were in a hurry. I didn't talk to them."

"Are you acquainted with a man named Villa?"

"No, Señor. I don't know him."

"Conoce Thomás Urbina?" The rurales now ringed the old man who looked up at them.

"No, Señor. No one named Tomás Urbina is known to me."

"That is fortunate for you. How are you called?"

The old man raised his chin. "Isidro."

"Fortunate, Isidro, because they are insurrectos."

"I do not know that word, sir." Isidro could hear the fear in his own voice.

"I think the riders who came through here yesterday were insurrectos."

"I don't know. I don't now what insurrectos are."

The rurales laughed. The rurale leader moved his horse closer to Isidro.

Isidro backed away to avoid the hooves of the big black. He backed into a rider behind him, lost his balance and fell. The gold coin given to him for his niece's birthday fell to the ground, and the hot sun glinted off of the coin.

Scared now, Isidro stood. "Sir, I don't believe they were insurrectos, they were only some vaqueros taking horses from Texas."

"If you don't know what insurrectos are...," The rurale leader stepped down and picked up the fallen coin. "What's this?" he asked. He turned the coin over in his hand.

Again Isidro felt the cold sweep through him

and he tried not to look at the coin.

The rurale spoke again. "They were not insurrectos eh? Manuel, see who is inside."

The rurales dismounted and two of them grabbed the old man, pinioning his arms. The rest searched the houses, prodding the unresisting people into the dusty street. One rurale dragged Juana into the square. She cried out when he twisted her arms behind her back.

Standing between two rurales, his arms pinioned behind his back, Isidro said. "Please, Señor, don't."

"Silence!" the leader said, and slapped Isidro across the mouth.

Juana bit the man holding her, in surprise, he relaxed his grip and she twisted out of his hands, running to her uncle. "Cobardes! You would hit an old man?"

The man whom she had bitten caught her by the hair, jerked her back and slapped her across the face. "You little whore."

"Cabron!" Isidro jerked free of the two rurales who held him. A knife flashed from his sash and before anyone could move, he plunged it into the throat of the man who had slapped Juana.

The knife stuck, and Isidro could not pull it

out. Jerking back, the man released his hold on Juana and reached for the knife. A look of panic crossed his face as he crumpled to the ground.

Another rurale hit Isidro in the head with the butt of a carbine, knocking him to the ground. Juana dropped beside him, holding his head in her arms. The rurale leader kicked her in the side. "Bitch! Tie him up! He will learn not to lie."

Juana doubled over and two rurales grabbed her. Two more pulled Isidro to his feet. This time, they tied his arms behind his back, dragged him over and roped him to the mesquite tree in the center of the square.

The leader pulled his knife and caught Isidro's right eyelid between his thumb and forefinger. The pain seared through Isidro as the rurale cut the eyelids from his eyes.

"Now, watch!" He grabbed the throat of Juana's dress and tore it down to her waist. He jerked it until Juana was naked before him. He removed his gun belt. "Hold her!"

Isidro tried to shut his lidless eyes. He could barely see through the blood as two rurales grabbed her and bent her face down across the well.

She seemed to be only partially conscious when the rurales spread her legs apart. They pushed her down with their hands and held her legs with theirs. Their spurs raked her calves, and she screamed as the rurale leader penetrated her.

Overcome by fear, one villager ran toward the brush. He was shot in the back as he ran. The shot set off the other rurales who began shooting the men of the village as they tried to run.

One man, faster than the others, made it to the brush. A rurale mounted his horse, pulled out his saber and followed him. The man didn't have a chance against the horse. The rurale swung the saber, hitting the man where his neck joined his shoulder, almost decapitating the running peon. The fugitive screamed and fell. The horse's hooves caught him in the middle of his back as the rurale rode over him. Isidro heard the sound of bones breaking.

They raped the women repeatedly. When it was over, the women huddled against the wall of one hut. Isidro could hear their whimpering. His niece, deathly silent, lay across the well, blood ran down her legs.

"Silence," the rurale leader shouted at the women. Most were too far gone to respond and continued to whimper.

He pulled his pistol, walked over to the nearest

woman, put the barrel of his pistol to her head, and pulled the trigger.

Her hair muffled the noise. As she fell forward, he shot the next woman. He continued to shoot until his pistol was empty.

One woman, a gaping hole where her left eye had been, tried to get up. The leader motioned and a rurale hit her in the head with the butt of his rifle. She lay still.

"What do you think now of lying, old man?" the rurale leader said. He pulled his knife and slowly plunged into Isidro's belly, twisting it as he withdrew it.

The pain was immense.

The rurale mounted his horse. "Vamanos."

Chapter Twenty-seven

A cold, gray, miserable dawn greeted the dejected riders as they rolled from their bedrolls. There had been no fire and there would be no breakfast. The sky was dark. Clouds blown in during the night shut out the sun and a cold west wind hurled dust and sand along the ground.

Padget pulled on his coat and thought about the warm cookhouse at the Rafter J. He took a brush from his saddlebags and swept the dust from Dynamite's back. He picked up each foot and checked the hooves. He thought of the Rafter J and could almost smell the coffee and hot biscuits. Satisfied with his work, he placed the blanket carefully on the roan's back and smoothed out the wrinkles. He swung the saddle in place, drew the cinch tight and jammed his Winchester in the saddle boot.

Stepping into the stirrup he eased his right leg over Dynamite's rump and gently talked him out of bucking. When he had settled into the saddle, he took a swig from his canteen. He swirled the water around and spat out the brown taste in his mouth. "Ochoa, when we get back to the ranch I'd like to go deer hunting. You want to go?"

Ochoa pulled on his coat. "Hunting's my middle name. I saw two pretty good bucks in Quitman Canyon when we were trailing those lions."

Padget turned to follow the posse back toward Texas. He looked over his shoulder at Ochoa. "There's a big, old mossy horned buck up near Eagle Peak that Shorty was telling me about the other day, said his rack looked like a Christmas tree."

The clouds piled higher as they rode on, and the darkness grew until Padget could barely see the horse in front of him. The wind moved around to blow from the north and a low moaning sound could be heard across the desert. He pulled his bandanna over his nose and tilted his hat against the wind blowing into his left ear.

Ochoa rode beside him, stirrup to stirrup. He removed his glasses and wiped the lenses with the tail of his shirt before putting them back on. Then squinting into the wind he turned to Padget. "I don't know what to make of it, doesn't smell like rain and it's not cold enough to snow...damned strange weather."

"Dynamite doesn't like it either. He's been hunting boogers since noon, and now he's acting like he was walking on eggs," Padget said.

They camped for the night in an arroyo, lit a small fire and made coffee. The night was cold and dark and long. Up before sunrise the posse saddled the horses and continued on.

The sun stood just above the horizon and would soon drop behind the hills. The shadows grew longer, and the day got colder.

"It seems like to me that we ought to be getting close to Talón pretty soon," Shorty McCorkle said.

"Back trail's always longer," Padget said. "Maybe we can get some frijoles and tortillas that haven't been packed all over creation."

Bill Matson held up his hand. The riders stopped, looking to see what caused the signal.

There, in the gray gloom Talón was just visible. Bill turned his horse and rode back to the posse. His face was stern and he spoke quietly to the riders. "Boys, I don't like the looks of this. Padget, you and Ochoa ride the flanks. Shorty, drop back a ways and watch the trail behind us. The rest of you boys come with me." He nudged his gray into a slow walk. The riders spread out around him.

Spurring his horse Padget rode to the north side of the trail; he glanced at Ochoa, pulled his rifle and broke into a lope. He placed his rifle across the pommel of his saddle and looked up at the sky. Vultures flew in a dark circle over the settlement of Talón.

The bodies lay broken upon the plain like rag dolls tossed aside, and the greasy odor of death hung like a cloud. Blue entrails trailed from lacerated bodies and white bones lay exposed to the cold. The old man hung from the mesquite where Padget had last seen him when he waved goodbye. The crows had been at work, pecking out his eyes and leaving lidless sockets to gape accusingly at the riders. Padget felt the gorge rise up in his stomach and he fought to keep from vomiting. He and Shorty McCorkle helped Bill Matson cut the old man down.

Chapter Twenty-eight

Numbed by the sheer savagery of the scene, Padget led Dynamite through the settlement, stepping around great splotches of blood, and looking closely at the mangled carcasses strewn unevenly up and down the street. He didn't know what he was searching for, but in the third hut he found her.

"Aaah, no," he said.

She lay sprawled on the floor, legs spread, her thighs red with blood from the rape. Embarrassed for her, he pulled off his jacket and spread it over her nakedness. He knelt and felt for a pulse. He saw the tooth marks where she had been bitten on her neck and face. Her left eye was purple and red, swollen shut. There was blood on her mouth and cuts on her lower lip.

He pushed a strand of sable colored hair out of her face and a faint quiver made him draw back. She was alive. She moaned as he lifted her head and her eyes flew open.

He rubbed her cheek with the back of his hand. "It's all right, Juana."

She screamed one long piercing cry and fainted. Her scream brought the other riders into the room, guns drawn. As they crowded around her, Padget pulled a serape off the wall. He covered the girl up to her chin. He stood as Bill came in.

Bill leaned down and examine her face, he shook his head. "I don't know, she's pretty far gone, probably won't make it through the night."

"Maybe not, but we can't just leave her here like this."

Bill pushed up his hat. "I guess we're going to have to, we can't take her with us, and we have to get back to the other side of the river before the rurales find us. It's tough, kid, but..."

Padget stared at Bill, thinking, you are one cold son of a bitch. He fought to keep control of his anger. "Well, you go on, Bill, I'm not going to leave her here."

Ochoa stepped around the group of cowboys. "I think maybe I'll stay with you, Mano."

Bill stood up. "You boys are grown men and can do what you want, but I wouldn't hang around here too long. Whoever did this may come back, she just isn't worth the risk." Bill turned to the other riders. "The best we can do is to bring those bodies into one of the huts and shut the door. The coyotes won't get to them. We'll make it back to the river before sunup if we hurry."

Padget watched the riders file from the room. He mulled over Bill's words. Bill wasn't afraid. It had to be that Bill considered most Mexicans just a little better than dogs and a raped, broken, Mexican girl just wasn't worth a gun battle.

Padget moved to the side as Ochoa brought a worn blanket into the hut and laid it over the unconscious girl. "She don't look so good, Mano."

Padget crouched by her side, holding her hand, talking softly, trying to ease her pain. The sound of the posse leaving subsided after a few minutes. This is bad, really bad, he thought. She is going to die if we don't do something. Feeling helpless, he looked up at Ochoa who was standing by the door of the hut clutching his rifle. Finally he made up his mind. "Dave, would you bring Dynamite? I can't just stand here and watch her die. I'm going to take her to Ojos Calientes. Mrs. Rudd has had plenty of practice doctoring people. At least there, we can give her a decent burial."

With Ochoa's help Padget wrapped the girl in the blanket and carried her outside. Ochoa reached for the girl. "Here, let me have her until you get on your horse."

Padget mounted and Ochoa handed Juana up to him. Padget took the girl across the saddle in front of him and held her in one arm. He nudged his horse and started off toward the river. Keeping the roan in a walk, he was careful not to injure the bruised and beaten girl further.

Ochoa mounted and followed. He carried his Krag in one hand, barrel up and the stock against his thigh.

The night wore on, the sky cleared, the cold intensified, and the girl shivered in her sleep. Padget clutched her tighter trying to protect her. His arm fell asleep from holding the girl. When Ochoa offered to take her, he shook his head in refusal. He was afraid that any move would drive her further toward death. A piteous moan, when he took her up on his horse, had been the only sound she had made that night.

They rode all the next day and still she did not wake. The horses were so tired that they began to stumble over the unevenness in the trail. Padget pushed on, trying against all hope to get her to someone who could help. Long after the sun had gone down the second day, they reached the river.

A wraith of mist hung over the Rio Grande, partially obscuring the far side. In the cold gloom of night, lit only by a sliver of the moon, the white stucco buildings of Ojos Calientes lay in dark shadows.

Unsure of his welcome, Padget handed the girl to Ochoa. He stepped back so that he could see the second story. He called out. "Mrs. Rudd! Pilar! Wake up!"

On the second story, someone lit a lamp. Padget could hear footsteps running along the balcony and Pilar appeared. Looking down she recognized the riders. "What are you doing here?" she asked.

"Pilar," Padget said, "open the door we've got a very sick girl here...from Talón. Please! She's hurt bad. I think she's dying."

Pilar disappeared and the front door opened. Jewel Rudd stood in the lamp light holding a shotgun. "Well, don't just stand there. Bring her in." She motioned them into the lobby.

Pilar appeared just as Padget lay the girl down on the couch. Pushing him out of the way she knelt down to examine the girl. Angrily she turned around, her eyes flashing. "This is Juana Paredes from Talón. What are you doing with her? Who did this?"

"Whoa, hold on," Padget said, "I don't know who did it. Whoever did it, murdered everyone there."

"What..." Jewel Rudd said.

"We were with Bill Matson chasing some horse thieves ... we talked to an old man, Isidro, her uncle, on our way in, when we came back we found everyone dead, except her."

"Who did it?" Pilar said.

"I don't know. It wasn't that bunch we were following. It had to have been another bunch of bandits," Padget said.

"Take her to my room, Pilar," Jewell said. "You," indicating Padget and Ochoa, "come with me. You can't do her any good." She walked toward the bar. The odor of stale smoke and alcohol was heavy and dense. "Sit down and have a drink," she ordered, and set a bottle and two glasses on the table. "I'll get Cruz to rustle up some food and put your horses away. Stay here until I get back."

Ochoa poured a double shot. They drank and he refilled the glasses. "We haven't been shot yet," he said. "For a while there I didn't know."

Padget picked up his glass; he was more tired than he could remember. "Maybe she's going through the change." He shook his head and drained his second drink

A woman, squat and dressed in black, came into the cantina from the kitchen carrying tortillas, salsa and beans and put them on the table. She left without a word. She returned with a pot of coffee and two cups. She poured the coffee. Again she left without speaking.

They were finishing the last tortilla when Pilar came into the cantina and motioned to them. "Come with me." Padget thought she was going to take them to the girl. He and Ochoa followed her into the hotel. Climbing the stairs, she opened the first door and motioned them into the room. Their saddlebags and rifles were stacked against the wall. Padget turned to Pilar.

"Where's the girl?" he asked.

"She's sleeping. I believe she has a chance... she is stronger than she looks. Sleep here and tomorrow you can go back to the Rafter J. We will look after Juana."

"Did she say who did this?" Padget asked.

"No, she didn't wake up. We cleaned her up

as best as we could, but she needs rest. No. NO! There is nothing more you can do for her tonight. Get some sleep and we will talk tomorrow." She closed the door behind her.

Chapter Twenty-nine

Padget woke with the sound of a rooster crowing somewhere off in the distance. He rolled over and watched Ochoa who was snoring on the other cot. He sat up, pulled on his pants and boots, tucked in his shirt, and shrugged into his suspenders. The movement caused him to break wind.

He went down to the kitchen and found the same taciturn woman who had fed them earlier. She might have smiled when handed him a cup of coffee, he couldn't really tell. He took the coffee and walked outside. He thought about the girl lying upstairs and wondered what would become of her, if she lived.

Padget found Dynamite and Blue in the big corral, separated from the other stock and eating hay put there by one of the hands. A young boy gathered eggs from the hen house. He would gently lift the hen and remove the eggs, set the hen back on her perch and go on to the next hen. Padget threw the dregs of his coffee on to the ground and walked back to the hotel. He sat on one of the two cane-bottomed chairs on the porch. Dawn was breaking; the day would be clear and bright.

A flock of geese flew over, honking their way south. A covey of blue quail ran through the yard, stopped, then started again, first this way, then that, calling to each other as they moved.

"They're beautiful birds; it's unfortunate that they taste so good."

Startled, Padget turned to face Jewel Rudd who was holding a cup of coffee and watching him. He got to his feet, feeling like he had been caught doing something wrong. "Good morning, Mrs. Rudd, I didn't hear you come up. Is Juana awake yet?"

She shook her head, "Still out of it. She's resting easy. The longer she sleeps the better. Tell me what happened down there?"

"I don't really know what happened. We got to Talón late Friday afternoon. Everything was okay when we left. Bill was in a hurry and we rode all that night. Next day we weren't any closer to catching the rustlers; they had split up in every direction, so we turned around. We got to Talón Monday afternoon late."

His voice slowed. "I've seen dead people before, but I've never seen anything like that. They didn't have a chance. Those poor folks in Talón weren't even armed. I doubt if there was a single barreled shotgun among the whole bunch. Whoever did it aren't human, they are a murdering bunch of cowards." He shook his head. He heard the sound of running footsteps on the stairs and looked up as Pilar appeared.

Pilar opened the screen door and beckoned. "Come on. She's awake."

Padget felt his throat choke up when he saw her and he stopped at the foot of her bed. Someone had brushed her hair and tied it back with a red ribbon. Her eyes had a vacant look and her face was drawn and haggard. She sat silent in her bed, her hands folded in her lap and Padget wondered if she could talk.

She looked around the room, and then the words tumbled from her mouth. She told them how the rurales had come, late on the day after the posse left. They said they were looking for insurrectos, arms smugglers. Then they found the gold coin the Americano had given her uncle and the rurales said they were all criminals, they would not listen when her uncle tried to explain. They cut out his eyes and shot the men and killed them with sabers. They laughed while they did it. They laughed as they raped the women, and laughed as they killed the women, and laughed when they left her for the coyotes to finish.

The tears rolled unchecked down her cheeks and she began to sob. Pilar shooed them out of the room. "You've done your part. Jewel and I will take care of Juana. You and Ochoa can come by to check on her in a week or so, if you want."

Chapter Thirty

Padget was downhearted and Ochoa was silent during the long ride back to the Rafter J. The shadows were long when they turned the horses into the corral and Padget could smell the warm odor of hot biscuits from the cook house. They were in time for supper. "Sure makes my mouth water," he said to Ochoa.

They threw their saddles on the corral fence and hurried across the yard to the ranch house. Walt and Claire sat at the kitchen table. Walt looked up from his bible, leaving it open between him and Claire.

In quick steps Padget went to his aunt, bent over and hugged her. He crossed the room and picked up the coffee pot from the stove where it had been warming. He filled two mugs, handing

THERE AIN'T NO MONEY IN IT

one to Ochoa. Hungry and tired he stood against the wall and sipped from his cup.

"You look tired, Son. Sit down. Maria, would you bring these boys some supper? How'd it go? I talked to Bill. He told me he didn't get his horses back," Walt said.

Padget dropped down into a chair. "We didn't even get close enough to smell their dust."

"Bill said there was some kind of mess down there and you boys stayed behind to clean it up."

"Did the girl die?" Claire asked.

"No," Padget said. "She's alive and most likely will recover. It's going to take a long time though, I'm afraid."

"Where is she now?" Claire asked.

"We left her at the Rudd place. Pilar and Mrs. Rudd are taking care of her."

"Was she hurt pretty badly? Bill didn't think she would last out the day."

"She was hurt a whole lot more than I want to talk about. Her outside hurt's healing. She was awake when we left this morning, but she's pretty tired. I don't know about the inside hurt."

Claire looked at him, the question left unspoken.

"I mean, I don't know what's going to happen

to her. She hasn't got any family to help her," Padget said.

"God will provide," Claire said.

"He sure as hell hasn't done a very good job so far," Padget said.

"Watch your mouth," Walt said.

"She just turned fourteen for Pete's sake," Padget said. "She doesn't deserve anything like what she got."

"That's pretty close to blasphemy, son. There are a lot of people who don't deserve what they get and some that don't get half what they should — good or bad," Walt said. He picked up the Bible and thumbed through it. When he came to the passage he was looking for, he put his forefinger on the page and moved it down. "For to him that is joined with all the living there is hope; for a living dog is better than a dead lion."[5] He turned to another passage. "And we know that all things work together for good to those that love God, to those who are called according to his purpose."[6]

He placed the Bible down on the table and gently closed it. "We don't always understand the

---

[5] Ecclesiastes 9:4
[6] Romans 8:28

ways of God, Wes. He has a plan and it'll work out for the best."

"Well, there are a lot of things in this world I don't understand. Just a whole hell..." Padget glanced at his aunt. "...heck of a lot. A blind man can see what's going on down there in Mexico and know that it's bad. I know that those folks in Talón were pelados, but they sure weren't hurting anybody. They were just trying to make it from one day to the next and keep from starving."

Maria came in from the kitchen and set a plate of food in front of him and Ochoa and refilled his coffee cup. Padget smiled up at her. "Hell—I'm sorry, Claire—it's just that one of them, the old man Isidro, used to work for Bill, at least he knew Bill and called him captain.

Bill gave him a twenty dollar gold piece for the girl's birthday, so they must have been pretty close at one time. It was that gold piece that got them killed. A damned twenty dollar gold piece! Juana, that's her name, said the rurales found it when it fell from Isidro's pocket. They thought it was from the bandits we were following.

They wouldn't listen to anything after that. I guess Isidro didn't tell them we were in the country. I can't help but believe the whole town would be alive, if we hadn't been chasing those horse thieves."

Padget placed his elbows on the table and rubbed his forehead and temples with both hands. Then he looked up, "Well, that's all water under the bridge and there's nothing we can do about it."

That night he and Ochoa field-stripped, cleaned, and oiled their guns. Padget picked up a rag and wiped the grease off the cartridges he had loaded. He looked at Ochoa who was sitting in one corner of the bunkhouse saddle-soaping his revolver holster. "Mano, I don't know if I can just sit back and watch what's taking place down there or not."

Ochoa finished soaping the holster. He put his revolver in it and hung it on a peg over his bunk. "What do you think you are going do about it?" he said. "There isn't a living soul in Texas, who gives a hoot about what's happening across the border and I sure don't see anyone forming up the Rough Riders to go down there and straighten things out."

Padget unbuckled his spurs and took off his boots. He hung his hat on a peg. "It's just that I feel like we ought to be doing something. I'm going to turn in."

Chapter Thirty-one

Two days later Padget was getting the kinks out of a long legged roan colt when he ran across turkey tracks in Wild Horse Canyon. A rush of excitement thrilled him as he read the sign. He picked up a twig fallen from a mesquite, stirred through the turkey droppings, and looked closely at the content.

The birds were feeding on fiery little peppers the locals called pequeños. The tiny red and green chili peppers flavored the meat, making it hot and spicy. His mouth began to water. Maybe it was time to go hunting.

Back at the bunkhouse, Ochoa had his boots off, lying on his back with his hands under his head and staring at the ceiling.

"Hey, Mano I ran into some turkey tracks."

"A blind man could find turkey tracks, they're all over the ranch," Ochoa said, still lying on his back.

"They are feeding on pequeños," Padget said. "It's time to go hunting. Christmas isn't too far away; fresh venison and a turkey or two would be welcome in the cook shack."

Ochoa sat up and reached for his boots. "Now you've got my attention."

Sitting in front of the stove in the bunkhouse that evening, Padget and Ochoa honed their skinning knives, cleaned their rifles and reloaded rifle cartridges. "Did you ever kill a moose?" Padget asked.

"No. I saw one though, up near Big Piney, Wyoming. How about you?"

Padget filled the empty loops in his cartridge belt. "Yeah, I shot a moose, in Alaska. They're not hard to bring down."

"Big as they are, you'd think it would take cannon to drop one," Ochoa said.

"Well it doesn't. I put one down right on his nose, up near Soldatna, with one shot from my Winchester. He stuck his nose in the dirt and just stopped, didn't fall over-just stayed upright on his belly, looked like he was taking a nap...he was dead on his feet before he even hit the ground."

"How close were you to him?" Ochoa asked.

"Not far, about forty yards. I caught him just behind the right front leg. The bullet went through both lungs, clipped the top of the heart, broke his left front leg and lodged just under the skin on the off side."

They put the reloading equipment away, rolled out a small wall tent and checked it for wear. After sewing up one small hole and brushing the canvas clean they re-rolled it and turned in.

The sky was dark and stormy and great purple and black clouds piled up menacingly in the west. A cold north wind brought the hint of snow when they saddled their horses and loaded the pack mare.

Padget noticed the clouds, but thought it was too early in the year to mean much. He knew that there could be buildups, days before a storm. He motioned to the southeast. "The place I want to hunt is just under Panther Peak and a little to the south. It should be chocked full of turkey and deer this time of the year."

Carrying his saddle to the corral, Ochoa scanned the sky. "We're going need that tent we packed."

They slipped through the corral poles and loaded the hunting gear: tent, bed rolls, Dutch ovens, cooking gear and food on a chunky little gray mare named Mouse. They caught their horses and saddled them.

The chill of the morning made the horses inclined to buck. Padget laughed, welcoming the contest between the horse and his ability to ride. Happy, he stepped into the saddle and slacked up on the reins. The dun ducked his head and jumped high in the air, coming down stiff legged with a spine jarring impact. He made a few more jumps, then as quickly as he started, he stopped.

Riding across the corral Padget picked up the lead rope, led Mouse to the gate, and turned in the saddle to watch Ochoa.

A sorrel gelding named Scorpion stood quietly while Ochoa rubbed him down and put the blanket and saddle in place. The horse shifted in his tracks when the cinch was pulled tight. As soon as Ochoa hit the saddle, Scorpion bogged his head, lunged forward and started to buck.

Ochoa laughed and yelled, as the bronc started pitching. He pulled off his hat and slapped the sorrel alongside its neck, his spurs raked the sorrel from shoulder to flank and Scorpion began to sun fish. Ochoa dropped his hat and held his arm up for balance while the sorrel continued to buck around the corral. When he finally quit bucking Ochoa stepped down and retrieved his hat. Jamming it on his head he pulled the stampede straps tight.

"Are you ready to quit showboating now and go hunting?" Padget said.

"I was ready when I walked out of the bunkhouse this morning, so talk to Scorpion if you want to nag. It was all his idea."

"Maybe, but you sure seemed to be enjoying yourself," Padget said.

Padget led the way through Goat Canyon and south up over the ridge at the top of Horse Canyon, following the same path they had when trailing the jaguars. The morning wore on, and the wind steadily increased in velocity. Half way up Horse Canyon, snow started falling, intermittent at first, and then steady as they rode on. It was swept across the trail by the wind and began to pile up in drifts against the sagebrush.

Through the driving snow, Padget caught sight of a small bunch of brood mares and their colts. They were near the rim of the canyon, bunched up and facing west into the wind and blowing snow. As he watched them, the wind died and the snow flakes became huge; floating straight down to the ground. A hush covered the land with a particular stillness that precedes the first snowfall of the year.

Padget turned in his saddle. He cupped his ear with his left hand. "It is so quiet right now I believe you could hear a mouse break wind. The area I want to hunt isn't far from here; it's on the southeast side of the Eagles and a little higher up." As the words died on his lips he saw Ochoa draw his revolver and shoot twice. Immediately, he heard the flurry of powerful wings beating the air.

Button ducked his head and crow hopped a couple of steps. Padget jerked his head up. He looked in the direction of the shots and saw six wild turkeys flying off through the falling snow. Flopping on the ground, were two young toms.

Padget laughed, "I thought we would at least get out of Wild Horse Canyon before we started hunting. This'll make Claire happy though." He got down from his horse and picked up the birds and carried them back to the pack horse. He tied their feet to the crossbucks on the pack saddle, letting them hang; one on each side, so the blood would drain.

Eagle Peak loomed off to the southeast,

towering over other peaks in the range. As Padget looked, the clouds moved in from the west and Eagle Peak disappeared from sight.

They skirted the southern end of Horse Canyon. The terrain grew more rugged; cut through with arroyos and box canyons whose sides were nearly vertical.

Climbing steeply, they began to encounter Douglas fir and aspen. The canyon narrowed, then widened out as they climbed.

They crossed Frenchman's Canyon, climbed the trail along the rim and rode down into Cypress Canyon. The snow was now three inches deep and continued to fall. The quietness made the sound of crunching made by the horse's hooves loud on the trail.

Padget pointed to the head of a shallow feeder draw west of Cypress Canyon. "We'll set up camp near that seep spring right over there."

Chapter Thirty-two

Padget hung a flour sack full of cold baking powder biscuits, slab bacon, coffee, salt, dried apricots and beans Maria had prepared in a cedar tree to keep it off the ground.

They would be hungry when they came in from hunting and to Padget there was nothing as bothersome as having to rustle up firewood when he was tired. He gathered up an armload of dry branches and laid them under a tarp by the tent. Gathering up several large rocks, he built a stone wall to reflect heat from the campfire toward the tent. Next, he put up a canvas fly to cover the front, making a dry place to sit, and stacked the saddles under it.

The clouds were so close to the ground that he could almost touch them, and the snow was coming down hard and thick. Padget watched the snow pile up on Ochoa's hat brim. If they are going to get any hunting done today, they would have to get a move on. The temperature dropped rapidly, as the storm closed in around the camp.

They removed their spurs and picketed the saddle horses and put the packsaddle on Button. Padget started up the ridge behind the tent. Ochoa walked downhill from him about twenty five feet, fading in and out of sight as the falling snow swirled around him.

Padget approached the top of the ridge and looked into the storm. Across the draw, through the swirling snow, a movement caught his eye. He squinted dimly in the fading light, and could see an enormous mule deer lying under a mesquite tree. At first, Padget thought it was a doe, and then as he watched, the deer moved his head and he could see its huge antlers.

Cocking the hammer, Padget glanced over to make sure Ochoa had not moved into the line of fire, and looked back at the buck. In one silent movement the buck unfolded, and like a ghost, faded into the storm.

Padget stood there with his rifle half way up to his shoulder, willing the buck to show himself through the snowfall. When he didn't, he lowered his rifle and let the hammer down. He hadn't gotten those big horns by waiting for some dumb cowboy to make up his mind, he thought.

Ochoa's Krag went off over to his right. Padget ducked when he heard the shot, and then moved through the deepening show to where Ochoa stood.

Ochoa pointed. Barely visible across the draw lay a deer. Padget looked at the antlers and thought for a moment that Ochoa had shot the buck that slipped away from him.

They walked slowly, digging in their boot heels to keep from slipping on the wet snow as they slid down the steep side of the draw and climbed up the other side. Feeling under the snow with each step, Padget managed to stay upright and finally reached the rim of the draw and the buck.

Ochoa handed Padget his rifle and pulled out his skinning knife. Working rapidly in the snow, he soon had the buck opened up and spread out. The bullet had gone through the throat, breaking the neck before exiting the other side.

Padget guessed that the buck would probably weigh over 200 pounds. It took both of cowboys to get him loaded across the packsaddle and head back to camp.

THERE AIN'T NO MONEY IN IT

The snow storm increased its onslaught. The tent was a quarter mile away and uphill. By the time they stumbled into camp, it was completely dark.

Padget put Button on a picket line, and started a fire. Ochoa hung the buck in a cedar tree and propped the carcass open to air out. He then salted and rolled up the hide and hung it alongside the buck. By the time he was through, the coffee was boiling, the bacon was frying and the biscuits were warming in a Dutch oven.

Ochoa rubbed his hands clean with snow and wiped them on his Levi's. He picked up the coffeepot and poured a cup.

Using a mesquite limb Padget lifted the lid off the Dutch oven. He put bacon and several biscuits on two tin plates and handed one to Ochoa. "That's a pretty good sized buck; Claire will sure appreciate the fresh venison." He picked up the coffeepot, "Want some more?"

Ochoa nodded and as Padget refilled his cup asked. "In Arizona, did you like being a Ranger?"

"Oh, I don't know, it's about like any other job. There were a lot of outlaws and we were pretty close to the border. The roads were all bad and it was hard to get word of anything, rough country."

Ochoa chewed on a piece of bacon. "Yeah, but did you like it?"

"I don't know if I liked it or not. Chasing down outlaws was hard work. Catching them was damn near impossible. You almost had to run one outlaw down and tie him to a bush, while you went after another. Hell, I guess it wasn't any worse than riding for the Hash knife. Most of the time, you couldn't tell an outlaw from an honest cowboy. We did all right I guess." He pitched the dregs of his coffee into the snow and got ready for bed.

Sitting on his bedroll Ochoa said, "When did you start shooting that Thirty Government?"

"When I rode for the Hash-Knife outfit; it was just after my first run in with some rustlers," Padget said. He pulled off his boots and placed them between the bedrolls. "There were three hombres who appropriated some Hash-Knife cows and we trailed them into a canyon where they holed up. One of them had a Sharps. He kept us far enough away with that damn buffalo gun that we couldn't get close enough to fight. We got the cows back. He was a cool customer though, just stood there in plain sight and poked away at us. We couldn't do anything about it. He shot my horse and I had to ride double back to the line shack. Anyway, next day I rode into Flagstaff, looking for something with a little more range than a .44-40 and they had this Thirty Government so I bought it."

Padget sat on his bedroll and looked out through the tent flap. The snow had stopped falling and the wind was starting to blow. It was going to be a cold blue Texas night. Bandit lay in the middle of his bedroll soaking up the heat from the campfire. Padget looked over at Ochoa who was pulling off his boots. "If this wind keeps up, the drifts will pile up deep and trap that bunch of mares and colts we saw earlier. We're going to have to push them back to the ranch."

The sound of the wind increased in volume and became a prolonged howl echoing through the canyon. Bandit burrowed further down into Padget's bedroll. He was soon asleep and dreaming. His nose twitched and his right front paw ran in place. Over the howl of the wind, Ochoa asked, "That girl, what's going to happen to her?"

Surprised, Padget thought about it. "I don't know Dave... My guess is she'll stay at the Rudd place. Not much future though. No family — all busted up that way — maybe it would've been kinder to leave her, like Bill said."

When Ochoa didn't say anything, Padget

continued, "Folks down there in Mexico, the poor ones anyway, don't have a snowball's chance in hell. They're ignorant, dirty. Most of them are sick, one way or the other... I'm going to turn in. We're going to have a long, hard day tomorrow."

Ochoa banked up the fire and lay back on his bedroll.

Just before Padget went to sleep, he heard Ochoa say. "You will forget your misery; you will remember it as waters that have passed away."[7]

That night Padget dreamed about Juana. He was back in Talón by himself, unarmed. He was huddled in one of the adobe huts, holding her as rurales surrounded them. He could hear them searching through the huts. He tried to keep her quiet, but Juana kept screaming and screaming. He awoke, wringing wet with sweat.

It was still dark and the wind still blowing hard. Awake now, he felt silly that the dream caused him to panic. After all, it was only a dream and he was awake now. It wouldn't bother him anymore. He rolled over and went back to sleep, but the dream stuck with him. The specter of her battered face would not go away. He sat up. The dream, for some reason, brought back memories

---

[7] Job 11:16

of the death of his mother.

He had never had a chance to know his father, who died when Padget was a year old and his mother died of scarlet fever when he was four and he felt abandoned by his parents. If he went back to sleep he was afraid the dream would return.

With the wind still howling outside, the night dragged on.

Chapter Thirty-three

Padget woke up to find a fine powder of snow over everything, even his boots were white. Reluctant to leave the warmth of his bedroll, Padget shivered and pulled on his jeans while lying in bed. Throwing back the blankets he grabbed his boots and shook the snow from them; stiff from the cold they were difficult to pull on, and right spur strap broke when he pulled it through the buckle. "Damn." He stepped out into the night to relieve his bladder. "Lord its cold."

Ochoa came to stand beside him. "You're shaking like a dog crapping peach seeds."

Padget ducked back inside the tent. Bandit had not moved off the bedroll; the blue heeler lay on his stomach with his head on his forepaws watching him. "Come on you lazy rascal." Padget pushed him out of the tent and found his heavy sheepskin coat and went to check the horses.

Ochoa inspected the frozen deer carcass, still hanging in the cedar tree. "I'm going to need some help getting this quartered and packed."

Padget grabbed the camp axe and split the deer into quarters, small enough to get into the panniers. By the time they packed up and broke camp it was full light and white as far as you could see.

The wind had swept the trail clean in some places, in others; drifts were piled up, covering it with several feet of snow. It was easy going until they reached the ridge separating them from Horse Canyon where snow blocked the trail.

Padget stood up in his stirrups and peered at the drift. "That's got to be waist deep, and I don't know how far it goes. The trail looks blocked all the way to where it bends around to the west, after that I can't tell."

Unable to see how far the drift extended, Padget got down off his horse and walked into the drift, stamping down the snow. Breaking trail, he struggled in the snow for what seemed to be hours. When he looked back, he was barely twenty yards from where he started. Ochoa took over lead and broke trail for the next two hours. Mid-day came and they were still fifty yards from the top of the ridge.

Padget took over the lead the again, fighting through the snow with all his strength. Abruptly, he fell forward landing on his hands and knees onto a portion of the trail that had been swept clean by the wind. Now he could see all the way to the summit. When they reached the ridge top, the trail was visible for the entire length of the canyon. He could that only two more drifts blocked the trail: the first drift near the head of the canyon, the second about a half way down.

The brood mares and their colts were visible, bunched up near the far end and Padget looked at them through his field glasses. He could see that their flanks were sucked in from lack of water. The blowing snow had trapped the horses as effectively as a fence. He knew the only water in the canyon was beyond the second drift and the horses had been without water for the better part of two days. The mares looked to be in fair shape, but he couldn't tell about the colts.

By the time he and Ochoa fought through the drift to the stranded horses it was dark. Loosening the cinches they put nosebags on Button, Scorpion and Mouse. They built a fire and melted snow to water the trapped horses. As midnight approached the temperature began to plummet.

Padget doubted if the colts could survive another night out. "We've got to get these horses to shelter," he said. It was three a.m. and bitter cold, when they broke through the last drift. A pack of coyotes howled on the ridge to the west and were immediately answered by another pack to the south.

Padget pulled his hat down. "The jackrabbits are going to catch hell tonight." It was a cold, miserable, toe-freezing ride. A small triangle of snow on the leeward side of every creosote and rabbit bush marked the wind's passage. When they broke over the ridge into Goat Canyon the trail was open.

They arrived at the Rafter J just at first light and turned the horses into the pasture. Miguel and Shorty were pitching hay to the livestock. They waved and kept working.

Padget and Ochoa put the venison in the smokehouse and hung the hide in the barn. They went back to the cook shack and ate pancakes, eggs, biscuits, cream gravy, and beefsteak. Padget leaned back in his chair. "It sure is good to be back."

That evening over supper, Claire told them

she wanted to go shopping. "Walt and I decided to adopt Juana. I spoke with Jewell and she agreed Juana would be better off here at the Rafter J. She's going to bring her to the ranch as soon as she is able to travel."

She said that a young girl would need clothes, shoes and other things, and that she and Walt would take the buckboard into Sierra Blanca and the train to El Paso. There were dozens of things Juana would need when she came to live with them.

"I always wanted a daughter and now that I have one, she is going to have a good home and an education. I'll make sure she gets a good education. It won't undo what she's been through, but it's a whole lot better than she would have if she went back to Mexico. No one is going to hurt her here," Claire said.

Walt poured more coffee. "Those colts you've been working on are ready for market; you and Dave can take them to Fort Bliss tomorrow and come back on the train."

Chapter Thirty-four

Feeling the cold leather in the early morning air, Padget threw his saddle on the back of a chunky bay gelding and checked the saddle strings. He was going to have to restring his saddle soon. The horse he rode, and the one Ochoa was riding would be sold to the Army.

They left the ranch at sunup and pushed the horses downhill into Eagle Flat where the trail flattened out. They turned the herd west along the Southern Pacific Railroad tracks and arrived in Fort Hancock at sundown. They turned the horses into the holding corrals along the railroad tracks.

Up and moving before daylight, they drove the horses toward El Paso. Ten miles east of Fort Hancock, they turned aside to water the horses in the river. Padget was bent over, making coffee on a small mesquite fire when Ochoa said, "Looks like we got company, Wes."

Padget pulled his Winchester from the scabbard and looked at the dust rising further west. The red and white guidon of a cavalry troop could be seen whipping in the wind. "Army patrol."

The lieutenant didn't look old enough to shave. He threw up his right arm. "Troop halt!" he called.

Padget gestured toward the fire. "Morning, lieutenant, get down and have some coffee."

"Sergeant, dismount the men. We'll take a ten minute rest." He had New England twang.

Padget handed him a cup of coffee, "Don't see much of you men out this way."

The lieutenant took a sip of his coffee, "You'll see a lot more of us in the future with your governor downsizing the rangers, and bandits out of Mexico crossing into the United States all along the river. Someone has to secure the border."

"Where are you headed?" Padget asked.

"To the Matson Ranch, near Sierra Blanca. Mexican bandits ran off some horses."

"Hell, lieutenant, that was four weeks ago and those hombres got plumb away. Dave and I were in the posse that chased them across the river. We chased them way to hell and gone into Mexico. Then they split up and we couldn't follow them," Padget said.

"News travels slow I see. Where are you taking these horses?" He motioned toward the colts with a wave of his arm.

"To Fort Bliss, you may be riding one of them pretty soon," Padget said.

The lieutenant nodded, tossed the dregs from his cup on to the ground and handed it back to Padget. "Duty calls." He mounted his horse. "You men be careful." He led his troop downriver.

Padget and Ochoa sold the horses to the Quartermaster at Fort Bliss, Friday, December 17th, 1909. They checked into the Sheldon Hotel and put the voucher for the horses in the hotel safe. Done with business a few hours before the train arrived, they walked downtown to take in the sights.

El Paso was decorated for Christmas and jammed packed with people. There were soldiers in khaki, teamsters driving wagons loaded with goods, cowboys on horseback, and townspeople on foot hurrying along, in and out of shops.

Black smoke from several automobiles lingered over the street. Unused to the strange contraptions, horses jerked at their tethers. They sidestepped and rolled their eyes whenever one came too close. A cowboy on a blaze faced sorrel arrived at the intersection of Main and Oregon at the same time as a touring car. The driver honked his horn which startled the horse. The horse jumped sideways, bogged his head and started bucking.

Pedestrians scattered from the intersection and onto the boardwalk. Wheeling, the horse reversed its course and the next jump carried him onto the boardwalk among the people who had taken refuge there. They ran back into the street and the sorrel stampeded under an awning, knocked off the rider's hat and came to a quivering halt. The people in the touring car cheered and waved at the cowboy as they continued down the street.

Padget stopped in front of a shop that sold women's clothing. Embarrassed, he stood gazing at the two mannequins in the window.

"You need a new dress?" Ochoa said.

"No. I don't need a new dress," Padget said. He pushed open the door and entered the shop.

Ochoa followed him and watched as Padget picked up a chocolate colored scarf and took it to the register. "May I look at those?" he said, pointing to a pair of earrings inside the display case.

THERE AIN'T NO MONEY IN IT

A slender, dark headed sales clerk held the earrings up to the light. "The woman who gets these will be a lucky girl."

"Well, I'm sure glad you cleared that up for me," Ochoa said. "My Pard's been acting kind of strange lately, and I was beginning to wonder." He grinned at Padget, "I wouldn't be surprised if these weren't for that little dark eyed gal down on the river."

Padget swung around to look at Ochoa who held up his hands in mock surrender. "On second thought, one of those through your nose might fit your personality."

They left the store and walked to the plaza in the center of town and joined a group of tourists looking down into a circular pit. Brick walls encircled a man made enclosure that was filled with alligators.

"How did they get here? Surely not from the Rio Grande," Ochoa said.

Padget leaned on the rail. "Nobody knows for sure," he said. "I've heard that someone in Louisiana sent them to a friend here, as a joke. They've been here since I was a kid."

"They sure are ugly." Ochoa said.

"Only if you're not another alligator." Padget said.

"I read in the National Geographic Magazine

that they have man eating crocodiles in the Nile." Ochoa said. "Even had pictures of them."

"Are they much different than these?" Padget asked nodding toward the alligators in the pond.

"I couldn't see much difference, a little skinnier in the snout, but all in all, pretty much the same."

Growing tired of the alligators, they pushed away from the rail and started walking down the street. Ochoa stopped for a moment in front of Jones' Hardware and Mercantile store. He looked at the guns in the display window and walked in. Padget caught up to him at the counter.

"Would you mind letting me see that hand ejector?" Ochoa said pointing to a Smith and Wesson double action revolver in the display case.

"This is the newest design in revolvers," the clerk said. He removed three revolvers from the case and placed them on the counter. "I've been selling every one I get in, almost before I can take it out of the box. All I've got right now are these two thirty-twos and this forty-four forty."

Ochoa picked up the forty-four forty and opened the cylinder. Satisfied it was unloaded, he closed the cylinder and cycled it twice to test the trigger pull. He opened the cylinder again and motioned to Padget. "Come over here a minute,

Mano, and take a look at this."

Padget looked up from the rifle rack and walked to the counter. Ochoa handed him the revolver.

Padget examined the revolver closed the cylinder and cocked the hammer. "Shape of the hammer is all wrong."

"You're not supposed to cock it," Ochoa said, "And quit looking at it like a chicken looking at a snake."

"If you don't cock it, how are you going to shoot it?" Padget said.

"That's what you call a double action. All you have to do is pull the trigger," Ochoa said.

Padget pulled the trigger and cycled the revolver. "Pretty stiff," he said. He cycled it again. "That's pretty fast all right, but it sure is ugly."

"Ugly? What do you mean ugly? This has to be the most beautiful bit of perfection I've laid eyes on since I left Colorado."

"You're carrying two pistols now. How come you want another one?" Padget said.

"Some people just don't appreciate the finer things in life," Ochoa said. He reached over and took the revolver back from Padget.

Padget arched his eyebrows. "And you were worried about me?"

Ochoa opened the cylinder and looked through the bore. Closing the action he spun the revolver in his hand and cocked it when it came level. He let the hammer down, shifted the revolver to his left hand and spun it again. Without cocking the hammer he rapidly pulled the trigger twice. After checking the action, Ochoa asked the proprietor if he could try it out.

The clerk put a box of ammunition on the countertop. "Out through the back there and do your best."

Ochoa picked up the ammunition and walked to the rear of the shop and into the fenced back yard. Standing at the far side of the yard was a plank with a bull's eye painted on it. He loaded the revolver and with deliberate aim, pulled the trigger. There was a loud report and a hole appeared just to the right of center. He pulled the trigger again and a hole appeared beside the first. Rapidly, he fired the remaining four shots.

Padget walked to the plank and spread his hand over the bullet holes. With his fingers spread out, he could cover all six holes with his hand. "Well, you sure haven't lost your talent, Mano."

Ochoa paid fifteen dollars for the revolver.

Padget bought four boxes of ammunition for his Winchester.

At S.D. Myres Saddlery, they looked at new saddles. Padget paid thirty-five cents for a new pair of straps for his spurs.

Ochoa sketched the design for a holster he wanted made for his new pistol. "I don't want a hammer thong. Just make sure it's deep enough; so I won't lose it when I'm riding."

As they were winding up the transaction, a long low whistle signaled the arrival of the westbound train. Discussion swiftly ended, Padget and Ochoa hurried to the train station. They were in time to meet Walt and Claire as they were coming out of the depot.

Chapter Thirty-five

Later, Padget carried bundles stacked up to his chin and listened to his aunt talk about how happy she would be when Juana came to live at the ranch. Following Claire from shop to shop was like following a whirlwind. They met Walt at Doctor Bush's office where he examined Claire and pronounced her healthy. He invited them to a formal dinner party the following evening.

Leaving Walt and Claire after breakfast the following day, Padget and Ochoa walked across the international bridge into Juarez. They were stopped on the Mexico side by Federal Troops, questioned and passed through Mexican Customs.

The city was filled with soldiers who stood in groups of three or four on every street corner and glowered at the American tourists. Mexican peons scurried along the streets, staying as far away as they could from the soldiers. Eyes downcast, they gave the soldiers wide berth.

Padget and Ochoa stopped in a clothing store and bought new suits, shirts, socks and underwear. Carrying the paper wrapped purchases they walked down the avenue in search of a cantina. Rounding a corner, they came upon a crowd of people watching a squad of soldiers.

Three men were standing blindfolded against an adobe wall, their arms bound behind their backs and tied to three poles set in the ground. A squad of soldiers with rifles at their sides, stood waiting.

At the officer's command they raised their rifles and took aim at the three men. The man in the center trembled. It was obvious he was terrified of what was about to happen.

"Tira!" the officer called out loudly. Eight rifles went off and the three men jerked. Padget saw the dust bounce off their clothes as the bullets hit them.

Despite being hit several times, they were still alive. They raised their heads and turned towards the sound of the footsteps of the officer, who now approached them with his pistol drawn. He walked to the nearest man and put his pistol close to his head, cocked the hammer and pulled the trigger. The impact slammed the man's head to one side blowing his brains out through a hole in the opposite side of his skull.

The officer walked to the next man and repeated the process. The third man, sensing what was about to happen, tried vainly to pull away. Bound tightly, he could not move. The officer laughed, slowly cocked his pistol and placed the barrel against the victim's face so the he could feel it.

The man flinched.

The officer waited a moment, and then shot him through the right eye.

"That son of a bitch likes it," Ochoa said.

Feeling anger well up inside, Padget pulled his hat down on his forehead. "That's a mean, heartless way to kill a man." He wanted to vomit. He turned to the Mexican next to him. "What did they do?"

"They are insurrectos. They printed papers against El Presidente." The man edged away from Padget.

Depressed, angry, and sickened Padget said, "Come on, Ochoa, let's get done and get on back to Texas."

At the corner to The Sixteenth of September

Street two Mexican soldiers stepped into their path. One held up his hand. "Hey, gringos, where do you go in such a hurry?"

Padget moved his coat tail aside and dropped his hand to his pistol. "Step aside greaser."

Ochoa moved to one side, his hand near his shoulder holster.

The second soldier looked at Padget' face and grabbed his partner's arm and pulled him to one side. "Por favor, Señor," he said to Padget. "My friend, he is drunk."

The first soldier struggled to pull loose. His companion would not let him go. "Calmasé. You are very close to getting your head blown off by this Gringo."

"I'm not afraid of no damned gringo."

"Sí, sí. I know, but just the same, have much care with these two."

Padget and Ochoa turned their backs and walked on toward the bridge.

Back at the Sheldon Hotel Ochoa picked up the black suit he had purchased that morning. "I usually wear these to funerals." He pulled on the pants and stuffed in the tails of his shirt.

"Then you should have been wearing that suit this afternoon," Padget said.

"Si, por supuesto. That's for sure."

Padget buttoned his shirt. "You know something, Mano?"

"What's that?"

"The gates of hell are wide open and they're right over there in Mexico. Here, give me a hand with this damned tie will you?"

Chapter Thirty-six

The dining room was decorated for the season. A highly polished table reflected images of the dinner guests illumed by the light of a dozen candles lining the center. Bush sat at the head of the table. Phillips sat at the other end. Ten guests sat around the long table between them. Waiters moved among the diners, pouring wine and removing empty plates. The tinkling sounds of wine glasses and silverware clinking against fine china were clearly audible through the hubbub of conversation.

Padget felt vaguely ill at ease sitting among the guests in his new suit, but couldn't help smile at the scent of bayberry coming from the candles that stood like sentinels down the middle of the table. He heaped butter on his baked potato and looked around for the salt and pepper.

"They were anarchists for Christ's sake and deserved what they got." Padget turned to look at the man who was speaking. He recognized the tall heavy officer with a large nose. He was Major Daniel L. Reed, the officer from the Remount Service at Fort Bliss who signed the payment voucher for the horses.

A tall dark mustachioed man seated across the table stared at the officer. "Anarchists? Crime? Since when, is it a crime to publish a paper asking fair treatment for the peons?" Padget found out later that he was Abraham Gonzales and worked for Francicso Madero.

"Fairness?" The big nosed officer said. "Those people can't even spell the word, much less understand it. They need and want a firm hand."

Padget surprised himself by interrupting the conversation. "I saw that firm hand you're talking about today, Major. That firm hand, as you call it, stood three men up against an adobe wall and shot them. And just because of some damned paper they printed against the government — they shot them like dogs. So don't talk to me about a firm hand. What I saw today was murder — plain and simple murder."

The room got quiet and eating stopped. Padget

looked around. Everyone was watching him and he could feel the tension.

"Speaking of governing themselves; I've read Mr. Madero's book." Walt's calm voice broke into the conversation. "It's certainly a pragmatic way to go about changing the government, and I do believe Mexico needs a change, however, I don't think it will happen until Diaz is dead. That old vinegaroon isn't going to give up anything so long as he can sit up and take nourishment. I don't hold out much chance of Mr. Madero being elected - not this year anyway."

Gonzalez seemed to bristle and his face turned red. "Señor Johnson, we must have land reform in my country, and whether or not you choose to believe it, we have an excellent chance of winning the election. If we don't, the people will revolt. Of that I am confident. In your own country you opened up the land for settlement. Homesteading, I believe it is called. I submit that is the real reason your country is so powerful." Everyone around the table looked at him. Some people appeared quizzical, others annoyed.

Undaunted he placed his fork quietly down on his plate and continued. "There is great unrest, across the river. For years, here in Chihuahua, anyone who would fight the Apaches received land in exchange for his services. But now that the Indian threat is over and the government does not need them to fight the Indians, it is stealing the land from them by chicanery and legal manipulation."

"What do you mean stealing?" asked the major.

"There was a time when the only people who stood between Mexico and the Apache were the common people who had no place to go. They fought and held the Indians at bay while the hacendados abandoned their estates and ran back to the security of civilization."

"Indian fighters, huh? Well we don't have an Indian problem now," a middle aged man across the table from Padget said.

"My point exactly, and now that the Apache are no longer a threat, the people who shed their blood in defense of their homeland are no longer needed. Crooked politicians, like Luis Terrazas and his son-in-law Enrique Creel, have taken over the state and are passing laws to steal the land back from the very people who kept it out of the Apaches hands," Gonzales said.

The man across the table shook his head. "Oh, come now, those are pretty strong words."

Gonzales scowled at the remark. "They've already replaced the elected leaders with their cronies. The common man no longer has anyone to prevent the theft of land. Land they fought for is now being taken from them. They are left to starve."

Padget watched Gonzalez's face. The man sounded like he knew what he was talking about.

The big nosed major's voice rose. "That sounds like Bolshevik talk to me."

Walt lifted his wine glass. "Spoken like a true despot, Major. Have you ever been to Mexico to see how the peons down there live? We called it slavery, and fought a war to stop it, not too long ago."

"When did you become an advocate of rebellion?" the major asked.

"Since I was in Coahuila last year. Times are getting pretty tough on both sides of the border. There are a lot of people out of work down there," Walt said.

"So?"

"Well, I know for a fact that Madero's been using his own money to feed the people on his ranch and it doesn't matter if they work for him or not," Walt said.

"Surely you're not suggesting that we should feed the poor? We would go broke in a fortnight," the Major said.

Walt set his wine glass on the table. "We've always fed anyone who comes by the Rafter J. You should read the bible, Major. Start with Matthew 19:21. How can you not feed someone if he's hungry?"

Bush, in an apparent effort to change the line of conversation before it got out of hand, broke into the conversation. "Speaking of dictators, what is the latest from Europe? Are we going to get sucked into that fiasco? Ah, here is dessert."

Padget watched Bush disarm the argument. He owed that man a lot for saving his aunt. Later that evening as the guests were filing out, Padget told Bush that if he wanted to go deer hunting there was a big old mossy horned buck hanging around under Eagle Peak with his name on it. Bush smiled and said that sounded good. He hesitated, and then said, "Why don't you and your friend join me for breakfast at Mae's Café tomorrow. There is something I would like to discuss."

Chapter Thirty-seven

The aroma of frying ham and baking powder biscuits greeted Padget as he pushed through the doors into Mae's Café. The room was crowded with the breakfast rush. Bush and Phillips sat at a table in the rear, away from the other customers. Bush raised his hand and waved them over.[8]

Padget and Ochoa squeezed their way though the early breakfast racket to the table. Bush motioned toward chairs on the opposite side of the table. "Here, please sit down, I hope you slept well."

Ochoa pulled off his coat and hung it on the back of a chair then plumped down into it. A petite brunette poured coffee into thick china mugs. She took their orders and left.

---

8 This would be Saturday, 19 December 1909.

"Padget, I've been giving some thought to what you said last night," Bush said.

"Well, I hope so. We've got some of the best hunting in west Texas on the Rafter J," Padget said.

"What I mean is...last night you were quite outspoken with Major Reed."

Padget set his cup down and looked at him. "I don't know if I was outspoken with that pig headed son of a bitch or not."

"Don't get me wrong, I agree with you. Reed is, as you put it, pretty pig headed, but you called the execution in Juarez yesterday, murder," Bush said.

Padget leaned back in his chair, folding his arms across his chest. "I don't know where you're going with this Doc. And I don't know where you stand, but my words were straight. It was murder, plain out and out murder, and yesterday wasn't the first time I've seen it with Diaz's bunch."

"Not the first time?" Bush said.

"Just after Thanksgiving, Ochoa and I were in a little place called Talón; across the river in Chihuahua. The rurales slaughtered an entire village — except for one little girl they raped and left for dead."

"We hadn't heard anything about that," Bush said, looking at Phillips.

Padget told them about the chase down into Mexico after the stolen horses and the trip through and back to Talón and about bringing Juana back to Ojos Calientes. He told them about the hangings at the Cananea Mine when he was an Arizona Ranger.

"Ochoa and I were in Cuba with Colonel Roosevelt when he put the quietus on the Dons. I don't know why we don't just do the same thing and put an end to this mess down there in Mexico."

Harvey Phillips set down his coffee cup. "That was a different matter altogether. Cuba was occupied by a foreign power — Mexico is not."

"What difference does that make? It's six of one, half a dozen of the other. Whether it is a rattler or a copperhead that bites you, if you don't get some help, you're probably going to die." Ochoa said. He was clearly agitated by the question.

"Truly spoken," Doctor Bush said. "But surely you understand that the United States can do nothing overtly?"

"I don't know what you mean by overtly—we ought to be doing something." Padget said.

"Openly." Doctor Bush said.

"I don't care how we do it," Padget said. "We need to do it."

Phillips shifted in his chair. "There are people in the United States with investments in Mexico, powerful men who believe a change to a democratic regime would cost them money. Those same men have a great deal of influence in Congress. Consequently, I don't believe that the United States government will intervene."

Padget leaned forward. "So, we're going to sit back and watch while a bunch of people get slaughtered because some rich people back east are afraid of losing a few bucks?"

"There are some who are unwilling to sit idly by and watch innocent people get killed," Phillips said.

Padget and Ochoa looked at Phillips, waiting for him to continue. Phillips picked up his cup and motioned to the waitress. No one spoke while she poured coffee.

When she left, he continued. "You've seen what is happening down there. In my opinion there will be a revolution, and it will happen soon."

The more Padget thought about it the more he agreed. "When the shooting starts the peons won't have a chance unless they're armed," he said.

"You could be a big help, if you really meant what you said about doing something," Phillips said.

Phillips wanted something from him and it was probably something shady. "Well, sure I meant it, but how can we help?" Padget said, and glanced at Ochoa. "I'm speaking for myself here."

Ochoa rubbed his nose and pointed at Padget. "My pard's talking for me too."

"What I'm saying is, when the time comes, we must make sure the insurgents have the arms they need to fight Diaz's soldiers," Phillips said.

Padget shook his head. "If you are talking about running guns, let me pass on something to you that I heard from Jose Griego. Back in October, Ochoa and I were chasing jaguars all over the country. I rode down to the river and stopped at the Griego Farm. It was after we split up, so Ochoa wasn't with me. While we were eating supper, Don Jose tells me that a friend of his with the rurales knows all about the arms smuggling that's going on."

"Exactly what did he tell you?" Bush asked.

"What he said was that this colonel friend of his knew that Madero supporters in El Paso had purchased some rifles and ammunition from an arms broker up in New York. And that the shipment is on the way down here and that an attempt would be made to smuggle the stuff into Mexico. So if that is what you are talking about, forget it. They know about it already. Anybody who tries to run those guns into Mexico is going to have a pretty tough time getting over the river without getting shot."

"Yes, his intelligence apparatus is good," said Phillips. "But not as good as it might be."

The waitress set their plates on the table and refilled the cups. When she left Phillips resumed. "The shipment your friend was talking about is a load of Mauser rifles and ammunition captured in Cuba when you men were there. Subsequently, they were purchased by a man named Bannerman in New York and stored in his warehouse. The bad part is that the storage was damp and the arms are pretty much useless. Anyway, the Army intercepted the shipment and it will probably never reach Mexico. The confiscation of the arms established the intent of the United States with regard to the Neutrality Act. They're discouraging anyone from helping the insurgents. By the way, those guns were confiscated last night — while we were having dinner."

"So what is it you are saying?" Padget asked.

"The information passed to Colonel Kosterlitzky was a ruse. What he does not know and what he probably does not suspect, is that there is another shipment: Mausers, brand new and straight from Germany. This shipment is sitting on a Southern Pacific siding, until it can be moved into Mexico."

"Excuse me, Mr. Phillips, but how do you know all this?" Padget asked.

"This is all confidential of course. I use to work for the Secret Service and still maintain close connections with my friends there. We also have agents in the field, people who work for me and not any government agency. There are people in the United States who believe as you do, Mr. Padget. My job is to get the shipment of arms to the right people in Chihuahua. That is where you come in, if you are willing to help us. There is five hundred dollars apiece in it for you and Ochoa, if you can get those rifles into Mexico."

Padget rubbed his mustache with his thumb and forefinger. "Why us?" Padget asked. "If you have the rifles, why don't you just move them across the river? There are a hundred places to cross between here and Indian Hot Springs."

"Well, the problem is not so much finding

a place to cross. We need to move them from where they are to the river. And there is one other proposition."

"What is that?" Padget said.

"The insurgents are just getting organized; the groups are quite small. The largest is somewhat fewer than one hundred men. The rifles will have to be moved in small batches, and we can't store them in Mexico," Bush said.

"Sounds like you're damned if you do and damned if you don't," Padget said. "You can't leave them where they are and you can't take them into Mexico. So what's your plan?"

"I'll need your word that you are with us before we go any farther." Phillips said.

Padget shook his head. "I'll give you my word this conversation won't go any farther, but until I know what you want Ochoa and me to do, I won't agree that we'll do it."

Phillips looked at Bush who nodded his head. "There are 1000 brand new 7mm Mausers and 100,000 rounds of ammunition in a box car near Sierra Blanca. We need to move them to Indian Hot Springs and store them while we take small lots into Chihuahua when they are needed."

"Whoa, hold on, are you telling me that Mrs.

Rudd is in on this? " Padget asked.

"Jewel Rudd is one of my agents and knows about the shipment. There is another person, a young lady who teaches the local children. Her name is Pilar Martinez. We will store the load in Jewell Rudd's barn until we can move it on down."

Padget was stunned. He would never have guessed in a hundred years, that either of these women would be involved in smuggling. Women weren't supposed to get involved in this kind of stuff, they kept house,cooked, washed, and taught school, but smuggling arms was unheard of.

The table was silent as Ochoa and Padget looked from one to the other and back again. Finally Padget broke the silence. "Well, I guess I'm in. But you better tell us exactly what we have to do; we have a train to catch."

The car was empty except for Padget, Ochoa, and an ancient Mexican lady wearing a black shawl over an equally black dress. She huddled against the cold in the front of the car.

Padget pulled his coat up over his ears and

watched the jackrabbits. Sitting along the railroad, they appeared to be watching the train as it sped along the tracks.

Ochoa leaned back in the seat. "It's going to take more than one wagon."

"I've been thinking about the weight of that shipment. It will be slow going; it won't be too bad from Eagle Flat to the Rudd place, from there I figure we'll pack the guns on mules if all we're only going to take is a hundred rifles and ammunition at a time." Padget scrunched down in the seat and pulled his hat low over his forehead.

"We should be able to get ten rifles and a thousand cartridges on a mule without too much trouble," Ochoa said.

"We'll string them together. You take five and I'll take five...move pretty fast that way. Be in and out in two days at the most," Padget said.

"That's the easy part. Got to make it through the Army first," Ochoa said.

Padget pushed his hat back. "It's our Army we have to watch out for, the federales stay pretty much away from the river." He shook his head. "I wasn't drunk when I agreed to do this, hell I hadn't even had a drink, but you'd damn sure think so. You think maybe I'm getting senile in my old age?

Why I let Phillips talk us into this beats the hell out of me."

"He didn't have to talk too hard after he laid those double eagles on the table," Ochoa said.

"Well you could have jumped in and said something anytime," Padget said.

"Won't make me rich, but the money ain't bad," Ochoa said.

Chapter Thirty-eight

The west Texas sandstorm was doing its best to batter down the town of Sierra Blanca. The wind bounced a tumbleweed across the depot platform with a force that almost blew off Padget's hat. He watched the tumbleweed pause against the handrail for a moment and continue on east where it came to rest against a barrier of mesquite and catclaw at the edge of town. He jammed his hat down on his head and turned to help an elderly lady down from the train. Holding on to her arm, he walked her inside the depot.

The wind caused the clapboards to slap against the side of Griego's store. Against the howl of the wind it sounded like someone shooting off a pistol. Keeping a hand on his hat Padget walked into the store and out of the wind. The noise of the clapboards was louder inside and Padget looked up to make sure the roof was still holding firm.

"Well, if you two don't look like something the cat dragged in."

Padget turned. Intent brown eyes examined him from behind the counter. "Are you working for Don Jose now, Pilar?" Padget said.

"Just for the Christmas season; Robert's in Fort Worth and Hector's down with the flu. He asked me to fill in. How was El Paso?" Pilar asked. There was the merest hint of a smile at the corners of her mouth. Her long black hair was done up in a ponytail and tied with a red bandanna. The effect was one of youthful beauty. She was the prettiest woman he had ever seen.

"How's Juana?" Padget and Ochoa asked at the same time.

"Lots better. She's getting over the physical damage. Holding her own with the other," Pilar said. "She is eating well and learning to read. She's here in town with me. We're staying with Uncle Bill and Aunt Dorothy. Your aunt and uncle were by yesterday to drop off some things for her. They will be back tomorrow to take her home for Christmas. Come over for supper tonight, Bill and Dorothy will be glad to see you and I know Juana will be delighted. She's been asking about you."

"Count on it." Padget said.

The wind died at sundown and silence fell over the town as they sat down to supper. Juana sat quietly with her eyes downcast, leaning on Pilar. Padget noticed, that through her dark eye lashes, she kept glancing at him and Ochoa.

"Hola, Miel, Hi Honey," Padget said.

She blushed and looked down at her plate, then back up again and smiled. Padget made small talk with Pilar and the Matsons. When he thought Juana wasn't looking, he examined her face closely for any sign of distress; seeing none he relaxed. Praise the Lord for miracles. He felt the sting of tears and turned to look at Ochoa who seemed to have something in his eye. I swear to God. As long as I live no one will ever hurt her again.

After dinner Pilar put Juana to bed. There was no protest. It was evident to Padget that it would take some time for her to regain full strength. It would do Claire good to have someone to care for.

The dishes were washed, wiped and put away. Ochoa and Bill were discussing the merits of the Colt Lightning against the Smith and Wesson hand ejector. Dorothy excused herself to correct mid-term exams from her class. Pilar pulled a shawl down from the wall. "I'm going to take a walk; do you want to come along, Wes?"

Padget scrambled up out of his chair. "I sure would."

"I usually walk down by the depot and back," she said.

Anywhere you want to go, and anything you want to do lady, he thought. "Sure, that sounds fine," he said.

Pilar walked through the gate he held open and Padget could smell the faint aroma of lilac about her. Side by side they turned south along the Del City-Sierra Blanca Road walking toward town. A jack rabbit sitting alongside the road started and casually hopped off into the chemise. A coyote began tuning up somewhere to the east; it was immediately answered by several more away to the south.

They walked in silence until they came to the railroad tracks. Holding her hand, he helped her over the rails and she did not pull her hand away. At the depot they climbed the steps to the platform and stopped to watch the station clerk hang a mail sack alongside the track.

Padget inclined his head toward the bench outside the waiting room and said, "Would you care to sit for a spell?"

Pilar laughed softly. "Sure, that sounds fine." She took his hand in both of hers and led him to the bench. He had been around women before, but none made his throat ache like this one. They sat with shoulders touching, silently watching the stars come out one by one.

A freight train passed through without stopping. Someone threw a mailbag to the platform, and a hook on the baggage car caught the hanging mailbag on the fly. The click-clack of the wheels lulled Padget further into his own thoughts. The train was a mile from town before either spoke.

"What was it like in Cuba when you were there, Wes? I mean the people. Were they glad when we beat the Spaniards? Did it make a difference? Was there a change in their lives? Was it better for the poor people?" she asked.

He paused and thought about the questions and remembered Cuba and the war. "To tell you the truth I don't really know. Yeah, I suppose they were glad to see us... at least there were plenty of people giving us information about the Dons. Most of them were dirt poor and starving. We, that is my troop, gave most of our rations to those hungry kids. Just some beans and hard tack, but they were glad to get it. It's kind of like Mexico I guess.

THERE AIN'T NO MONEY IN IT

Rich folks seem to make out, no matter what the deal is and the poor folks just keep on getting the dirty end of the stick."

The talk about the war seemed to break the spell and gloom settled in where pleasure had been. He stood, pulling Pilar up with him. "You mind if we walk a bit farther?" he asked. She shook her head, looking closely at him.

They left the depot platform and circled the stockyards, walking into the chaparral outside the town limits. She didn't take her hand away and as they walked, her presence soon dispelled his gloom.

The moon was high in the eastern sky and Sierra Blanca Peak loomed large in the west. They stopped to admire the grandeur of the mountain. The night was silent and he turned to look at Pilar. She was watching him. His throat tightened. He pulled lightly on her hand and she came into his arms. He bent his head and kissed her.

She parted her lips and he felt the soft touch of her tongue and her arms reached up and caught him tightly around the neck. How long the kiss lasted he could never remember, but she broke off and pushed him back and looked into his eyes.

"Whew! Cowboy, let a girl catch her breath."

Chapter Thirty-nine

It was the last day of 1909 when, stricken by anxiety, Padget presented the bill of lading to the clerk who worked for the Southern Pacific Railroad at Sierra Blanca. It read: *FARM MACHINERY AND WINDMILL PARTS- HOLD, WILL CALL.*

It was a cool day, but Padget could feel the sweat under his arms. He had a strange premonition that the Army had discovered the ruse and was just waiting for someone to try to claim the shipment. They would arrest him any minute now. "How do. We're here to pick up some farm machinery." He pushed the paper across the counter.

The clerk glanced at it and said, "Well, it's out at Eagle Flat — it's about time someone picked it up. What's the Rafter J going to do with all that farm machinery?"

"Actually, we're just hauling it up to Dell City for some people in El Paso," Padget said.

"Why didn't you have us bring it into town instead of leaving it on the siding?"

Padget felt the panic inside. "If it was up to me, I wouldn't even have ordered it at all. I told you we're just getting paid to haul it."

"Well the railroad's not going to pay to have it brought in. You'll just have to go get it yourselves. I'll send Curt out to cut the seal for you," the clerk said.

Padget felt the cold sweat roll down his sides. They were undone; Curt was the railroad detective and would arrest them as soon as the car was opened and he saw the guns. "Hell, we can cut the seal ourselves. You don't need to bother Curt. That'll save him a trip all the way out to Eagle Flat and back."

The eyes of the clerk narrowed; a look of suspicion showed plainly on his face. "Nope, can't be done that way. The railroad has to remove the seal," the clerk said.

Padget stomach knotted and he wanted to turn around and walk out of the station and forget he had ever heard of Phillips or Bush or the insurgents

DELBERT GILBOW

in Mexico. Maybe if he left now he wouldn't have to spend the next ten years in a federal prison. He wiped the sweat off of his forehead with the back of his hand.

The clerk stared him straight in the eye.

Ochoa broke in. "How about if we sign a paper that says we accept the goods just as they are. That way you and the railroad will be off the hook, the detective won't have to make a long dusty ride and we can load the stuff ourselves and get on the road. I'd like to get this job over with and get back to riding for a living."

The clerk looked at Ochoa for the first time. His face plainly showed that he thought Ochoa was the smarter of the two. "Well, if you want to take responsibility for the shipment..."

"Oh, we take responsibility," Padget quickly said, "and that way we can get on the road and Curt won't be put out any." Ochoa, you are a coyote.

"Damn, how many cases of this stuff did they send? There are enough guns here to start a..." Padget stopped and laughed.

Working in the warm January sun, it took

nearly five hours to load two hundred cases of ammunition marked FARM EQUIPMENT and one hundred cases of rifles marked WINDMILL PARTS. They divided the arms between the two wagons and covered the loads with sacks of corn and oats. They stretched canvas tarps over everything and roped the cargo securely. Padget drove one wagon, Ochoa the other. They headed east along the south side of the railroad tracks.

"Anybody who knows me will think I'm crazy," muttered Ochoa. "Nobody will believe, that instead of eating black eyed peas and side meat, I'm spending New Years Day running guns."

Padget flicked the lead mule with a jerk line. "What are you carping about now?"

Ochoa's voice carried back to Padget. "If someone had told me last month that we'd be starting a revolution, I would have told him he was as full of crap as a Christmas goose. Now look at me."

"I sure do hate to hear a grown man cry." Padget felt a lot less anxious since covering the wagons. "Just think of what you can do with all that dinero you're getting for this."

"All we got was a down payment and it will be pretty hard to spend any money from a prison cell." Ochoa whistled to the mules pulling his wagon. "We'll be on the road for two days, just getting to the river. If anybody comes along, we'll be up to our eyebrows in brown smelly stuff."

"We'll stop at the Macadoo place for the night, and then go on in the morning," Padget said.

The sun was down behind Sierra Blanca Peak and gray twilight filled with bull bats swooping and diving at insects. A coyote howled behind Devil's Ridge and was answered by another off to the east. It would be dark in a few minutes.

"The moon will be up about midnight and we can get an early start."

"You sure you don't want to just keep on going?" Ochoa asked.

"There shouldn't be anyone out and about on Sunday. We ought to be able to make it to the Rudd place by tomorrow afternoon late, if we don't run into the Army," Padget said.

"You think the Army is this far out?"

Padget felt like he was whistling his way past a grave yard. "Not on New Year's Day. We shouldn't have any problem, once we get to the main road running south. Anyway, if they are out, they're not likely to be this far from the river."

"You always did talk a good fight," he heard Ochoa say.

Chapter Forty

Tired and hungry they reached Ojos Calientes just after sundown. Jewel Rudd stepped out of the shadows. "Get down; I see you boys took up honest work for a change. Supper will be ready pretty soon, go on into the hotel and I'll have the boys put these wagons in the barn. Pepe, Manuel, ven"ca," she said to two young Mexican men standing by the corral. Jewel inclined her head toward a large corral alongside the barn. "The mules are in there and ready to go. The boys worked all week getting the kinks out. The others will follow that bay jenny with the crook in her ear. You better put your horses in the other corral."

After supper, there didn't seem to be any sense in going to bed. Padget and Ochoa stayed up drinking coffee, cleaning their rifles and replacing the cartridges in their shell belts. Ochoa inspected each cartridge as he removed it from the box. He wiped it clean with a rag and with his pocketknife, cut a thin slice of lead off each bullet. It gave it a blunt end.

Padget was amused at his obvious concentration. "You must be reckoning hard, Mano, because I see the smoke coming out of your ears."

"I am," Ochoa said. "Chances are pretty long that we'll run into that Urbina hombre down there and he'll have a lot more of his crowd with him. I don't care what Bush and Philips say. Villa may not be able to hold him back."

"Them Mexicans bother you some?" Padget said.

Ochoa grimaced. "He'd give his right arm to shove a knife in your guts, Wes. I've got a hunch he'd like to get his hands on me."

Padget nodded. "I admit I've been thinking about that some. Sometimes, I think that we're crazier than a pet coon for running guns across the border."

"It's a little late to start thinking," Ochoa said.

Padget picked up his cup and drained it and set it on the table. "Say what you want, but lately I've been thinking a lot about some of the choices I've made in my life."

"So?"

"Not many of them showed any smart, but none of them was this dumb," Padget said.

"About like the day Bucky O'Neill got it and you led the charge up Kettle Hill to pick him up. I thought that was pretty dumb."

"If you thought that was so dumb, why did you come along?"

"To keep your butt out of trouble," Ochoa said.

"And what does that make you?"

Padget picked up his Winchester and began to wipe the dust from the action, thinking about the fight with Urbina in the cantina. "I suppose that before I get too much older I'm going to have to kill that Mexican son of a bitch." Padget saw Ochoa looking over his shoulder and turned. Pilar was watching him from the door. There was a stricken look on her face; she looked like she had just been slapped.

"I didn't know you were here, Pilar," Padget said.

She turned and walked away. Padget quickly got up from the table and followed her into the yard. "Pilar. Where are you going?" As he caught up with her he put his hand on her shoulder.

She jerked away, "Don't touch me."

He stopped and dropped his hand. "What is wrong?"

"We're wrong, Wes. You and I."

"I don't know what you mean, Pilar. I thought..."

"So did I for a while, but we could never work out..."

"That's the craziest thing I've ever heard. What have I done?"

"It's not what you've done, Wes, it is what you are."

"I'm a cowboy, always have been, always will be."

"That's not what I mean."

"I know I'm a little rough around the edges, but…"

"The rough I can handle. It's the way you feel about Mexicans."

"What do you mean, the way I feel about Mexicans?"

"You don't like us, Wes."

"Pilar, that doesn't make any since at all. I love you, and David Ochoa is Mexican. He's the best friend I've got in this world." He searched her face for any sign of emotion. He found only pain.

"Dave has a Mexican name. You speak better

Spanish than he does. Anyway it doesn't have anything to do with that. Did you hear what you said?"

"What are you talking about?"

"When you were in the kitchen talking to Dave. The vehemence you put on the word Mexican scared me. It still scares me...as if you think that Mexicans are a different species."

"Pilar, I...that isn't what I meant at all. It's just that after the fight we had, I don't know of any other possible outcome."

"No, Wes, you said it twice. You asked Dave if those Mexicans bothered him, and then you said I'm going to have to kill that Mexican son of a bitch. You should listen to yourself, Wes."

Padget stood helpless as she walked into the darkness.

Chapter Forty-one

Still confused about Pilar's reaction to his words; Padget sat with his back against a clump of willows and watched the far river bank. He wondered if they were riding into a trap. A match flared across the river. Someone lit a cigarette and in the glare of the flame Padget could clearly see the lines in the man's face. Through his field glasses, Padget watched the man throw back his serape and urinate into the river. Buttoning his pants the man turned and walked back toward a jacal that showed dimly against the night. Padget waited another hour. When nothing moved he returned to the hotel. "It's time to go."

"Damn, it's dark as the inside of a mine," Ochoa said. He stumbled as he stepped down from the hotel porch, almost dropping his rifle. Padget reached and steadied his friend, "The moon will be up in a little bit." He could hear the mules eating hay near the barn. The smell of the hay, mixed with the odor of mule crap wafted across the yard.

When he got to the corral he found ten mules, with their tarp covered loads of rifles and ammunition. They were tethered head to tail in two rows along the south side the barn. Padget walked among the mules, inspecting the packs. He pulled on a quarter strap here and loosened a breeching there. He made sure the ropes that tied the guns down were tight and that nothing would come loose. He didn't want to lose anything on the trail. Pepe and Miguel appeared from the barn.

"Cuantas por mula?" Padget asked.

"Diez rifles y mil cartuchos. Como me dijo." Ten rifles and a thousand cartridges, like you told me.

The moon had risen and the coyotes and night hawks were quiet as Padget stepped aboard Skeeter. He reached out his hand and took a lead rope from Pepe. "Gracias," he said.

Padget looked around the ranch for any sign of Pilar. If she was there, she wasn't letting him know it. He touched the dun with his spurs and started toward the river with five mules in his string. Each mule behind the leader tied to the tail of the mule ahead with a line from its headstall.

The bells on Ochoa's spurs jangled softly as he mounted his horse. Manuel handed him the lead for the remaining five mules and touched his hat with his left hand. "Cuidado."

"Por supuesto," Ochoa said. He waited until the last of Padget's mules passed him, then fell in behind with his string.

The moon rose just as they reached the Rio Grande crossing. Padget stopped at the water's edge on the United States side of the river. He peered through the mist and tried to see the far bank. After several minutes he continued across.

The swish of the water against the legs of the horses and mules seemed loud enough to wake the dead. Padget continued to strain his eyes, looking for federales that might be lying in ambush on the Mexico side. Reaching the south bank of the river, they began the steep climb to the mesa that ran along the river channel.

Bending over the saddle and looking at the ground, Padget found the main trail about a mile west of the crossing. Silently he touched Skeeter with his spurs and turned south along the beaten path. He looked back to make sure Ochoa didn't miss the turn. He wanted to stay together because it wasn't far to the rendezvous. They traveled slowly, watching and listening for any sign of trouble.

A lighter band of sky began to show on the eastern horizon. Padget reined in Skeeter and waited for Ochoa to catch up. He placed his forefinger over his mouth for silence and stepped down from the roan. He handed Ochoa the reins and lead rope. "Notice anything?" he whispered.

Ochoa nodded and swept his right hand out from his left shoulder in an arc to the right and touched his ear. The quiet beat down upon them. There was not as much as one bird chirp. It was as if the night was waiting for something to happen. Ochoa eased his Krag from the saddle boot and placed it across his knees.

Padget could just distinguish the gray-blue color of the chaparral from the night shadows. It was too damn quiet. "I'm going to scout on up the trail a ways," he whispered.

He knelt in the sand to unbuckle his spurs. Buckling them back together he hung them on his saddle horn. He slipped his carbine out of his scabbard and moved off into the darkness. Forty feet away he slipped down into the arroyo running along the road and disappeared from sight. An hour passed before he returned.

"It looks like the bunch we are supposed to meet, is up there waiting for us on up the trail. Five of them and they look like bandits. They damn sure don't look like federales," Padget said. He put his spurs back on, mounted Skeeter and took the lead rope from Ochoa. The roan started forward in a walk with the mules trailing along.

It was getting light when they reached the junction of a trail that led off to the west and into the hills. A group of riders, motionless in the brush, watched them as they approached. The crowns of their sombreros stuck up like fingers in the pre-dawn light. Bandoleers of ammunition crossed the chests of the riders. One man wore a single cartridge belt that contained both rifle and pistol ammunition and instead of a sombrero, wore a much abused narrow brimmed old derby.

The first thing Padget noticed was a sandy red cavalry moustache that hung down over a wide smiling mouth, and a pair of pale blue eyes that looked at him in the early morning light. A double action Colt Lightning hung in a homemade holster on his right hip. It was balanced by a long skinning knife on his left. Both were suspended from a wide cartridge belt with a double row of cartridges.

The man with the cavalry mustache was sitting

with his right leg thrown over the saddle horn rolling a cigarette with one hand. He stuffed the tobacco sack back into a pocket in his leather vest. He left the round Bull Durham tag hanging outside the pocket. Without taking his eyes off Padget and Ochoa, he licked the paper, shoved the cigarette between his lips and lit it. He sucked the smoke in lustily and exhaled. "Hello, boys, I'm here to show you the way into camp." He pulled his horse's head around and led the way down into the arroyo.

The riders traveled single file for about a mile behind a thicket of catclaw and into a ravine surrounded by tall, vertical walls of sandstone. Here the trail widened and two riders could now ride side by side.

The Mexican riders formed an escort around the mules and started into the ravine. The man with the mustache reined his mount down until he was riding beside Padget. "Frank McComb," he said, reaching out his right hand to shake with Padget. "Bush says to say hello."

"Wes Padget. Glad to know you." He motioned to the rear with his left thumb. "David Ochoa."

Padget was surprised to find a gringo this far from the border who seemed to be in charge of an aggregation of Mexican bandits. After the first exchange of words, nothing more was said as they worked their way up the trail. Two hours passed and McComb raised his arm to stop the riders. "Soy McComb con rifles y cartuchos," he yelled out. The yell of an unseen sentinel immediately answered him.

"Bueno. Pasen, Francisco. Bueno, Frank. Pasa. Pancho espera." McComb dropped his arm and spurred his horse on up the trail. The rest of the convoy followed.

Chapter Forty-two

From somewhere up ahead Padget heard a dog bark. Another immediately joined it, and others soon joined in to shatter the early morning silence. The pungent smell of burning greasewood drifted down to the riders. The trail opened into a broad canyon. Down through the center of the valley a line of cottonwood trees marked a stream course. In the shade of the trees tents and make-do shelters were lined up along both sides of the stream.

Padget looked down into the faces of a hostile, silent group of men and women who stared at them as they rode into camp. Padget counted twenty-eight men and ten women. One woman held a naked baby on her hip while it sucked on her exposed breast. He scanned their faces, looking for Urbina.

The procession pulled up in front of a dirty wall tent that might have been white somewhere in the far distant past. It was pitched in the shade of a tall cottonwood tree that stood alone.

McComb motioned the riders down off their horses. "Rest your saddles, boys." He swung down from his horse and nodded in the direction of two riders across the canyon floor, "That's the jefe over there."

Padget could see the two riders across the valley floor on the far side of the stream, but could not determine which of the two riders McComb indicated. Turning back to the mules he dropped the lead. The mules stood, ground hitched, and began cropping the short grass growing along the stream. "Where do you want the guns?"

McComb motioned to one of the men who then unrolled a tarpaulin and laid it out on the ground. "Right over there."

Ochoa untied the pack ropes on one mule and unloaded ten rifles and ammunition onto the tarp. He walked to the next mule and began to untie the pack. McComb stopped him. "I don't know where they will want to stow this stuff, so why don't you wait before you unload the rest?"

Padget and Ochoa picketed the mules on a line

that allowed freedom to graze, but kept them together. They could be caught easily. No one spoke to Padget and Ochoa.

McComb demonstrated how to remove the bolt from the rifles and clean them. He handed a rifle to one of the Mexicans and looked at Padget. "These will help. We can get horses from the rancheros here about, but we're always short of rifles and cartridges."

The two riders, McComb had pointed out to Padget, rode in under the cottonwoods and let their horses drink. Padget recognized one of the riders. He nudged Ochoa, "That's Abraham Gonzales, Madero's man."

The riders crossed the stream and rode into camp. Gonzales smiled as he rode up. "Señor Padget, Señor Ochoa, bien venido." With a motion of his right hand he indicated the other rider. "Let me introduce to you to my friend, Francisco Villa."

Padget looked at the man. A round face with coal black eyes stared out from the shadow cast by his sombrero. "Hola, señores," Villa said. He stepped down from his horse and stood beside McComb. He was shorter by a half foot. He had a large mustache that drooped at both ends and wore silver mounted spurs with rowels that were larger than silver dollars. The spurs jingled when he moved. He wore a double bandoleer of ammunition crossed over his chest and an ivory handled Colt stuffed into the waistband of his trousers. A smile crossed his face. "Bein venido. Soy Pancho."

Without waiting for a reply he turned to a woman standing at a nearby campfire. "Comida. Tengo hambre." He motioned to an emaciated Mexican whose deeply pock marked face reminded Padget of a lava flow. The man brought one of the rifles to Villa. Villa worked the bolt and squeezed the trigger. The clear snap of the firing pin falling on an empty chamber seemed loud in the stillness.

"Bring some cartridges, Pablo," Villa said, opening the bolt. Holding the rifle in his left hand he took a stripper clip of cartridges from him and loaded the rifle with one swift downward push of his right thumb. He closed the bolt with one fluid motion, raised the rifle to his shoulder and pulled the trigger. The sharp report of a high powered rifle filled the air. The recoil rocked Villa backward and a puff of dust flew from a rock across the canyon. He handed the rifle to Padget and nodded toward the target.

Padget threw the rifle into his shoulder and

fired. Without taking the rifle from his shoulder he worked the bolt and chambered another round. Dust from a rock alongside the one hit by Villa, marked his shot.

As he took the rifle down from his shoulder, Frank McComb's rifle went off. Padget looked at the hillside and saw a rock breaking into pieces some fifty yards farther than the ones he and Villa had hit.

Before anyone could say a word Ochoa fired and hit a rock even farther away.

Laughing, Villa took the rifle from Padget and handed it to one of the Mexicans standing nearby. "Hold this for me. We shall now discover the rooster. Pepe, blanco a que si tira." A short Mexican trotted across the valley floor and placed some tin cans in a line against the canyon wall.

Villa signaled nine of the bandits to step forward. The pockfaced bandit handed each of the nine a new Mauser and a bandoleer of ammunition. McComb spent the next hour with them in rifle practice.

Padget tightened the cinch on Ochoa's horse. Then he caught Button, replaced the headstall and tightened the cinch on his saddle. He looked for Ochoa and saw him drinking a cup of coffee, talking with one of the bandits.

He raised his hand to motion to Dave. He caught the sound of someone yelling and looked around. He could hear men shouting near the mouth of the canyon. There was some kind of commotion. He saw a group of riders coming in fast. Padget felt the hair on the back of his neck stand up. He put his thumb and forefinger in his mouth and whistled to Ochoa. Ochoa looked up and trotted toward him, carrying his Krag in his left hand. Villa and the other bandits were looking intently at the approaching riders. Something was definitely wrong.

Chapter Forty-three

Padget mounted his horse. He didn't want to be afoot if this was trouble. The dun danced sideways, sensing the excitement. "Whoa, settle down."

Ochoa mounted his horse, still holding his Krag. He rode up alongside of Padget and the two of them watched the arrival of the men racing across the valley floor. The riders pulled their horses up and skidded to a stop in front of Villa.

"Rurales! Rurales!" they shouted as they pulled up

"Donde?" Villa asked.

"Alli, alli," one rider said. "En la sendera detras." He pointed to the trail behind him. Padget saw a group of riders pouring into the canyon. Without slowing, they spread out into a line abreast.

A trumpet sounded and they charged straight at Padget and Ochoa across the level valley floor.

"Oh, crap," Padget said, as he recognized the precision of seasoned troops in action. The rurales were halfway across the valley before anyone moved.

Villa, the first one to act, threw up his rifle and fired. The foremost horse went down, throwing the rider over his neck and somersaulting over him. Puffs of smoke erupted from the charging line. The flat whip of a bullet passing close caused Padget to wince. It was followed by the plop of a heavy projectile hitting flesh. The pock marked Mexican grabbed his chest and crumpled to the ground.

A woman, holding a baby girl, started to run toward the trees. Padget watched her dart between the tents, picking up speed as she raced across the open ground. She reached the stream bank, fell, dropped the child, and sprawled headlong on the ground. A heavy caliber bullet had gone through the woman's body hitting the child in the head. He turned back to the fight.

Now, Villa's men began to return fire, ragged at first, and then with increasing regularity as the bandits overcame their initial astonishment.

Firing from the rurales increased in volume. A man on Padget's left fell to his knees, the lower portion of his face shot away. Padget felt the air whip his shirt and heard a grunt behind him. He glanced to his rear. A bandit abruptly sat down on the ground holding his stomach. He put one hand to his belt buckle as if he wanted to undo it, and then slumped to the ground, blood gushed from his mouth.

They were shooting them to pieces. When Padget looked back at the attackers he saw a yellow flickering off to one side of the soldiers and heard the sound of automatic weapons fire.

The federales had a damned machine gun. He wondered idly if it were a Vickers or a Colt.

The rurales were almost upon them; their horses loomed large in the morning sunlight. The sound of the hooves on the hard packed ground hammered in his ears as they pounded closer. Suddenly, the line of rurales swerved out of the path of the automatic fire into a line oblique.

"A caballo," Villa shouted. "Vamanos!" Instantly, the scene turned from confusion to chaos. Men ran to their horses. Two raced toward a woman that was running across the valley. One rider fell behind; using his body as a shield he screened her from the shooting.

The other bandit grabbed her arm and without slowing his horse swung her up behind him. She grabbed him around the waist and the three raced toward the far end of the canyon. The rearmost rider emptied his revolver at the approaching rurales.

Padget heard McComb shouting, "No, no! Aqui! Pepe, Jesus, Edon, Guillermo, to me, to me." Eight men armed with the new Mausers ran to McComb. He motioned them to spread out and return fire.

If this doesn't tear it...well, hung for a sheep, hung for a lamb. Padget pulled his Winchester from the saddle boot and stepped down from the dun. Holding the reins in his left hand he fired at the machinegun crew, three times, as fast as he could work the lever.

The loader for machine gun pitched forward, knocking the gun down. The gunner stood and picked up the machine gun. Oh, no you don't! Padget shot him through the head. He reached into his jacket pocket and stuffed rounds into the Winchester.

Glancing to his rear he saw the loaded pack

mules shying away from the sound of the gunfire. They were dragging their lead ropes and moving down the valley away from the commotion. "Grab those mules, Dave," Padget shouted.

When he turned back to the fight the machine gun was back in action. The muzzle swung from left to right and the bullets began to fall among the bandits. Padget threw his Winchester to his shoulder and shot three more times. The machine gun stopped.

One man got up on his knees and started to reach for the gun. Padget shot again. The man fell forward on top of the machine gun. Padget shouted, "Dave, catch those mules." He continued shooting at the oncoming riders. Ochoa spurred his horse after the retreating mules.

Taking deliberate aim, Padget shot twice. Two rurales, riding in the forefront of the charging line, fell off their horses.

After what seemed like and interminable time, he heard rifles going off. McComb's group was finally getting into action. He chanced a quick glance to his side and saw McComb and Gonzales standing behind eight bandits who were kneeling and returning fire. They were shooting as fast as they could work the bolts on the Mausers. The concentrated rifle fire was murderous.

The rurales slowed, but kept coming straight at them.

A second fusillade from McComb's men tore a gap in the charging line of rurales as the rapid rifle fire from the new Mausers emptied more saddles. Two of McComb's men fell.

Padget went down on one knee and took aim and pulled the trigger. Another rurale fell back off his horse. The man hit the ground just as a bugle sounded across the valley. The charging line turned and raced to the rear and began to regroup for a second charge.

Padget glanced toward the direction of Villa and his bandits. A dust cloud was the only sign he could make out. He saw Gonzales say something to McComb, who trotted over to him.

McComb was holding his rifle in his left hand and pointing to a trail leading over the hills. "Padget, I don't know how long this is going to take. Right now, we've got them slowed up enough for you to get a head start on getting those rifles out of here. But it isn't going to last, it may get pretty ugly, pretty quick, and we're going to need all those rifles. I don't want to take the chance of the federales getting them; so why don't you and your amigo take those mules and get the hell out of here. Somebody will be in touch with you pretty soon."

"I'm not much on quitting a fight," Padget said.

"Oh, we'll be all right. We need those guns, and with those mules you won't be able to outrun the rurales. I'll see you in El Paso," McComb said.

Padget stood, reloaded his rifle, shoved it into the saddle boot and stepped aboard Skeeter. He touched his hand to his hat and smiled at McComb. "Adios, amigo."

McComb raised one arm briefly and said, "Adios." He turned back to the fight.

Padget loped Skeeter to where Ochoa was holding the mules. "Pardner, let's get on back to Texas, I guess this isn't our fight." Leaning over he took some of the lead ropes from Ochoa. He touched his spurs to Button and they climbed the slope out of the canyon.

Reaching the crest of the first hill, he turned to Ochoa. "From the tracks it looks like Villa's bunch headed east — we had better head west."

A few yards up the trail he found a small unused path leading toward the northwest and down through a steep ravine. He spurred the roan down hill, pulling the mules along behind.

The sound of firing behind them continued for a short time, stopped, started again, and then stopped completely. "That doesn't sound good for McComb. We better get a move on," Padget said. He turned in the saddle and could hear the sound of horses running past on the trail they had been on.

"Maybe it isn't all that bad. Sounds like some of them got away," Ochoa said.

Padget shook his head. "If they're really interested in these guns it won't be too long before somebody will notice there aren't any mule tracks going east."

Chapter Forty-four

Padget looked back over his shoulder and scanned the trail behind them. So far-so good, he thought. The steep chaparral covered slopes of Hueso Canyon rose above them. The height of the mountains shielded them from the late afternoon sun. The mules were lathered up from the fast pace and wanted to slow down.

Padget wrapped the reins around the saddle horn and removed his hat. He wiped his forehead and then the sweatband. He shoved the wadded up bandana back into his pocket and turned in the saddle. "The river's not too far ahead, if we can make it, we should be able to catch our breath…" He caught a movement on the trail behind them. "Damn!" He pointed back up the trail.

Ochoa looked up hill where the dust from

several riders could be seen. "I knew it wouldn't last, let's get out of here." He leaned low in the saddle and spurred Bear into a gallop. The lead mule balked, jerking the lead rope out of his hand, almost pulling him from the saddle. Free from being led, the mules stopped to crop the few weeds left over after the winter storms.

Padget picked up the leads and handed them to Ochoa. They started again, this time in a walk to get the mules moving. The lead mule balked again and refused to follow. Padget looked up the trail. The dust was getting nearer and he could hear the sound of pursuing riders. He dropped his lead rope and raced around behind the rearmost mule and swung the end of his lariat. The end cut an inch gash in the mule's rump. She brayed, jumped, and began running through the bunched up mules toward the river. The other mules followed her at a dead run.

Padget heard a shout and turned to see a dozen rurales burst out on the flat behind them. He shouted, "Keep them moving, Pard." He pulled his rifle from the scabbard and threw it to his shoulder. Button danced sideways. Padget shifted his rifle and patted him on the neck. "Whoa, settle down boy." The dun, hearing the calm voice, stopped moving.

Padget raised his rifle and sighted on the foremost rider and pulled the trigger. The recoil pushed him back into the saddle. He saw a puff of dust behind the rurales and watched as the leader slipped forward in the saddle and fell off his horse. It went right through the son of a gun. Damned if he didn't love his Winchester. He levered another cartridge into the chamber.

The rurales paused momentarily, and then spurred their horses forward, shooting as they rode. Padget felt the whip of concussion as a heavy bullet passed very close, and triggered off four more shots as fast as he could work the action on the Winchester. The foremost two riders went down. The riderless horses kept running with the rest of the rurales.

Padget reined Button around and spurred him into a run for the river. Bent low in the saddle he urged his horse on. He could see Ochoa stopped ahead in the trail kneeling, taking aim at the pursuers with his Krag. Padget heard the crack of the bullet as it passed him. He glanced over his shoulder and saw one of the rurales fall from the saddle. He saw Ochoa shoot once more. He reined in Button.

"That will hold them for a while," Ochoa said, and remounted his horse.

Padget looked back over his shoulder as they loped down the trail and around a bend. He scanned the ridges on either side of Hueso Canyon. "Dave, maybe we better put the fear of God into that bunch before we go much farther." He motioned up hill. "Tell you what, why don't you take your Krag and ease on up that ridge right up there. I'll take the other side."

He pointed to a scattering of boulders about three quarters of the way up the hill. "You'll have the sun at your back. I'll take the mules and mosey on north a little bit. When I get up the trail a piece, I'll slip back on the other side. You remember that Sunday when we broke the Dons from sucking eggs?"

Ochoa nodded his head and pulled his Krag from the scabbard and reached into his saddlebags. He pulled out a bandoleer of cartridges and slipped it over his shoulder. Touching the brim of his hat, he slipped from his sorrel and scrambled up the ridge.

Padget took the leads of the mules and Dave's horse and started down the trail in a short lope, raising as much dust as he could. When he rounded the next bend, he tethered the pack animals and grabbed his Winchester and a belt full of rifle cartridges. He remounted Button and rode over the hill. Near the top of the ridge he started back, riding just under the rim.

He stopped just under the crest of the ridge and left the dun tied to a mesquite tree. From there he crawled up to the ridge top on his hands and knees. Lying behind a clump of rabbit brush he looked across the canyon for Ochoa. It took him a while to locate him concealed behind a granite boulder.

They had worked too many fights together in Cuba for it to be necessary to signal that he was in place. He pushed the barrel of his Winchester through the rabbit brush making sure it was in the shade and not giving off a reflection.

The first rider appeared in view. Padget thought, Ochoa will take the lead and I'll close the back door, and then we'll just squeeze them up close.

Eight rurales appeared, one riding out about 20 yards ahead of the others. Behind him rode two men, side by side, then two more, and finally three strung out in the rear. The furthest rider was perhaps three hundred yards distant.

Looking through the vee of his rear sight, Padget centered the front blade of his rifle on the last man and took up the slack in the trigger.

Ochoa's rifle cracked on the other side of the canyon. The echo made it difficult to pinpoint the origin of the shot and the riders started to bunch up and look around them.

Padget pulled the trigger. The man in the rear threw up his hands and fell over the rump of his horse. Working the lever of the Winchester Padget heard Ochoa shoot again and was aware of three riderless horses running back up the trail. Moving his sights again to the most distant man, he pulled the trigger and the rider pitched over the head of his horse. That left four.

He heard Ochoa's rifle the third time and another saddle was emptied. The three remaining riders turned around and spurred their horses back up the trail. They were four hundred yards away bending low over their horses and fast disappearing down the trail. His front blade centered on the low profile of the retreating rurale. He thought that may well be the son of a bitch hurt that Juana. Padget squeezed the trigger and watched the rider spill sideways from his horse.

Just as the last rider passed from sight, he heard Ochoa's Krag go off again. Eleven out of twelve wasn't bad. He walked to Button and mounted. Gathering the mules, he rode down to the canyon bottom. By the time he got there, Ochoa was waiting for him. "That last shot was a little bit long, Mano, but I think I may have hit his horse."

"It would take too long to dig him out, let him go. We've got enough dead Mexicans now to dam the river," Padget said.

Ochoa nudged one of the dead rurales over with his boot. "There are probably more where these come from."

Padget glanced back up the trail. "Yes, and we'd better move on before the rest of that bunch comes this way."

"Are we going get these guys off the trail?"

"Well, only if you think we've got time?"

Ochoa looked at him and laughed.

Padget handed him a lead rope. "We've got to do something with these guns before the Army comes along. I don't know about you, but my hind end is dragging. We'll stop at the old Henshaw place and water the horses. It should be dark by then and we can make it on home before sunup."

"What about those horses?" Ochoa asked.

Padget peered at the dead rurales horses. "We might as well gather them up. Those are good mounts. Maybe take them to Bliss and sell them to the Army when things cool off a bit. If not, I wouldn't mind owning a few more horses."

The Mexican horses, tired from being ridden hard all day, were caught quickly. Padget and Ochoa dumped the saddles into the chaparral and bunched the horses with the mules and drove them along the road toward the Rio Grande.

Ochoa watched the bank of the River. "Moon won't be up for a couple of hours."

The damp fishy odor of the Rio Grande permeated the air as they sat on their horses and watched for any sign of movement among the willows that lined the banks. Padget pulled his field glasses out and scanned the far bank. "Nothing I can see," he whispered. He waited, and then pulled his Winchester out of the boot. He held it barrel up, the butt against his right hip. He nudged his horse into the water.

The current against the legs of twenty-three horses and mules made soft swishing sounds, clearly audible, but surprisingly quiet. They crossed without incident.

The moonrise cast a pale light over the prairie. Riding Button at a trot, Padget pushed the mules through Quitman Canyon and Ochoa followed along with the horses. They stopped to water the stock at the Henshaw ranch and rode on; it was after midnight before they reached the Macadoo place. They stowed the guns under a layer of loose hay in the barn loft and turned the captured horses out to pasture. They led the mules into the corral.

Talk about being caught between a rock and a hard place, what in the heck were they going to do with all those rifles and mules?

Chapter Forty-five

I should have known. I should have known. My mother is right. You just can't trust men. Pilar felt the hot tears roll down her cheeks. The empty feeling in her stomach was almost too intense to withstand. She threw the skirt she was holding into the suitcase, slammed the top down and buckled the straps. She wiped the tears from her cheeks with the back of her hands and hefted the packed case and grabbed her purse as she walked out of the door to the train station.

I can live without him. I know I can. Pilar stared out at the mesquite as the train rolled past Fort Hancock and watched an army patrol, off in the distance, paralleling the railroad tracks, heading in the direction from which she had come. The rattle of the wheels on the tracks only made her feel lonelier.

Absorbed in her misery she didn't realize that someone had spoken to her until she felt a light touch on her shoulder. She looked up.

"Your ticket, miss?" the conductor said.

"Oh, I'm sorry." She handed him her ticket and smiled weakly.

Pilar felt alone and far from home as she stepped down from the train in El Paso into the West Texas wind blowing down from the Franklin Mountains. She clutched her suitcase and hurried into the railway station to get out of the wind and the acrid fumes it brought in from Smeltertown. A young lieutenant of the U.S. Cavalry touched the brim of his hat and offered to carry her bag. She refused with a smile and said, "Thank you, lieutenant, but I am perfectly capable of managing on my own."

Later, holding her skirt down with one hand, she walked to a small clapboard building where a small hand lettered sign proclaimed that this was the office of Ira J. Bush, MD. She pushed open the door into a small, neatly decorated room. The sun, coming in from a window on the left, cast its light across a leather bound journal on a desk which stood along one wall. Several papers were stacked neatly along one side of a silver mounted secretary. Pilar wrinkled her nose at the odor of alcohol and iodine as she glanced around the room. Her gaze came to rest on the door in the corner, from where voices could be heard.

She recognized the voice that came from somewhere behind the door, "Just have a seat. I will be with you in a minute."

She did not sit; instead she walked to the wall opposite the desk and examined a framed photograph of three men, huge grins on their faces, holding rifles, and standing behind several deer and one mountain lion laying in the foreground. She heard footsteps enter the room and turned to see Dr. Bush escort a woman from the back room. He handed a matronly woman a bottle.

"Just take two tablespoons of this before going to bed." He opened the front door, "Now, Henrietta, be sure to take the whole bottle. I will come by the ranch next Thursday and check up on you," he nodded in the direction of the bottle, "but that should do the trick."

He closed the door and turned back to face Pilar. She watched a smile play across his face. "Pilar, it is good to see you. Won't you sit down? Are you well?"

"I'm fine, Doc. Thanks, but I've been riding since early morning, standing feels good. I recognize you behind that beard," she said, pointing at the photograph.

"That is Abraham Gonzalez on the right and the shorter one is Francisco Madero. What brings you to El Paso?"

"Oh, I decided to get away from Sierra Blanca for a while and this seemed like a good place to do it."

He knitted his brows and she watched him look closely at her face.

He thinks I'm ill. She laughed quietly. "Really, Doc I never felt better, but I would like to talk to you…look, if I'm imposing upon you. I'll leave." She arched her left eyebrow.

Pushing back his suit coat he pulled a watch from his vest and looked at it. "That is utter nonsense, you are not bothering me, but I do have to be somewhere right now. Do you have a place to stay?"

"Yes. I'm staying with Dorothy… Mom Matson's sister's family — you may know them — the Greenlees?"

"John and Laura? Of course, he has the hardware store. Look, if you can come back here tomorrow," he walked behind the desk and looked at the journal, "how about nine o'clock, I'm free until eleven; we can discuss whatever you want."

She felt relief flood through her. "Thanks, Doc." She swallowed. "I was hoping you could use a nurse or a bookkeeper. I need a job."

Pilar's room, a dimly lit rectangle, was on the second floor. It had lace curtains and space enough for one tenant. On one wall, hung a sepia photograph of a street scene in Mexico, against another stood a dresser with a mirror, along the third, a bunk bed, and on the forth wall was a window that looked out over San Antonio Street.

The noise of the ore wagons rumbling along the street made her feel like a castaway. She sat in a wooden rocking chair, her brow wrinkled in concentration, memorizing the muscles of the human body from a copy of *Gray's Anatomy*. The enticing aroma of tea arose from the cup on the table at her side. Next to the teacup was a copy of *A Life in Medicine and Bacteriology.*

She had been at Doctor Bush's office all day learning to fold bandages, steaming surgical instruments and cleaning the office with carbolic acid. She was tired, her eyes burned and she was sleepy, but she did not feel that she had a right to sleep. There was a lot more to becoming a nurse than she had thought.

It was still dark when she woke up next morning and there was a thin glaze of ice in the water pitcher on the table. Picking up her towel, she pulled her robe close about her body and walked down the hall to the bathroom she shared with other roomers.

Pilar pulled the string to turn on the light and looked at her image in the mirror, noting the dark rings under her eyes. Well, it was up to her. She blew her breath out to test the temperature and watched the fog wisp away upwards.

The face staring back at her from the mirror was a stranger. Her mouth was pulled down, and lines showed around her eyes. She was going to be an old maid, and she might just as well face up to it. The thought troubled her in some unidentifiable way, she tried to ignore it. The problem with her was that she wanted it all.

Her first day as a nurse-in-training had begun with a young cowboy who had broken his shoulder the evening before. A mustang threw him into the hitching post in the center of the corral and he spent the night in misery. One whole side of his torso was swollen before his boss finally put him in a wagon and brought him into El Paso.

When he saw Pilar, the cowboy tried to smile. It turned out to be a grimace and sweat broke out on his forehead when Bush examined his shoulder.

Pushing and probing with his fingers, Bush picked up the cowboy's arm and held it for a moment. When he moved the arm to test the rotation, the cowboy passed out. He tugged the arm with one swift jerk and the shoulder snapped in place.

Bush showed her how to bandage the shoulder to minimize the movement. He then demonstrated how to make a sling and pinned it to the cowboy's shirt with safety pins. They left the young man to wake up on his own and turned to other patients lined up in his office. They worked through the day without stopping for lunch and finally, long after suppertime, closed up shop and went home.

This morning she was not going to skip

breakfast. She was a healthy girl and had a good appetite. She walked through the morning-chilled air three blocks to Mae's Café. She hesitated a moment, and then went into the warmth of the diner. She ordered ham and eggs and placed her copy of *Gray's Anatomy* beside her plate to read while eating.

A petite brunette waitress, wearing big hoop earrings came over with the coffeepot and refilled her cup. "Are you new around here, honey?"

It didn't sound like a question so Pilar did not respond immediately.

As the waitress started to turn Pilar said, "I'm sorry. I don't mean to be rude. Yes. I just arrived day before yesterday."

"My name's Beth," the waitress said, "I'm pleased to meet you."

"I'm Pilar."

"Let me see if your breakfast is ready."

Pilar drank a second cup of coffee before the waitress came back with her breakfast. She motioned with the coffeepot and Pilar covered her cup with her hand. The waitress laid the bill on the table and left.

Pilar finished her meal and paid the tab; thinking she would have to start cooking her own food because she couldn't afford to eat out.

The day grew warmer as she walked to work. The Franklin Mountains, normally a dull tan, were turning red and yellow in the early morning sunrise. Traffic consisted mostly of freight wagons laden with ore, headed toward Smelter Town. There were a few pedestrians hurrying along the boardwalk.

Chapter Forty-six

Feeling the need for coffee, Padget walked into the cook shack. He pulled off his gloves and massaged his hands. They were cold and stiff from the long ride. He pulled a match from his pocket and dragged it across his jeans; it flared brightly in the late night darkness. He raised the chimney and lit the coal oil lamp. He almost spilled the coffee beans, putting them into the grinder and he held his hands over the lamp chimney to warm them.

Dave stomped into the room and dropped down into one of the kitchen chairs. He shoved his boots out in front of him, the rowels of his spurs raking the wooden floor. "I don't know if I want to go through that again."

"You notice that hombre who rode in just ahead of those rurales?" Padget asked.

Ochoa nodded. "You mean the one who kept looking at you like a bull at a bastard calf?"

"Urbina."

"You couldn't have missed him if you were blind in one eye, and couldn't see out of the other. He recognized us too." Ochoa said.

Pouring coffee into two cups, Padget sat down in the chair across the table. "Wonder if that bunch we left strewed all over Hueso Canyon was part of the outfit that slaughtered all those folks at Talón?"

"Put money it," Ochoa said. "It's probably the only bunch of rurales in this part of Mexico."

"They weren't there by accident, that's for damn sure." Padget sipped his coffee.

"And that pretty much settles that," Ochoa said.

"Settles what?"

"The fracas back at Villa's camp. You can bet your hind end that when word gets back, the river will look like an ant hill that's been stomped on. There will be federales swarming all over the place."

"Villa will be on the run for a while, maybe a long while. I wonder what they'll do now," Padget said.

"If the federales catch up with him, and those

are pretty good odds, they'll stand him against a wall like they did those poor bastards in Juarez," Ochoa said.

"I mean about those rifles."

"Villa?"

"Bush and Phillips. What are they going to do about the rest of those rifles? The ones we have and those left at Ojos Calientes?" Padget said.

"I don't know. And another thing I don't know, Villa's supposed to be the jefe down there, but McComb seems to be pretty much his own boss."

"He's got to be working for Gonzales. It was his orders that we take those mules and leave. Just before McComb came over I saw Gonzales nod in our direction and say something to him."

"McComb is a cool customer all right," Ochoa said.

"He doesn't seem to care whether school keeps or not," Padget said, and mimicked McComb's gravelly voice. "We'll be needing those rifles not too long from now. So why don't you boys take those mules and get the hell out of here. Somebody will be in touch with you pretty soon."

"One thing's for sure," Ochoa said.

"What's that?"

"Now that the federales know we are running

guns in this part of the country, they're going to do everything they can to keep the rebels from getting them," Ochoa said.

"You can sit up if you want," Padget said, "but I'm going to sleep for about a week. I'm so tired my butt's making one big wide track."

Padget was making coffee next morning when he heard a horse approaching from the direction of the Rafter J. He finished spooning coffee into the pot and set it on the stove. He walked out on the porch just as Billy Shakelford rode into the yard.

"Padget, those lions were seen down at the old Sherman place last night," he said.

"Get down, Billy and tell me about it. Coffee's on," Padget said.

Chapter Forty-seven

Late that morning Ochoa and Padget rode west toward the Sherman ranch. Other than a Red Tailed Hawk high overhead, nothing moved in the landscape. They reached the wagon road that led south from Sierra Blanca to the river. Here they crossed Red Light Draw and rode southeast toward the Rio Grande. Padget nudged the blue roan with his spurs and rode down into the bottom of the draw covered with animal tracks. Ochoa followed.

"Sometime, Pard, before you head back to Colorado, we'll take a ride into Quitman Canyon and look at the Indian paintings there," Padget said.

"I saw some of them when we split up after the storm."

They arrived at the wagon road that ran

alongside the river in the middle of the afternoon. They turned east. Relaxed in the saddle the cowboys rode down river. Suddenly, Belle bayed. Padget looked up the road at the hound. She was standing stiff in the middle of the road, her tail straight up. As he watched, she disappeared into the willows and salt cedars that lined the riverbank.

Padget and Ochoa spurred their horses and loped to where she left the road. There, side by side, the lion tracks led south to the river and Mexico. Belle bayed again, excited now. She was somewhere close, but still hidden by the cedars.

Ochoa reined Bear into the willows and jabbed her with his spurs, riding fast toward the sound of Belle's baying. Padget followed and they broke out of the brush together at the water's edge. Padget could see Belle in the water; she was almost half way across the river. She was swimming hard, but the current was carrying her downstream to his left. Out ahead, one of the jaguars was swimming fast and pulling away from the hound.

Ochoa jumped down and jerked his rifle from the saddle scabbard. The lion neared the far bank with Belle hot on her tail. Belle's excited baying finally got the lion's attention. Reaching the bank she turned and bared her teeth.

Belle was still in the water between Ochoa and the cat. He didn't shoot. The lion rushed Belle so fast that Padget thought she was done for, but the hound darted to the right, barely missing the lion's claws, and bayed again.

Ochoa pulled the Krag hard into his shoulder and squeezed the trigger. His shot took the lioness just behind her ears and broke her neck. She dropped like a rock.

Belle charged in and caught her throat in her jaws and held on pulling and jerking the cat back into the river. Ochoa called her off with a shout.

Padget scanned the far riverbank for the second cat. There! The big lion was already on the other side. He was crouched on his belly behind a driftwood log, his attention on something on the far bank.

Padget glanced to his left and saw two Mexican women washing clothes in the river and he could hear the sound of children laughing, coming from somewhere near. He located them; they were between the women and the lion. Three children were making mud pies and playing at the water's edge. None of them had seen the cat. The women looked at Padget.

Padget swore. He dropped into the wet sand

and took up a sitting position. He pulled the rifle hard into his shoulder. The lion moved, shifted his weight, and prepared to spring. Padget worked the lever of his Winchester, jacking a cartridge into the chamber.

The big lion shifted his front shoulders again, and his tail whipped back and forth as he watched the children. A small girl emerged from the brush lining the bank. She was to the right of the other children and about ten yards from the lion. The lion sprang from behind the log and charged directly toward the small child.

"Please, Lord," Padget said as he pulled the trigger. The lion went down, hit through the paunch, but kept moving. Screaming in pain and anger the lion dragged his hindquarters toward the girl. Damned, too far back, Padget thought.

The girl stood petrified, watching the jaguar. Padget chambered a second round and pulled the trigger. The big lion was knocked sideways by the heavy bullet. It went down.

Padget chambered another round, sighted on the motionless lion, waiting for any sign of movement.

The women were screaming, the children were shouting, the little girl was running toward the other kids. The women ran to the children, gathered them together and stared at the jaguar lying dead, so very close to where the children had been playing.

Padget and Ochoa mounted their horses and rode through the water into Mexico. Padget waved and reined Skeeter toward the dead lion that lay in a crumpled heap. The roan balked. Padget jabbed him with his spurs. He smiled at the women. "Buenos días, señoritas."

Ochoa roped and dragged the other lion onto the bank. Slowly, the women and children came up to where they were working, grateful, but still wary. The little girl, who came so close to death, cautiously put out her hand and touched the head of the male lion. The other children came up and began touching it. They rubbed its pelt and laughed courageously.

Ochoa pulled a sack of gumdrops from his vest and held them out to the children.

Chapter Forty-eight

For three interminable months, while El Paso slipped from spring into summer, Pilar lived in a state of near exhaustion, her time spent either in Doctor Bush's office or in her room, where she spent most of each night studying the *Merck Manual* and *Grays Anatomy*. Her German dictionary was always open.

Sometimes on Fridays, just for the opportunity of watching people laughing, she went to Mae's and had coffee before trudging on to work. On Wednesdays she had supper with Dorothy's sister and her husband who owned the hardware store over which she roomed. Mostly, she stayed by herself, miserable and lonely, denying the aching emptiness inside.

Tonight, she stared into the lamp on the table

and saw Padget's face smiling at her across the table in Ojos Calientes as she held his hand to light her cigarette. Why did he have to come back from Arizona? She was doing all right and holding her own before he showed up at Ojos with those sky blue eyes. Would she ever get him out of her life? He was out! No more of this! But still…

Chapter Forty-nine

Spring passed quickly into summer. The mesquite bloomed and the political problems in Mexico, though unsolved, seemed far away. A rugged economy emerged and rustling declined. People minded their own business; living out their lives in unruffled peace.

The crew at the Rafter J separated the new bunch of colts from the mares, and ran them into a horse trap close to the ranch to be sold to the Army at Fort Bliss. Fences were mended, windmills serviced and a new garden put in by Maria and Claire. Life at the ranch went on much as it had for thirty-odd years.

Padget rode the colt he was training through the mesquite flats along the railroad tracks. The sun dropped behind Sierra Blanca Peak and darkness spread over the land. He took a shorter grip on the reins, reached down and patted the little grulla filly he was training for Juana. "What's the matter, girl? Are you seeing boogers?"

A jack rabbit suddenly darted from the base of a creosote bush directly in front of the filly. She jumped sideways. Padget squeezed together with his knees, pulling her head up sharply to keep her from bucking. "Whoa, girl you've been over this trail after dark before. There's nothing out here to be afraid of."

The filly, wall eyed with apprehension, spun half around and danced sideways. When she did, Padget caught a glimpse of a strange streak of light over Apache Peak

Padget gazed in amazement at the night sky and a shiver raced up his back. He reined the filly around and started back to the ranch. When he unsaddled the colt and turned her into the corral the strange light was still visible.

The cookhouse was warm and the cowboys were all sitting around the supper table when Padget came in. "Anybody notice that streak of light in the sky?" he asked. There was a murmur, followed by a questioning silence around the table. Everyone looked up from his plate, waiting for someone to speak.

"If you mean that long streak of light over Apache Peak, that's Halley's' Comet," Walt said.

"A comet?"

"According to the Farmer's Almanac, it comes every seventy years or so and is supposed to be a sign of bad things to come," Walt said.

Claire arched one eyebrow as she looked up from reading her Bible. "For then there will be great tribulation, such as has not been from the beginning of the world until now, no, and never will be."

"Is that from the almanac?" Shorty Davidson asked.

"No. It's from the Bible, Matthew 24, and you ought to know that, Shorty Davidson, or you would if you'd read it once in a while," Claire said.

Billy Shackelford raised his voice. "By the way, as long as we are talking about trouble; I heard this story about a Mexican bandit named Pancho Villa. He showed up on a ranch down in San Isidro posing as a cattle dealer and murdered the owner and his son — pass those biscuits down this way will you — Maria, do you have any more gravy?"

Walt said, "Tomorrow, Wes, I want you to ride into Sierra Blanca. Jonas Brothers finally sent those lion skins back. They're at the post office, take Ochoa with you."

"I need you to pick up a couple of things at the store too," Claire said.

Maria put a coffee mug in front of Claire. "Maybe you'd better take the wagon. There are some things I would like you to get for the pantry."

"We'll have those colts ready to take to El Paso by the time you get back," Walt said.

Claire glanced over at Padget. "Dorothy got a letter from Pilar Martinez; she's training to be a nurse."

The sound of her name struck Padget like a punch in the solar plexus and he felt his throat squeeze shut. His voice sounded strained when he spoke. "Did she say where she was?"

"No, only that she's training to be a nurse."

Chapter Fifty

Stretched out in two straggly lines on either side of the Southern Pacific Railroad, Sierra Blanca sweltered in the late afternoon heat. At the far end of the hot dusty street two cowboys could be seen, loading barrels and sacks into a freight wagon. A pair of gray draft horses hitched to the wagon stood hipshot in front of the general store.

Padget shouldered the last sack of beans into the wagon and climbed into the seat. He pulled off his hat and drew his sleeve across his forehead. Replacing his hat he kicked the brake loose and turned the team around in the street. He drove to the east end of town and stopped in front of the Stockman's Saloon. He reached behind the seat and picked up the rolled up Jaguar hides, threw them over his shoulder and jumped down to the ground.

"Come on, compa I'll buy you a beer."

"For awhile, I was afraid you'd joined up with the W.C.T.U.,"[9] Ochoa said, climbing down from the seat.

Padget pushed open the swinging doors into the dimly lit pool hall. Shorty McCorkle and three other cowboys were shooting billiards. Sauntering to the table he threw down the hides and rolled them out. "Wade, how about a couple of beers over here," he said to the bartender.

Wade Moore, the bartender, drew two beers and set them down on the bar. "You're not crippled as far as I can see. What have you got there?"

Padget motioned him over. "This is what's left of those two lions that Ochoa got last year. Just came in from Jonas Brothers."

The cowboys crowded around the pool table. "Wouldn't those make a beautiful pair of chaps?" Joe Holloway, a bronc rider for the Diamond A ranch, said.

"You might want to talk to Walt before you go cutting them up," Ochoa said, "they're his."

---

[9] Women's Christian Temperance Union (WCTU) was organized in 1874 by women who were concerned about the problems alcohol was causing their families and society. The members chose total abstinence from all alcohol as their life style and protection of the home as their watchword.

"The green felt sure makes the yellow stand out," Shorty McCorkle said.

"There's a full mount in the Fifteen Leagues in Chihuahua," Bill Matson said, from the back of the room where he was sitting.

"Well, hello, Bill, I didn't see you. Where've you been keeping yourself? I haven't seen you since we got back from Talón," Padget said.

"Well, you've been busy and I was down in Chihuahua City for a while," Matson said.

"Are you still trying to find those horses?" Ochoa said.

Bill shook his head. "I've got some mining interests there and with the political situation being what it is, I have to keep a sharp eye on it."

"I hear that they threw Francisco Madero in jail, anything to it?" the bartender asked.

"I heard that too, it's pretty much all the talk down there." He laid a ten dollar gold piece on the bar. "Buy these boys a beer." He turned to Padget. "Do you remember the outlaw Pancho Villa, we was talking about after that run-in at Ojos?

"I do."

"Well, I saw Villa while I was in Chihuahua. I saw him once before in Ysleta."

"You saw Villa?" the bartender said.

"I did," Matson said.

"Did he have anyone with him?" Padget asked.

"He was alone. It was a Saturday, the second of July. I was coming out of the bank with a business associate. He was right across the street, I saw him coming out of the ice cream store on the corner. I don't know what made me notice him; there were dozens of people on the street. Maybe it was because he had this great big ice cream cone."

The bartender set the beers on the counter top. "That's pretty audacious, even for him."

"Nobody ever accused Villa of being shy," Matson said. "He shot a dude right there on the street."

"In broad daylight?" Short McCorkle asked.

"Right on the Paseo Bolivar," Matson said, "and Chihuahua was full of people, all dressed up in their Sunday best. Young cocks walking their girls up and down, arm in arm, talking and taking in the sights. Villa was leaning up against the wall of an ice cream shop, eating the biggest damned ice cream cone I think I ever saw. Hell, it must have been three, four scoops."

The room was quiet, the lion skins forgotten.

Bill continued, "He just stood there licking

his cone and watching the couples strolling along the street. It was about noon and hotter than blue blazes; and the ice cream was running down the cone. He would stick one finger, then the other into his mouth, and lick the melted ice cream off his fingers. He was about half way through the cone when this young couple came out of the Fifteen Leagues and headed in his direction. The woman was laughing and hanging on this dude's arm while he rolled a cigarette. They were pretty much wrapped up in each other and didn't notice Villa until he could almost touch them.

Villa came away from the wall where he was leaning and said something to him. You could tell this dude knew he was in trouble because his eyes flew open and he dropped the cigarette he was trying to light.

The woman sure as hell didn't know what was going on. She looked at Villa, and then looked back at the man with her." Bill motioned for Wade to fill his glass.

"What happened then?" Shorty McCorkle asked.

Bill took a sip of beer. "Anyway, he didn't answer. So Villa cussed him for a traitor and told him to draw his gun. The dude sure didn't want any of that and raised his hands; put them in front of his chest, palms out. He kept his hands away from his gun and I heard him tell Villa that it wasn't him. Villa told him that was bad luck, because he was going to die for it and told him to pull his gun or die like the coward he was.

The dude shook his head like he was trying to shake off a bad dream, and then before anyone knew what he was doing, he grabbed the woman, pulled her in front of him and shoved her into Villa, and took off like a scalded cat and ran back up the street. Cool as a cucumber and still holding the ice cream cone, Villa caught this gal by the arm and steadied her until she had her balance. I swear he touched his sombrero brim and bowed to her. And then, casual as could be, he stepped around her and drew his revolver. He cocked it and waited until he had a clear view of Reza and there wasn't anyone in the way.

By this time, Reza was running full out, up the street away from him, shoving people aside that got in his way. When Villa got a clear shot he pulled the trigger. Reza pitched headlong on the sidewalk, flopped around on the ground for a while like a chicken with its head cut off."

"What do you suppose that was all about?" Wade asked.

"I found out later that the dude's name was Claro Reza, a one time friend who led the federales to Villa's camp. It seems there was a big shootout over a delivery of guns. They got some of the bandits, but the federales lost more than half of their men, and they didn't get the guns either."

"They arrest Villa?" Padget asked.

"You mean after he shot Reza? I don't think anybody had the nerve. Villa holstered his gun finished eating the ice cream cone and nodded to Reza's woman. Then he wiped his hands across the legs of his pants, bowed to her and mounted a big bay gelding. He saluted a bunch of people that was staring at him across the street. No, nobody made a move to stop him."

Padget felt as if someone had just walked over his grave. He whispered to Ochoa, "We need to get to El Paso."

"Claro," Ochoa said.

Padget rolled up the lion skins on the billiard table. "We can swing by on the way, pick up those horses, and throw them in with the colts we're taking to Fort Bliss." Throwing the skins over his shoulder, he left the saloon.

Chapter Fifty-one

The headquarters building lay under a hot July sun, flies buzzed against the windows and the air was stifling. A cavalry troop exercised on the parade ground. Dust from the horses' hooves hung over the fort in a dense pall. Wes trailed Ochoa from the office and walked to his horse. He tightened his cinch, looking over his saddle at Ochoa who had already mounted. "Let's look up Bush and see if we can't get rid of those rifles."

Ochoa glanced at the door of the headquarters building and back at Padget. "First, I want to buy me a bath, a shave, and a haircut; I'm pretty ripe. And then I would like to get around the biggest t-bone in El Paso before I do anything that requires me to think."

They entered into an almost empty Mae's.

There was one patron sitting alone near the back reading a newspaper. Padget glanced at him took a second look and nudged Ochoa. "Do you recognize the mustache?"

Frank McComb was hunched over the El Paso Times and looked up only when Padget and Ochoa stopped at his table. "Well, I'll be damned. Drag up a chair and sit down."

Except for a fresh shave and haircut, he didn't look much different than he had in Villa's camp, and Padget could smell a faint odor of bay rum. "What you see when you don't have a gun. Well at least you smell a whole lot better than the last time I saw you," he said.

"Good to see you too," McComb said.

Padget pulled a chair out and dropped into it. "I wasn't at all sure you'd make it out. What the hell is going on down there anyway? The story is that Madero was arrested and the revolution is dead."

"Well, the story is wrong. War is building down there fast and furious and whether they've got Madero in jail or not, the revolution is alive and well," McComb said.

Padget took the coffee mug a waitress handed him and ordered a steak. "When we heard the shooting stop, we figured you'd been rolled over."

McComb sipped on his coffee. "Not as bad as you would think. Those federales must all have been married men, or else wanted those guns pretty bad. Just after you topped the ridge, they rode around us and followed you on out of the valley. We vamoosed the way we came in, and then hightailed it out of there. You boys were the ones we were worried about."

"What happened to Villa and his bunch?"

"They got away, and split up; I know that much because Urbina and his bunch caught up with us down near Banderas...he was looking for you."

"So what do we do about that pack train of rifles and ammunition we brought back?" Padget glanced around the room. "I've got other things to do in life besides sitting on top of a load of rifles until someone decides to do something."

McComb shook his head. "You're asking the wrong man. I just work for Gonzalez. He is the honcho around here."

The steaks arrived and for several minutes the conversation ceased while they ate. When they finished, McComb stood up and signaled for the check. "Come on, I'll take you over to where Gonzalez, Bush and Phillips are having a pow wow."

Two very large Chinese Elm trees cast dark

shadows across the front yard of a two story house set back from the street and surrounded by a white picket fence. McComb knocked and a Mexican woman opened the door. She took their hats and with a wave of her hand, directed them into the dining room where three men stood near a sidebar. They were off to one side of a large room illuminated by a pair of coal oil lamps. Bush turned at the sound of their entry and motioned them over, "We're having a drink before supper, gentlemen, whiskey or bourbon?

"Whiskey," Padget said.

"As long as I have a choice, I'll take bourbon," Ochoa said.

Bush poured from a cut-glass decanter and clinked his glass against theirs. He raised his class in salute. "Salud."

"Salud, pesetas, Y mujeres bonitas," Ochoa said.

"Salud," Gonzalez said. "I am told that you and Urbina had a misunderstanding."

"You might call it that." Padget said.

"Tomás doesn't seem to like you very much," McComb said. "He said you two killed three of his men down in Ojos Calientes; plumb put out about it. He wants the chance to even the score some."

Padget narrowed his eyes. "Any time he wants." His voice sounded flat. "I was overly generous last time; it won't happen again."

"That poses something of a dilemma," Phillips said. "It seems we have an unanticipated problem here, gentlemen. We can't very well have our comrades in arms killing one another."

"Things have changed somewhat," Bush said. "Things have taken a turn for the worse. You may have heard that Madero is under arrest?"

"We heard. But what I want to know, is when we're going to do something with those rifles," Padget said.

"How many rifles did you bring back?" Gonzales asked.

"Nine mule loads, we left ten rifles with Villa's bunch. The rest are hidden where we're staying, and I don't remember anything being said about riding herd on a load of rifles."

Phillips rocked forward on his toes. "Like Doctor Bush said, our plans have changed somewhat. We are now forced to wait for a more propitious time to move the guns into Mexico, at the moment we have a more important concern and that is getting Madero out of San Luis Potosi."

"Why is it I have this feeling that I'm not going

to like what you're about to say?" Padget asked.

"If we don't get Madero out of prison the revolution will be delayed and we can't afford the time loss," Bush said.

"If it were me, I would be afraid that Diaz would have him killed while he's in prison," Padget said.

"Yes, there is a distinct possibility of his being assassinated; the only thing that keeps him alive now is his social station. His father is a hacendado," Phillips said. "But that can change at any time."

"So, where do you think we fit in the scheme of things?" Padget asked.

"Will you and Ochoa accompany McComb to San Luis Potosi and bring Francisco Madero to Texas?" Phillips said.

"You're serious? You want us, three gringos, to waltz down and break him out of prison?" Padget said.

"You won't have to, as you say, break him out. Madero is under house arrest. He is free to move about as long as he stays within the city. If it weren't for the guards that go with him everywhere, he could just walk away," Phillips said.

"And that's where we come in," McComb said. "It shouldn't be too hard to persuade those guards that they have business somewhere else. Then we'll just put Mr. Madero on a train and bring him back to San Antonio."

"Easy as pie; all we have to do is get past the prison guards, the local police, the Army, and any blockades they throw up along the four hundred miles we would have to travel to get him to the United States," Padget said. He shook his head. "No, thanks; this time I'll pass if you don't mind. Walt always said that if you go over a fifty miles from home to fight you're just looking for trouble. We'll bring the guns in, like we said we would, whenever you want them, wherever you want them. But breaking Madero out of jail; forget it I'm not even going to try."

Phillips rocked back on his heels. "You won't go?"

"Right. If it's as easy as you say, you won't have any trouble getting it done without our help."

Gonzalez spoke, "He is right; we can't afford to have anything that smacks of a breach of the Neutrality Act."

Feeling somewhat out of place, Padget picked up his hat, put it on and nodded at the group of men. "Thanks for the drink, and I think I'll skip dinner."

As he and Ochoa headed for the door, McComb spoke. "If you boys don't mind, I'll walk back to the hotel with you." Padget and Ochoa nodded and the three men walked out into the warm El Paso night. They approached the Blue Moon Saloon.

"Come on I'll buy you both a drink," McComb said.

Chapter Fifty-two

Mid-summer in El Paso was stifling. There wasn't a breath of wind when she arrived at the office for work. Pilar surprised Doctor Bush in conversation with a tall Mexican male, who looked oddly familiar. Doctor Bush bid her good morning, but did not offer to introduce her. No name, no rank, no title, no occupation. That was queer because he normally went out of his way to acquaint her with patients.

Bush and the man with no name moved to the back room and continued the conversation. She tried not to listen, but from behind the closed door she heard the town of Ojinaga mentioned.

The mellow voice of the man with no name had the tone of a military officer, insistent and commanding. Bush's voice was calm, but she could not hear his reply.

She took off her coat and was hanging it in the closet when the door opened and the stranger strode from the back office. He touched the brim of his hat and nodded to her as he passed through the door. Bush followed closely behind the man and shut the door when he left. He turned to Pilar. "Come," he said. "We have much to do and not very much time to do it."

He sat down at his desk and picked up a pen and paper and wrote furiously for a few minutes. When he finished, he folded the sheet of paper and stuffed into an envelope. Leaving it unsealed, he wrote *Angus* across its face.

"I want you to take the train to Van Horn, there; you can hire a buggy to Presidio. When you get to Presidio, give this to Angus McMann. He owns the dry goods store there."

"Presidio? What about my work here?"

"I'll be along in a few days. Angus will take you to my place, just up the river. Ruidosa."

"I don't understand. Why am I going to Ruidosa?"

He smiled broadly at her. "The revolution is about to commence. We need to set up an aid station."

"Why Ruidosa? What's there? Who's going to start the revolution?"

"That man who just left was Abraham Gonzalez. If they are going to succeed, the insurrectos need a border town with access to arms and supplies and perhaps with a little customs revenue."

"Ojinaga," she said. Understanding what she had overheard at last.

"We will set up the aid station at my ranch. They will bring any wounded to us. We won't be in the line of fire," he said.

She left that afternoon. Her trunk, in the baggage car, held medical instruments and supplies Doctor Bush thought necessary to handle battle casualties.

Pilar sat alone in the empty coach, the stale cigar smoke from the last passenger who got off in Fort Hancock, permeated the air. Through the grimy windows, mesquite trees seemed to hurry past. She leaned back against the hard wooden seat and closed the Bible she had been reading. Weary, she stared out past her reflection and watched the barren landscape rush by.

After a while she closed her eyes and thought about the upcoming fight; it had taken a long time coming, but now she would have an active part, close to the action, and men's lives might well depend upon how well she performed her duties as a nurse. For years she had prayed for this day and now it was here.

The train pulled into Sierra Blanca, stopping in a rush of steam and boiling dust. Through the window she watched the children playing in the schoolyard. There, in that same playground a hundred years ago, she had met Padget for the very first time.

Staying in her seat, she pulled her head scarf down around her neck, feeling the soft silk as she stared out the window at the one room schoolhouse with its hard dirt playground. It looked the same as she remembered on the morning of her first day at school. She had walked from the Matson home, happy, looking forward to a whole new world of books and learning; instead, she found ugliness.

She let her memory travel back. She cringed against the schoolhouse wall, holding her books against her heart as a barrier. Four loutish boys, larger than the other kids, ringed her like a pack of dogs. "Hey, tortilla," the red head with crooked teeth said. "What'chu doing here? We don't want no frijoles in this school." A second boy, towheaded and taller than the first, pushed her hard against the wall. "You don't need book learning to make a living on your back."

She felt the hard wall digging into her shoulder and her fright changed to panic; she clutched her books closer to her breast.

"What's the matter, cat got your tongue?" crooked teeth said. He leaned forward until his nose almost touched her; his foul breath caused her to turn her head.

She spat in his face and ducked under his arm, darting toward the corner. Just as she reached it, she felt her head yanked back and she fell to the ground. She pulled her knees up to her chest for protection; her skirt fell down around her hips, exposing her thighs and underpants.

The boys whooped and leered at her naked thighs.

She straightened her legs and dropped her books and pulled her dress down. She held it around her legs, fighting back tears of pain and frustration. Help me. Oh, God, please help me. She tried to get up.

Towhead dropped down on her chest. He grabbed her arms, pinning her to the ground.

Shame and revulsion flooded her mind as she twisted under his weight. She shut her eyes to keep from crying, waiting for what would follow. She heard a thump and a grunt of pain and suddenly the weight was removed from her breast.

She opened her eyes just as a blond-headed boy she didn't know, hit towhead in the chin, twice, so quick she barely saw and so hard that towhead dropped to the ground, out cold. Then the blond-headed boy turned, grabbed crooked teeth and slapped him twice across the face. "Don't you know that hurts, you sorry excuse for a human? How do you like it?" He slapped him a third time and let him stumble and fall to the ground. The boy climbed to his feet and ran.

The blond-headed boy leaned down, took her hand and helped Pilar to her feet. He brushed the dirt from her book pack and handed it to her. Then he touched the brim of his cap, "My name is John. I don't think they'll bother you again. Come with me, Miss. I'll take you to class."

Pilar glanced sideways at him as they walked, he looked so relaxed, but at the same time, poised for action.

They found Mrs. Matson cleaning the chalk board. She hugged Pilar and called him John Wesley Padget. She thanked him for looking out for Pilar on the first day of school and said that she would make sure it never happened again. From that day forward Pilar became utterly, hopelessly, and irrevocably in love.

She never confided it to anyone. She would stop reading just to watch him, and kept as close to him as possible when walking home from school. She drew pencil sketches of him in the margins of her books and cried the day he left for Arizona. Stop it girl. You only make it worse.

She didn't remember the train leaving Sierra Blanca, yet found herself in Van Horn, her Bible lay on the seat beside her. She watched her trunk of supplies being unloaded onto the dock, and then walked across the street to the livery barn where she hired a buckboard and driver to take her to Presidio. She instructed them to pick up her trunk and be at the hotel at sunrise.

Dressed in a heavy coat, Pilar climbed into the buckboard and nodded to the driver. The vegetation became sparse as they traveled south. Creosote plants and rabbit brush replaced the mesquite. They traveled all that day, reaching Marfa after sundown. In a lonely hotel room, too exited to sleep, she spent the night in Marfa thinking about the upcoming battle for the liberation of Mexico.

Tired and hungry and sore after the long ride from Marfa to Presido, she was glad when the driver coaxed the horses onto a squalid side street and pulled up in front of a clapboard building with a sign that read McMann's Dry goods and Hardware. The door had a glass pane in the top half and hanging by string from the window shade in the middle of the glass was a sign that read — *OPEN*.

Once on the ground she stretched, rubbed her backside and fished her shoulder bag from under the seat. Stepping gingerly across the board walk, she pushed open the door and entered the store. A big rasping man, with a ruddy face and a gray suit with a half-smoked cigarette hanging from his lips stood behind the counter.

She produced the letter. Holding it in her hand she asked, "Angus McMann?"

"That would be me." A slight inclination of his head was his only movement.

She handed him the letter.

When he read it he bowed slightly at the waist and said, "I beg you pardon, Miss. I didn't know you worked for Doctor Bush." He dropped his cigarette to the floor, ground it under his shoe and peered closely at her face.

"I was told that you would arrange for me and my trunk to be taken to Doctor Bush's ranch," she said.

"Aye lass, that I will."

"Can you do it this afternoon?"

"Aren't you tired?"

"That can wait. Please. I would like to go as soon as possible."

The ranch lay two miles from the border, in a hollow of boulders and ocotillo. Sad and deserted, with windows boarded against the weather, the low rambling house stood in the middle of a courtyard surrounded by a six feet high adobe brick wall. There were cracks in the stucco and a well. The ground was grown over with sand burrs and a tin bucket hung from a frayed rope coiled around the crossbeam.

McMann pulled a lantern from the wagon and lit it. "No one's lived on the place for years." Tramping to the front porch he pulled a key from his vest and unlocked the huge wooden door and pushed it open and stood aside for Pilar to enter.

The furniture was covered with sand, evidence that boarded windows could not withstand the west Texas wind. McMann started a blaze in the fireplace. He went back to the wagon and brought her trunk into the living room. "I have some coffee in the wagon. I'll leave that and if you make a list I'll send Manuel out tomorrow with supplies." He motioned toward the rear of the living room. "The bedrooms are across the hall. I've got to get back. Let me know if you need anything."

She went to bed that night with a clear conscience, without undressing and without supper. She fell instantly asleep.

Chapter Fifty-three

They pushed their way into the Blue Moon saloon through a crowd of cowboys, soldiers, and miners drinking up their pay. The odor of raw whiskey, cigarette smoke, and sweat permeated the stale air. They ordered, and standing shoulder to shoulder with their backs to the bar, drank Canadian whiskey, watching the noisy assemblage.

Padget sipped his whiskey. "So, who's running the show here, Frank? It seems like there's a lot of chiefs and not enough Indians."

Frank set his glass on the bar top. "Madero is, in a strategic sort of way, Bush and Phillips are bit players and Gonzalez is the one who gets things done. He runs the day to day operations. Is that what you mean?"

"The wolves are gathering," Ochoa said. "This

crew looks tougher than Urbina's bunch down at Ojos Calientes."

The noise grew louder and a fistfight started near the door. The brawlers spilled out into the street. A cowboy, wearing a red checked shirt, threw a wide roundhouse punch, missed, lost his balance and almost fell. The second combatant, a miner, grabbed him around the waist in a bear hug, but was so drunk he couldn't hold on and the two broke apart. They staggered back into the crowd who had gathered to watch the fight.

"Go get him, Red," someone yelled. The crowd laughed. The miner dodged a punch thrown by the cowboy and fell down.

"Get up, Frank," someone yelled. The man on the ground rolled over in the street and tried to rise. The effort was too much; he slumped down in the street and went to sleep.

"Looks like you win, Red." The crowd drifted back into the saloon.

Padget opened his eyes. The sun shone through the window lighting up the dust particles floating in the air. He clamped his eyes shut against the blinding flash of pain that shot through his head. He sucked in his breath. Still holding his eyes shut he ran his tongue around the inside of his mouth and spat.

He forced himself sit up, and then with a groan he stood up. Holding on to the wall he grabbed a towel from a peg on the door and held it to his head. With both eyes closed against the pain he walked down the hall, using his shoulder against the wall to guide him to the bathroom.

The sound of his bare feet on the wooden floor sounded like someone beating a kettledrum with a hammer. He opened one eye and leaned against the wall with one hand. He urinated into the porcelain bowl and pulled the chain hanging down from the tank overhead. The rush of water exiting sounded like a flood.

He rinsed his mouth and brushed his teeth. Now able to hold his eyes open, he ran his tongue around the inside of his mouth checking to see if his teeth were clean and walked back to the room.

The noise of Ochoa snoring shook the windows. Padget kicked the foot of the bed. "Rise and shine, Mano."

There was a pause in the snoring. Ochoa rolled over on his stomach and pulled the pillow over his head. The snoring continued.

DELBERT GILBOW

Padget grabbed the pillow and jerked it off. "Get up you lazy bum, there ain't no rest for the wicked." Ochoa rolled over, sat up and grabbed his head with one hand, with the other grabbed the bed stead.

"Whoa, hold on there. Quit spinning." He bent over and reached for his boots. He straightened up and caught his head in both hands. "Whew, better write home to Mama Ochoa, I don't think I'm going to make it out of here alive."

The sky was bright and clear when they finished breakfast and walked down the street to El Paso Saddlery. A tall man in an apron smiled when they entered. "What can I do for you?"

"I want to buy a saddle for my niece, but I don't see anything small enough though," Padget said.

The saddle maker nodded. "I can build whatever you want. When do you need it?"

"It has to be in Sierra Blanca by November."

"Full tooled takes about three weeks," the saddle maker said.

Padget took the toothpick from his mouth and pointed with it. "Full tooled, like that one there is what I want and in a three quarter tree. Cap the horn with silver, and make a matching martingale and headstall. It's for a young lady who turns fifteen this fall. Can you handle that?"

The shopkeeper wrote down the specifications. "I'll get right on it. Do you want to pick it up, or should I ship it to you?"

"Ship it to Wes Padget, care of the Rafter J, Sierra Blanca. Wes pulled a fold of money from his shirt pocket."

"Pay me when you get it. I've done a lot of business with Walt."

Leaving the saddle shop they walked to Jones Hardware where Ochoa purchased a thirty two-twenty Smith and Wesson revolver for Juana.

"Let me look at that Winchester 92 in the same caliber," Padget said.

"Hey, Mano, If you're thinking about getting that for Juana I'll split it with you," Ochoa said.

"You've got a deal," Padget said.

They went back to the saddler and ordered a saddle scabbard, a cartridge belt and holster.

"I'll get these out in the mail just as soon as they are done."

"No later than November twentieth," Padget said.

Chapter Forty-four

Juana turned fifteen on Monday, November 28, 1910. A year had passed since that ill-fated day in Talón. She was physically strong for a fifteen year old girl and her eyes were bright. She spoke English fluently, and read from the Bible. Often she would sit on the corral and watch the men at work.

Tagging along after Padget and Ochoa when they practiced their shooting, she became a proficient marksman. They encouraged her to practice with a revolver every evening. Practice consisted of shooting first with one hand and then the other until all shots hit within a three inch circle. On alternate days she practiced with a rifle at ranges out to two hundred yards. The amount of ammunition expended at practice required them to spend most evenings reloading the empty cases for the coming day, and so she learned how to do that too.

One morning before riding out for the day's work, Padget spoke to his uncle. "Walt, I'd like to buy that little filly I've been training."

"She sure is a pretty thing, but what do you want with a filly? She'll never be big enough to carry you around."

Padget shoved his hat back and rubbed his forehead. "Aw, she ain't for me. I want to give her to Juana when she turns fifteen."

"Well, in that case," Walt said, "she's yours."

Padget shook his head. "Then she wouldn't be a gift from me. I'll pay you market rate for three year olds." Walt agreed and the deal was made.

Padget spent most afternoons gentling and training the filly to take the saddle and head stall. When she would carry his weight, he taught her to stand with the reins down and not move. She learned to come to a whistle and search his pockets for the lumps of sugar he carried. She could be mounted from either side.

On Monday[10], just after sunup Jewell Rudd, Dorothy and Bill Matson arrived at the Rafter J in a buckboard. A red blanket covered the wom-

---

10 28th of November

en, shielding them from the cold morning air. Bill wore a sheepskin coat that allowed him to go unhindered while he handled the team.

Walt called to them, "Get down and come in, the coffee is hot and breakfast is on the table."

Later, on the front porch, Claire held her hands over Juana's eyes. "Don't peek," she said. Padget led the filly to the house and dropped the reins.

"Now you can look," Claire said, and moved her hands.

When Juana opened her eyes, standing in front of her was the little grullo filly, all decked out in new gear, including the rifle Padget and Ochoa had bought. Juana clapped her hands with joy and tears came to her eyes when Ochoa gave her the revolver and cartridge belt. She ran her hand over the tooled holster and touched the saddle horn where it was mounted with silver. "They match," she said.

Showing him she had learned her lessons well she opened the revolver's loading gate and rotated the cylinder to see if it was loaded. "Now, no one will ever be able to hurt me again." Reaching up she hugged Ochoa and ran to Padget and kissed him.

"I'm so happy." She turned and ran inside the house, still carrying the belt.

Padget watched her run up the steps and across the porch. She was so frail; he didn't believe she would weigh eighty pounds soaking wet.

"Where're you going, Honey," Walt called after her.

She stopped and turned around. "I want to change into my riding clothes. Is that all right, Mama Claire?"

Claire nodded and Juana disappeared inside the house. She returned wearing a divided skirt and a wide brimmed hat. She pulled the stampede strings tight as she walked across the porch. She buckled the cartridge belt around her waist and ran to the filly and mounted.

"Tio, Wes, tio, Dave. Won't you come with me? I want to ride all the way to Eagle Flat. Por favor."

"Supper will be ready at sundown," Claire called after them. "Be back in time to eat."

Padget and Ochoa turned and waved, nodding their heads.

"Not much chance either of those boys missing a meal if they have anything to say about it," Walt said.

"It's a long way back to town. We've got plenty of room to put you up for the night," Walt said, holding the lantern up shoulder high.

"Thanks just the same. I guess we need to get on back home, and Jewell says that she needs to get home too," Bill Matson said.

"It'll be midnight by the time you do," Walt said.

Bill Matson made a motion with his hand up near his face that might have passed as a wave. "Adios." He slapped the reins on the dash. "Get up."

They disappeared into the night and soon only the jingle of the harness and the clatter of the wheels against the hard packed road were all that could be heard.

Walt brought a decanter of whiskey and glasses to the front porch. "I believe I'll have toddy. Anybody join me?" He said.

"Thank you, sir," Ochoa said, and he indicated three inches with his thumb and forefinger.

"Sounds about right," Padget said.

Claire pulled her shawl around her shoulders and put her arm around Juana. "You all can stay out here if you want, but we're going into the house. It's cold."

The men followed her into the study.

Juana crossed the room to sit on the couch

between Ochoa and Padget.

"No you don't, Miss Mouse. It's way past your bed time, even if it's your birthday. Scoot on upstairs and I'll be right up to tuck you in," Claire said.

Chapter Fifty-five

Walt lifted his glass and watched Juana leave the study. When she was out of hearing, "Sure looks like Madero's bunch got him out of Mexico."

Padget looked at his uncle.

"What do you mean?" Ochoa said.

"I hear he jumped bail and is holed up over in San Antonio."

"Where'd you hear that?" Padget asked.

"Bill told me. He was talking to some old ranger pals. It seems the governor's got the rangers watching Madero pretty close."

"He's in San Antonio?"

"That's what Bill said."

Padget and Ochoa looked at each other.

Walt looked closely at them. "I know you boys

took two wagon loads of rifles and ammunition down to the Rudd place and then packed some of them into Chihuahua awhile back, and I'm pretty sure there are a lot of rifles stored at Ojos Calientes and I'd bet my bottom dollar that Bush and that hombre Phillips put you up to it." He took a sip of brandy from his glass, pulled his lips into a straight line, still looking closely at Padget and Ochoa. "Do you want to confide in me or do you want to go it alone?"

Padget was stunned. If Walt knew about running guns into Mexico, who in the hell else knows? "How did you know?" Padget said?

"Manuel and I were coming back from Sheep Peak and happened to see you two unload that box car last January. I don't know who else knows. But Tom, down at the wagon yard, asked me what we were going to do with all those windmill parts.

I knew I hadn't ordered any windmill parts. It didn't take much to figure out that you boys were up to something.

Manuel followed you the next day and watched you unload them at the Rudd place. After that it was easy to figure out what you were doing."

Padget was shaken. If it was common knowledge in Sierra Blanca it would only be a matter of time before it got back to the Army. Maybe he and Dave should pull their traps and head for Colorado, before someone came looking for them.

"Looks like you've got us dead to rights," Ochoa said. "Speaking for myself, I'd sure like to hear what you advise."

All Padget could do was to nod his head. "I'm glad that's out of the way. I don't believe anyone besides me and Manuel has a hunch what you're doing. But it would damn sure help, if you would confide in me on just what's going on. Getting mixed up in a revolution is serious business."

Padget released his breath and said, "You remember when we were in El Paso before Christmas and we all had that big supper party at Bush's?" Padget asked.

"Yes, as a matter of fact I do."

"Well, next morning Dave and I had breakfast with him and Phillips. They asked us to take the guns from the boxcar at Eagle Flat down to Ojos Calientes and from there, take a few rifles and some ammunition about five miles across the river. We were to make several trips, over several weeks, until the guns were all across."

"I was sure that they were behind this," Walt said.

"We took a thousand German rifles and one hundred thousand rounds of ammunition to Ojos Calientes and hid them in Mrs. Rudd's barn. Two of her riders took the wagons back to Sierra Blanca. That night we took ten mules, 100 rifles and 10,000 rounds of ammunition to a camp just over the river in Chihuahua."

Walt took their glasses and refilled them, then handed them back. "Go on."

"We were met by an American with a big walrus mustache, named McComb, who took us to a man called Villa. Pancho Villa, the bandit you've been hearing about. While we were there a bunch of rurales, the same bunch that hurt Juana, charged into camp shooting and raising hell.

Villa stood his ground for awhile then lit a shuck. The rear guard, under McComb, held. We were told to bring the rifles back to the U.S. and hold on to them. You might say we won that fight. Dave and I came home. The rest of the rifles and ammunition are still in Rudd's barn. When the time comes, Dave and I'll haul them to Ysleta if the time ever comes." Padget said.

Walt grunted. "That still doesn't explain why you were dumb enough to go through with the deal."

Wes shook his head. "Juana is part of it, the firing squad in Juarez is another, a feeling of helplessness, hell, I don't know, there ain't no money in it."

Walt was silent for a while, and then tossed a copy of the El Paso Times on the table. "Count your blessings; I don't guess they'll need those rifles now. It looks like any cause for a revolution is long gone. Diaz is even importing grain from Argentina to feed the peons..."

Padget read the headlines. *U.S. Investments Up in Mexico, Budget Surplus.*

"You two have been down there rubbing elbows with the rebels. Tell me; are they just a bunch of Bolsheviks and anarchists?"

"From what I've seen, I believe most of the poor people in Mexico don't give a damn, one way or another about politics. There're two kinds of people in Mexico. Most of them just want to be left alone with enough frijoles and tortillas to live. The rest are interested in power."

"You think Diaz's bunch is wrong?" Walt said.

"Wolves or watchdogs, it's hard to say from which the sheep have most to fear. They are all bandits who will kill you at the drop of a hat; the Diaz bunch just has the law on its side."

Chapter Fifty-six

Padget yawned and tried to keep his eyes open. He was full and sleep beckoned. The after dinner cognac didn't help. "If you don't mind I think I'll turn in, I've got a full day tomorrow."

"By the way there's a letter for you here someplace." Walt searched the papers on his desk. After much rummaging he produced an envelope and handed it to Padget who glanced at the return address and shoved into his pocket. When he got to the bunkhouse he threw the letter on the table alongside his gun belt, thinking he would read it later. He pulled off his boots, pulled off his shirt and removed his hat, throwing it on the table. It landed on top of the letter.

He lay down on his bunk, staring at the log rafters overhead. After a few minutes he got up and pulled the blankets down and crawled inside. He was barely asleep when a piercing scream from the main house broke the stillness. Rolling out of his bunk, he grabbed his pistol and ran into the yard. Ochoa was right behind him.

The other ranch hands tumbled out into the night holding revolvers and looking wildly around. Again the night was split by a scream. It came from upstairs in the main house. Padget ran across the yard into the house and up to the second floor, taking the stairs two at a time. He turned down the hall and almost ran over a wide eyed Walt who emerged from his bedroom at the same time. They looked at one another and ran down the hall.

The door to Juana's room was open and Padget burst in, looking wildly around. Juana was sitting up in bed against the far wall. Claire was sitting on the bed holding her. When Juana saw Padget she held out her arms to him crying. "Mano. Mano. Ayudame!"

Padget shoved the revolver in his waistband and moved to the bed and took her in his arms. Ochoa crossed the room and looked out the window. After a moment he came to stand beside them. Juana's body shook with sobs.

Padget held her tightly in his arms. "It's all right, little sister. It's all right." Claire stroked Juana's hair.

Juana looked up and saw Ochoa. She reached one hand out to him. Ochoa took it in his two hands and sat on the edge of the bed. "Its okay, honey," Padget said. "We're here." If he ever got his hands on the sons of bitches that did this he would open them up from belly to brisket with his skinning knife and pull their guts out on the ground and stomp on them. He looked at Claire and raised his eyebrows.

Claire said, "I don't know, Sonny, she woke me up screaming. There was no one in the room; she must have had a nightmare."

"Oh, I'm so sorry, so sorry," Juana said, tears streaming down her face. "I dreamed I was in Talón and the rurales were trying to find me. I looked and looked for you, and you weren't there." She held Padget tighter and pulled Ochoa closer until he put his arm around her. "Don't let them take me again. You won't will you, Uncle Wes? You won't will you, Uncle Dave? Please!"

"Nothing bad is ever going to happen to you ever again, sweetheart," Padget and Ochoa said together.

"There's no use in everybody being awake," Padget finally said. "It's just a bad dream, why don't you and Walt go back to bed. Dave and I will just sit here with Juana until she gets back to sleep."

Chapter Fifty-seven

It was early morning when Padget and Dave got back to the bunkhouse. No one was asleep; the cowboys were sitting around the stove talking. Shorty Davidson looked up as they came in. "Has she calmed down some?"

"She's okay; it was just a bad dream. She'll be all right now," Padget said, sitting down on his bunk. The Colt in his waistband gouged him in the stomach; he pulled it out and laid it on the table by his bunk. As he did he saw the unopened letter lying under his hat. "I'm just too damned tired to read that now," he said to himself.

Lying there on his back with his hands under his head, he stared at the ceiling. He could see the cracks in the ceiling and the spider webs in the corners. He rolled over and stuffed the pillow up and lay on his side. He squeezed his eyes shut trying to force the images from his mind. He could see Juana hurt and whimpering in his arms. He wrenched his eyes open and stared at the wall.

He sat up and ran his hand through his hair. "Damn," he said, and pulled his shirt down from the peg where he had hung it. Taking a match from his pocket he wiped it along the edge of the table and lit the lamp. Then picking up the letter, he tore off the end of the envelope and pulled from it a single sheet.

Padget,
Events have forced a change in plans. John McComb will arrive at the Rafter J with instructions within the next two or three days. He will act as your guide.
I.J.B

Holding a hand to deflect his breath he blew out the lamp and lay back down.

The clanging of the dinner steel broke into his consciousness. He sat up and put on his hat and took his jeans from the end of the cot where he had dropped them and pulled them on. It was still dark. Buckling his belt he pulled on his boots, reached behind him on the wall and pulled his coat down. He stuffed his shirt into his pants and walked to the cook shack.

Frank McComb rode into the Rafter J on a tall sorrel gelding that evening at sundown.

It was November 29th, 1910.

Chapter Fifty-eight

The route to Presidio skirted the southern end of the Eagle Mountains, across one arroyo after another, along a narrow two rutted wagon trail. They pushed the mules hard for four days along the foothills and along the riverbank. At sunup, the third day out, in an arroyo running south to the river, near the southern tip of the Eagles they met a rider sent by Frank McComb to guide them to the rendezvous.

Riding into a very bright sun they almost ran into the cavalry patrol before they saw it. The double column of khaki clad soldiers came from the direction of Presidio. The only thing that saved them from discovery was the failure of the lieutenant in command of the column to put out flankers.

THERE AIN'T NO MONEY IN IT

They whipped the mules around and drove the wagons down into a gully out of sight. The day was bitter cold, a wind blowing down from the Eagles sent shards of sand spinning along the ground that caused the horses to tuck their tails down tight.

Padget crawled back up the bank and dropped behind a clump of rabbit brush. Lying on his stomach with his elbows on the ground, and the field glasses wrapped in a gunnysack, he watched the patrol. He could make out the letter C on the pennant carried by the guidon bearer. The guidon was one he knew. It was that of C Troop, part of the Tenth Cavalry. His unit had served alongside them in Cuba. It had been a good outfit back then and he didn't know why the officer neglected to cover his flanks today.

Through the field glasses he looked closely at the soldiers. He could see they were wearing long coats over their uniforms to ward off the biting cold along the Rio Grande. It was obvious they were not expecting trouble because their carbines were tucked away in saddle scabbards. He could see the dust on their olive colored hats in the morning light.

The patrol, a thousand yards out, did not once look in the direction of the wagons. The wind began to blow and sand drifted over the ground. Padget waited until the patrol rode out of sight before he returned to the wagons.

It was midnight when they pulled into a ranch yard near a small settlement on the Rio Grande. Padget hauled back on the reins and hollered, "Whoa." Tired, the horses stopped without even so much as a tail switch. It was Sunday.

A six-foot high adobe wall surrounded the yard, and from underneath a gigantic mesquite tree near the house, in the glow of a cigarette, a group of men were sitting on the ground. Three men rose and walked to the wagons. They unhitched the horses and led them into a corral located in the ranch yard. Without pausing, they brought out a fresh team of horses and hitched it to one of the wagons.

Frank McComb walked. "You're just in time, we were about to start without you. Get down and have a bite to eat before we go. We'll be crossing the river pretty soon." He motioned them towards a clay pot sitting next to the fire. Padget rolled some beans in a tortilla and spooned crushed jalapenos over it and took a large bite. "My belt buckle must be touching my back bone," he said.

McComb talked while Padget and Ochoa ate.

THERE AIN'T NO MONEY IN IT

He told them that Madero was recruiting enlistees from around Shafter and Marfa. Consequently, it was known all along the border that a fight was coming. Several hundred Mexicans from across the river, whose land had been confiscated by the Diaz regime, were now living in Texas and anxious to join the fight.

Everyone knew about arms smuggling, and there was a rumor circulating that the insurrectos were going to attack the Army at Ojinaga. He told them that the U.S. Army had been put on alert to keep the fighting across the river. The Army had been ordered to stop all smuggling and arrest anyone who tried to give aid to the rebels.

There was a company of Texas Rangers and even some agents from two or three U.S. corporations patrolling the border between Texas and Ojinaga to keep anyone from getting arms across.

"We will take one of your wagons and move it down river. You and Ochoa will cross over here with the other one. When you deliver this wagonload your job is done. You can get back to breaking broncs," McComb said.

As he stood listening to McComb, Padget discovered he had been hearing sporadic rifle fire from the direction of Ojinaga across the river for some time. The noise of the shooting suddenly increased in volume.

"Okay, that's the signal," McComb said. "Let's get these rifles across the river." He mounted a tall sorrel and led the way from the yard.

Padget climbed into the lead wagon and picked up the reins. He hollered at his team, and swung the wagon around and out of the gate to follow McComb.

Half an hour later McComb leaned down close to Padget and pointed to the river. "There's a crossing right down there where the road meets the river. On the other side about a mile from here is a place called Vado de Piedra, that is where we should meet up with our guys."

Padget urged the horses into the water and started into the river. Just over half way across, one wheel sank in the sand; the wagon came to a grinding halt. Padget flicked the check line and snapped the lead horse on the rump. The horses squatted and leaned into the harness. The wagon didn't budge.

McComb shook out his lariat and roped the rear axle hub and spurred his horse forward. Padget snapped the lead horse again. Slowly the wagon regained solid ground. They were surrounded by men who led them to a camp in the bottom of a rock strewn arroyo encircled by cactus and chemise.

Padget was too tired to pay much attention to the men introduced to him and as soon as he could, without giving offense, he rolled out his bedroll and turned in. Ochoa pitched his roll nearby.

A commotion woke Padget. He looked over the sleeping form of Ochoa and could see that the rifles were being handed out. The men stood around the wagons waiting quietly for the ammunition to be distributed. They were smoking and talking, plainly elated with the new rifles and ammunition.

Padget guessed that before the arrival of the wagons last night, the rebels didn't have many guns and even fewer cartridges. Now they each had a rifle and one hundred rounds of ammunition. There was much laughter and joking about shooting federales.

McComb walked over and stood beside Padget. "We'll be on the road for the most part of the day. There won't be any breakfast. You might want to get some coffee." He walked back to the group of rebels.

A short time later, the procession left the arroyo. The rebels put several outriders on each flank and two men scouting ahead to avoid any federal troops that might be in the area. They crossed a road and a railroad, arriving early in the evening at a place called Venegas ranch. More of the rebels were gathered there and the rest of the rifles and ammunition were distributed.

Padget followed McComb into the ranch house and recognized Abraham Gonzalez in the midst of several men.

"We will attack tomorrow if the garrison does not surrender," Gonzalez said. He was standing next to the only table in the ranch house talking to two men. He introduced Padget to Jose de la Luz Soto and Toribio Ortega, who turned out to be the leaders of two rebel bands that Gonzalez had persuaded to join him in the assault on Ojinaga.

Gonzalez continued his interrupted conversation with the two men. "I don't think they will fight us, it is obvious that they cannot win now that we have the arms. I shall demand their surrender."

Gonzalez handed McComb a letter folded over and sealed with candle wax. "Frank, please take this letter to Colonel Dorantes in Ojinaga tomorrow morning. He is the officer in charge of the garrison. Be so kind as to await his response."

Chapter Fifty-nine

Still at the Venegas ranch that afternoon, Padget didn't know why he was waiting around. He and Ochoa had other fish to fry.

Bored, he leaned back against the wall of the house and stretched his legs out in front of him. His spurs gouged long lines in the dirt. Padget pushed his hat back from his head and promptly fell asleep.

He was awakened long after dark by the sound of McComb coming back from Ojinaga.

McComb handed Gonzalez a letter. "Sorry, Jefe. The Colonel didn't go along with your surrender idea. It seems that he's drafted all the men around town into the Army. They brought in troop of artillery while I was there."

"Very well," Gonzalez said, crumpling the letter

in his hand. "We will attack tomorrow."

Padget turned to Ochoa who was sitting beside him. "Pard, what do you say we turn in and get an early start back to Texas in the morning?"

Padget woke early the following morning rolled out of his bedroll and walked barefooted to the edge of the yard and stepped on a sticker burr.

He jerked his right foot off the ground and hobbled one legged, several steps and leaned against the wall. He raised his foot and pulled the sticker out and dropped his foot to the ground.

With his back to the open yard he urinated against the wall and listened for the night sounds. A pair of chaparral birds was chirping in the mesquite trees despite the darkness, and a lonely bee was starting to buzz around the yard.

Two women, probably the same ones who were grinding corn the night before, were preparing tortillas for the men who would be waking in a few hours. He could smell beans simmering over the fire.

Padget shivered involuntary as he emptied his bladder and walked back to his bedroll buttoning his pants. He picked up his coat and shrugged it on and nudged Ochoa with his toe. He buttoned the lower two buttons against the cold morning air and sat down on his bedroll to pull on his boots. A young girl appeared from nowhere and handed him a cup of coffee.

He took it. Instantly a surge of pain shot through his fingers. He jerked his hand, almost spilling the coffee. It was scalding. He rubbed his burned fingers against his Levis and glanced over to the east. The moon was full; in a cloudless sky it cast long shadows across the desert floor. There was no movement anywhere. Padget could hear the horses stamping in the corral. It is almost too quiet, he thought.

Ochoa hadn't moved, so he nudged him again, this time he pushed him with his boot. "Get up, Pard." He handed Ochoa the cup. "Here drink this; it ought to get your juices flowing."

At that moment, the federales opened fire on the ranch. The sound of cannon fire came from the east. While the rebels slept, the federales had marched around and gained the element of surprise. Now, with the rising sun at their backs they had the advantage.

A round from a howitzer hit next to the two women grinding corn.

They vanished in an eruption of dirt and debris.

The concussion knocked Padget to the ground.

A second round hit the house, punching a hole in the southeast wall. It exploded inside the house, killing four men sleeping there.

On the far side of the corral a third round landed throwing dirt and debris onto the horses.

The horses panicked and surged against the pole gate that closed the corral. It bent outward, and for a moment Padget thought it might hold.

Several rounds landed at once and the frightened horses lunged against the gate again. The weight was too much and the gate disintegrated.

The horses broke out and raced through the opening into the yard. Running around inside the enclosed yard they knocked over pots and benches and broke down the strings of chilies hanging from the arbor, and creating chaos among the frightened people there.

Padget got to knees and grabbed his lariat. He fumbled with the coils, stood up and looked for his horse.

The front gate was closed and the horses ran in a circle inside the yard.

He spied his horse and with a quick underhanded toss threw the lariat across the back of a line-backed dun. The loop dropped over the head of Button as he raced by.

Padget heard a whistle. Ochoa's horse, Bear, stopped, whirled around, threw his head up and down, and then stepped gingerly up to Ochoa.

They saddled their horses and held them by the cheek straps to keep them from bolting.

The rebels ran from the house, pouring into the front yard yelling to one another. Men who slept outside the enclosure scrambled to get back inside.

Padget could hear screaming from somewhere in the house.

The acrid stench of cordite filled the enclosure and black smoke from exploding shells hung like a dark fog over the ground.

As if from nowhere, Frank McComb appeared. He was hatless and carried a shell belt and revolver. His bald head shone in the morning light.

Just like a billiard ball. I wonder why I never noticed that before, Padget thought.

McComb yelled for the men to form up with their rifles and pushed them forward through the gate.

A few men straggled into line, followed by a few more, and then still more, looking wild-eyed toward the east.

The artillery rounds continued to rain down like gigantic hailstones, exploding as they hit the ground. The noise and smoke caused much confusion among the insurgents.

"They didn't buy into this," Padget said.

"Neither did we," Ochoa said.

Gonzalez emerged from the house. He looked confused. "They are attacking us?"

"Sir, could you speak to the men? They need you," McComb said. He waved his arm in the direction of the men crouched together inside the wall.

"What's that you say? Speak? Yes of course. What shall I say?"

"We need them to form up and get ready to defend against the attack that's going to happen when the artillery barrage lifts," McComb said.

Another round fell short, hitting just outside the compound. It threw dirt and gravel over the fence hitting a group of men bunched against the wall.

A yell started from somewhere in the group and men ran toward the horses.

An explosion just inside the compound gate blew two men into the air.

Gonzalez, drew his sword, raised it above his

head. "Follow me," he yelled, and ran toward the gate.

The men pushed through the gate, and were greeted by rifle fire from a skirmish line of federales. They were almost upon the rancho.

The rebels kneeled and began firing at the charging men.

The line faltered and a bugle sounded and the skirmish line wheeled to the south and regrouped.

Trapped, the rebels looked around for a way to escape. The federales seemed to be on the south. But north lay open to the rebels.

The federale rifles were taking a terrible toll and men in the ragged line in front of the ranch began to fall. One rebel fell backwards killed by a bullet through his head, a rebel rifleman screamed as a bullet hit him in the lower belly. Another shot through the foot, cut short the cry of pain and methodically worked the action of his new Mauser and continued firing. The federale artillery finally found the range and the middle of the rebel line became a slaughterhouse of wounded, crying and praying men.

Then as suddenly as it had started the cannon fire stopped. The skirmish line charged.

Padget stood with McComb and Ochoa near

the right side of the rebel line and poured fire into the skirmish line. The federales had somehow left the route to the north open. It led down to an arroyo.

Padget had an eerie feeling. It's a trap, he thought. The federales wanted them in the arroyo. The rebels would be butchered. Even as the recognition of danger struck him, Padget heard the staccato sound of a machine gun.

Gonzalez shouted, "Fall back. Fall back."

Padget turned to Frank McComb. "Come with me. We've got to stop this." He signaled Ochoa and sprinted toward the grouped federales.

McComb shouted for the insurgents to follow him. A few jumped up and he kicked more men to their feet.

"Run! On your feet! Move!" He roused others. "To me. To me," he shouted and ran after Padget.

Thirty insurgents ran with him. When they caught up, he shouted, "We've got to break this up or we're all dead. Line up in a skirmish line and on my command, charge."

Chapter Sixty

Padget's rifle grew hot in his hands as he continued reloading and shooting into the federale line. He located the machine gun crew who was frantically working on a stoppage. If they got the machinegun back in action they would all be dead.

Gonzalez stood in the rear of the rebel line. He kept glancing back toward the ranch house. Finally he shouted, "Back! Back! Keep in formation!"

The rebels began to edge back toward the ranch.

The federale bullets thumped home and the rebel ranks became ragged as the men stopped to fire at the charging line. The progress was slow, too slow for Gonzalez's frazzled nerves, "Run! Run!" he shouted.

"Charge!" shouted Padget.

The small contingent of men followed, firing as they charged the federales.

He knew they followed him because they believed he knew what needed doing, and the certainty of his knowledge was strong in Padget. They followed him because they trusted at him this particular time.

"Conmigo. With me," he shouted as he leaped a wounded federale. He twisted as a bullet fanned past his face and turned to his left. Shouting, he led the men into the ranks of the enemy. The rebels began to yell and the enemy line broke and ran, throwing down their rifles as they fled this pack of madmen. Padget picked up the machinegun and smashed it against a rock, bending the barrel.

"Spread out. Spread out," Padget shouted. "Front rank; kneel! Back rank; fire!" The men understood what he expected from them and obeyed. He knew they obeyed because suddenly they had found confidence in a gringo.

The charge gave the insurgents time to retreat past the rancho. Those who had horses mounted and spurred them into a run headed east.

"Fall back! Keep together! Front rank, to the rear, at a walk! Rear rank, let them through. Fire"

The men started an orderly retreat, carrying their wounded. Padget was the last to leave. As he turned he saw an officer wave a sword over his head, calling for the soldiers to attack the withdrawing men.

"Steady! Ochoa, shoot that man on the horse," Padget ordered.

Ochoa's Krag went off and the officer fell to the ground.

"Thanks, Mano. Its time to get out of here," Padget said. He watched Ochoa follow the retreating men. He looked toward the rancho and the fleeing insurgents. These men would fight; the right leadership was all they needed.

Padget heard hooves slapping the ground behind him.

He turned to see a federale officer mounted on a big black stallion and holding a saber outstretched. The officer held his saber high and was almost upon him.

Padget dodged to his right and swung his Winchester in a butt stroke into the horse's mouth.

The horse squealed in pain and reared, throwing its rider. When he fell, the officer's right boot caught in the stirrup and the horse bolted through the retreating men.

One of the rebels caught the animal by the reins, jerking it to a stop. The big black whirled around stamping on the officer as the frightened animal tried to dislodge the man hanging from the stirrup. Finally the boot came loose and the horse quieted down enough for the rebel to vault aboard. He jerked back on the reins to stop the fearful horse from bolting. He pulled his revolver and taking deliberate aim shot the officer between the eyes.

Padget heard Gonzalez shout a command in Spanish and the fleeing men paused in their flight.

Gonzalez must do what he thought best and Padget would do what he had to. A strange realization came over him. He was gripped in the exultation of battle. Here, in the midst of the stench of cordite, on a battlefield in Mexico he felt at home. He hadn't known it, but he had been preparing for this for the past fourteen years. Other men learned to farm and raise cattle. He had learned how to use a rifle, how to turn an opponent's flank, and how to assault an enemy ambush. He could conquer his own fear and use the enemy's fear to his advantage.

"Stop! Face the rear! Ready! Fire!" He was rewarded by the crash of Mauser rifles going off almost together. The fusillade tore a hole in the federale line that had started forward again. A bullet whipped by Padget.

"All right, fall back! Steady! Slow."

Then they were back at the rancho. Inside the walls, they were shielded from the wind that was increasing its velocity. Sand was blowing across the desert floor, making it hard to see the enemy. If we can't see them, they can't see us. A second bullet cracked past his head. Through the sandstorm he caught glimpses of the federales standing in line firing at the retreating men. Gonzalez with some the men disappeared into the storm.

He grabbed McComb and pulled him toward the rear wall. "Inside. Up, on the walls. Keep firing." He shouldered through the assembling insurgents and saw a horse on the ground, kicking and bleeding. Then he was aware of a whipping and cracking around his ears as bullets from the enemy's guns poured into the compound.

"Get that gate shut."

Two men slammed the huge wooden gate together. The bullets made thumping noises as they struck the now closed gate. Padget saw one of the insurgents lying on his belly. Blood from a head wound spread out into the yard. A rifle cracked behind him, then another. The rebels had found places on the walls and were returning fire.

"Frank. What's the best way out of here? Where will Gonzalez go? If we can hold out until dark we might just make it out of here."

McComb motioned to a tall Mexican man standing alongside him. "Padget, this is Toribio Ortega. He knows this country like the back of his hand."

Padget looked at the slender, clean shaven Mexican and waited.

"There is a settlement north on the river. El Mulato," Toribio said.

Chapter Sixty-one

The wind veered and now blew from the south. The skittering sand made visibility difficult. Padget took a patrol out north along the road towards El Mulato. He wanted to find out whether or not the federales held the road where it crossed the arroyo. In the dismal visibility, he almost stumbled into federale pickets placed across the road a mile from the compound.

"We're pretty well cut off this way," Ochoa whispered, offering his gloomy opinion.

Instead of answering, Padget motioned to turn west. They made a full circle, reaching the bank of the river and finding that Mexican cavalry patrolled the Rio Grande. The only way left open to them was southeast. When they got back to the Venegas ranch McComb sat by a small campfire with the other men. They were out of food. Most of the men were hunkered down under their serapes against the blowing wind.

"This wind is strange," Toribio said. "It usually dies down at sunset." He shook his head. "I've never seen it blow from this direction before."

"How many of the wounded are able to travel?" Padget asked.

"Where are we going?" Toribio said.

"To El Mulato," Padget said.

Someone said, "Why? Why not wait here until Gonzalez sends help. That will surely happen before daybreak."

Padget couldn't make out who was talking. So when he spoke, he made sure his voice carried to all the men. "I don't think Gonzalez will be coming back for us. They will have their hands full just getting away. We're on our own. It's up to us to catch up with them if we can, or get across the river to the United States on our own."

"Perhaps we can sneak around them," McComb said.

"No, the roads are held against us. Padget is right. We will have to head east and I think a little north. We could fight the whole Mexican Army with thirty men, but I don't think we would win,"

Toribio said.

They traveled throughout that day into the blowing sand, noses and mouths covered against the onslaught, climbing ever higher picking their way through the rim rock and blind canyons and always into the teeth of a wind that brought a chill from the upper slopes of the mountains. They were only about two thousand feet high, but snow covered the upper reaches. Past midnight, they reached a rocky spur and could see far off, a smear of watch fires along the valley bottom through which ran the road between Ojinaga and La Mula.

"Federales," Toribio said softly.

Three hours later they came to a narrow stream flowing down from the heights. Small bare chaparral brush sparsely dotted the banks. The water was icy cold. The men drank thirstily, filling their canteens before crossing. It began to sleet. The wind wailed about them whipping through their thin clothing. They pulled their serapes close about their heads. The wounded were miserable.

Chapter Sixty-two

At dawn they came to a saddle between two peaks and found a shallow cave where Toribio led the exhausted men. Ochoa got a small fire started near a pack rat nest. He pulled several sticks from the pile of debris and lit it. It was a tiny, stingy, wood saving fire; nevertheless it gave off a welcome heat.

The men huddled around the skimpy fire feeding it branches from the rat's nest and trying to get warm. They had not eaten since the night before the attack and after a long day and night climbing, the men sat mute, miserable, and exhausted, but each held on to his rifle like it was the staff of life.

Padget walked away from the fire and lay flat on the sandy floor of the saddle, his chin on his folded arms and overhead the wind blew sand down from the peaks. The mountainside sloped gently where he lay, but below it was steep and he could see the outline of the dusty road through the valley. There was a railroad track alongside the road and far down the road he saw a troop of cavalry riding southward along the railroad, their uniforms a dull olive in the winter morning light. Off in the distance he could see a collection of buildings and a corral and on the northern edge a small band of green marking a stream.

"Is that the ranch?" he asked of Toribio who followed him.

"Yes."

"We will have to cross the road to get there."

"Claro," said Toribio who lay beside him looking over his shoulder. He looked emaciated in the cold morning light. He wore the leather clothes of a charro, short jacket and tight pants with crossed bandoleers of ammunition, only a few loops had cartridges, forming an x across his chest and with a holstered revolver high up on his belt. He was breathing heavily from the climb and his hand rested on a rifle by his side, not a Mauser from the wagon, but a Marlin short rifle with a hexagon barrel brought with him from home.

"Then you cannot see the outpost from here," Padget said.

"No," Toribio said. "See where the road turns. The outpost is down past the bend in the road toward La Mula."

"Is there a trail?"

"Across this road and railroad is an arroyo which leads to the river."

"And where do they patrol?" Padget said.

"Everywhere."

Padget took his field glasses from his saddle bag wiped the lenses with a handkerchief and screwed the eyepieces around until the buildings in the distance showed suddenly clear and the horses in the corral behind the open shed.

"There is smoke coming from the ranch house," Toribio said. "There are also clothes hanging on a line."

"I see them, but I do not see any people."

"Perhaps they are inside," Toribio explained. "It is cold now. They would be in the house where we do not see."

"Probably. Where is the next post?"

"It is at the junction of the road to El Mesquite at kilometer five from Ojinaga."

"How many men are there?"

"Perhaps four and a corporal."

"And toward La Mula?"

"More. Perhaps a dozen."

"And at Ojinaga?"

"The Third Cavalry Regiment, and sixty fiscales, more or less."

"Where is El Mulato?"

"Behind those hills there." Toribio pointed to the northwest towards the United States.

They crossed the road and railroad at midnight on a trail that led northwest, two riders on each side of their wounded to keep them in the saddle. Those able to ride alone struggled along without help from their comrades.

Toribio hunkered down against the sand blowing without cease throughout the night, a serape pulled tight across his jacket and across his mouth, the stubble of unshaven whiskers showing pale in the darkness. He rode beside Padget who had turned up the collar of his coat and pulled his hat brim down low over his eyes. Unable to hear one another, they rode without talk and looked back at times to check on the men who followed. At noon the wind stopped and the men began to speak.

"How did you get involved in the revolution?" Padget asked.

"A long time before Madero or Gonzalez. From the time the government began taking away the land we won because we fought the Apaches."

"What were you doing before?"

"I raised horses and traded them here and in the United States. When they confiscated my land I crossed the river and was a vaquero for several of the ranchers near Shafter and Marfa. It was there that I learned to speak English. Last month we fought the federales in Cuchillo Parado," he said this with considerable satisfaction. "How about you gringo? How did you come to be involved in the revolution?"

"I'm just delivering some guns. I'm not involved," Padget said.

"Do you like to fight?" Toribio asked him.

It seemed a strange question to Padget, but he answered, "That is all I seem to know. I've been fighting since I was fourteen years old."

"Claro. I could see that back at the Venegas ranch and a man doesn't have to be involved in the revolution to lead a charge into the mouth of a machine gun." He smiled and pulled a sack of tobacco from his jacket and rolled a cigarette. Holding out the tobacco sack, he offered it to Padget who shook his head. Toribio stuffed the sack back in his pocket and pulled a match from his jacket. He struck it across his leather pants and lit the cigarette, sucking in the smoke and exhaling through his nose. "Claro," he repeated. A smile crossed his face.

A low line of hills appeared on the horizon. Toribio took a long drag off of his cigarette and lifted his chin toward them. "Just behind those hills is El Mulato," he said as he blew out the smoke.

Chapter Sixty-three

The outrider on the left raised his rifle above his head and pumped it four times. He turned his horse and moved behind a rocky crag where he stepped down and held his horse's nose to keep it quiet.

"Get down," Toribio whispered to Padget, and he turned his head and flicked his hand down, down, to the column of men riding through the gap strung out in a long line with heads down and bodies surrendered to the fatigue of a long retreat without rest or food. He saw the men drop from the saddles and pull the wounded down from the horses, and then they were out of sight in a small saucer shaped depression.

Padget looked ahead across the open space through the ocotillo. He saw nothing and heard nothing, but could feel his heart pounding, and then he heard the click of shod hooves on rocks.

"Fiscales," Toribio whispered.

Padget turned his head and saw a column of men in blue uniforms appear on the opposite side of the canyon coming through a saddle between two low peaks. One rider was ahead and three more behind. The one ahead was looking down and appeared to be following tracks. The three behind fanned out across the ridge. They were all watching carefully. Padget felt his heart beating against the ground as he lay, his elbows spread wide and watched them over the sights of his Winchester.

The man who was leading rode along the trail to where he could look down into the valley below and stopped. The others rode up to him and he motioned them down from their horses.

Padget saw them clearly over the sights of his rifle. He saw the faces of the men under the tall crowned sombreros, the sabers hanging from the saddles, the sweat stained flanks of the horses, the big roweled spurs, the short, strange looking carbines and the blue uniforms sprinkled with dust. The leader motioned the men to remount and turned his horse directly toward where Padget and Toribio lay.

His horse's head toward Padget, the butt of his carbine sticking forward from the scabbard on the right of the saddle, the leader pointed to where they lay.

Padget pulled the rifle butt hard into his shoulder and looked along the barrel at the four riders stopped on the ridgeline. The three behind had their carbines out and across the pommels of their saddles.

You first, he thought, looking at the blade of the front sight now centered firmly in the vee of the rear sight with the top of the front sight lined up on the leader's chest, a little to the right of where the jacket opened, showing blue in the morning sun. You are about to die and pushed his fore finger against the trigger guard to keep it away from the trigger. And you, he thought again, and you, and you, and you. He reached out his hand and put it on the shoulder of Toribio.

He felt Toribio start to move, felt him stop. He shoved the butt back into his shoulder, looked along the oiled blue of the barrel, he saw the leader turn his horse and point down into the valley where El Mulato lay. The four of them trotted off over the ridge. Toribio looked disgusted and spat on the ground. "Guardas Fiscasles. Border Patrol."

Padget looked behind him where the men were hidden and could see no one. He turned to Toribio who was now sitting up and putting his sombrero back on, pulling the stampede strings tight.

"We could have killed them all," Toribio said.

"Si, claro, but who knows what the shooting would have brought?" Padget said. "Why do they all wear beards?"

"To frighten old women and children, they try to stop the bringing in of arms for us."

Just then they could hear the noise of a body of cavalry coming from across the canyon. He looked at Toribio.

"They will pass as did the others," Padget whispered.

They came into sight trotting through the saddle and along the ridge in a column of twos, twenty two men and an officer, armed and uniformed in blue as the others had been, their sabers swinging from the saddles and their carbines in saddle scabbards. They went out of sight where the four had disappeared.

"Did you see?" Padget said to Toribio.

"There were many," Toribio said."

"We would have had to deal with those if we had killed the others," Padget said very softly. His respect for Toribio had grown since the battle. His heart slowed and he felt the sweat in his armpits though the day was cool. There was a hollow feeling in his chest. The outrider appeared from behind the crag and made his way back to the column.

Toribio asked Padget for the loan of his field glasses and gave them to the rider and told him to scout along the ridge, but to keep out of sight and quiet. The outrider rode off back across the canyon stopping just below the crest where he dismounted and crept to the top and lay down. Padget could see him looking through the glasses toward the valley. Then the rider walked back to his horse and rode back to where Padget and Toribio were waiting.

"Jefe, they appear to be headed toward El Mulato."

Chapter Sixty-four

They followed the guardas patrol at a distance, keeping out of sight until they could see El Mulato clearly in the bright sunlight. It was obvious that there were men on the low hills around the town. Padget could see them strung out along the hilltop sitting their horses and watching the cavalry patrol and beyond that the square gray adobe houses of El Mulato and a church in the center of town. Some one from down below took a shot at the patrol. The bullet threw up dirt in front of the fiscales. The only visible effect was that the patrol stopped and spread out to lessen the danger of being hit by a lucky shot. A bugle sounded and the patrol withdrew to the west in the direction of Ojinaga.

Toribio held his men behind a low hill until the patrol was past, and then sent one of his men into town to inform them they had wounded with them, he then took the band into El Mulato.

The streets were teeming with insurrectionists who parted to let them ride through the white dusty street to an old-fashioned windowless chapel in the center of town where an aid station had been set up. Padget looked over the rebels in town and thought there must be several hundred men lining the street and on the roof tops all armed with Mausers. So this is where they took the other wagon, he thought. Something didn't seem quite right. He was halfway to the chapel before it hit him. There were no women or children. They were expecting a battle.

They stopped in front of the chapel and willing hands helped the wounded from the saddles.

"Toribio. Where do you come from? Have you seen the federales?" Someone asked,

"Come. You must be starving."

Later, Padget and Ochoa were sitting along he wall of the chapel when Toribio, flanked by Frank McComb and a Mexican Padget did not know, walked up to where they sitting.

"I guess you boys will be going back to Sierra Blanca. The boss said to give you this." McComb held out a handful of bills. Padget took the offered money. He counted the bills, handed half to Ochoa and put the money in his shirt pocket.

Toribio stepped forward. "Amigo. I know you are uninvolved in our struggle, for you yourself told me so, but before you leave could you do me a favor?"

Padget could not help liking this man. "Sure. What can I do for you?"

Toribio was obviously the leader of men. He was a man who dealt only in things he had experienced. When he asked questions, you knew they were from a man who knew what to ask. When he gave orders, you knew he had obeyed orders of others. When he spoke of death, you knew that he had more than a nodding acquaintance with the grim reaper. "Back at the Venegas rancho my men took your orders willingly. That is unusual, for sometimes they don't take orders from me and they do not like gringos much, but they followed you when you charged the enemy line. It is clear to them and to me that you know what to do in a battle. You were in the American Army, yes?

"Only for about eight months," Padget said. "Ochoa and I were with Colonel Roosevelt in Cuba."

"Eight months, eight years, no le hace. You

know about fighting. We, those of us from Cuchillo Parado, are charged with defending the hilltops. Favor. Come with me and help place the men where they will do the most good," Toribio said.

Padget felt himself flush under the compliment and knew he could not turn this man down. The escape through the mountains had made them comrades. He also knew that he would do what ever he could, to assist him to locate the men for the best field of fire. He and Ochoa would then be on their way back across the river.

The town lay on a low finger of land sticking out into the valley of the Rio Grande. The terrain surrounding the town consisted of a series of arroyos running north and south, cutting through the northern foothills of the Ranchito Mountains. The high ground gave a clear field of fire to whoever held it.

Padget spoke to Toribio. "Have the men not on sentry duty stay below the crest and out of sight until the enemy has begun its attack. Put your best riflemen here and here, there beyond that point, over there where they can control the arroyo below. Have them lie down, but make sure that they stay awake."

His greatest concern was the amount of

cartridges each man had. One hundred rounds per man wouldn't last long in a fire fight, but that is what they had and they had to make do.

"Most likely the main body of troops will come at us from upriver and on the flat. The pass through the mountains we came over is another route. The patrol came that way and even though it is a hard trail, we have to assume the cavalry may do the same," Padget said.

"So we need to put some men on the slopes then?" Toribio said.

"Only a few, for sentries. Put them where they can signal to us if anyone comes that way." He walked with Toribio to the northwest of the hill where he could look down onto the flood plain of the river. He pointed in that direction. "That is most likely the way they will come. We've done what we can; now we will just have to wait it out."

"Claro. For one so uninvolved you are in no hurry to get back to the United States," Toribio said.

Surprised by the remark Padget thought, he's right. I don't have any stake in this fight. I have my money. What's holding me here? He said, "Amigo, there is plenty of time to make that ride and anyway I like the food down here."

Ochoa and McComb walked up to where they were standing. "Mano, we've got the men placed where you wanted," Ochoa said.

Toribio turned to McComb. "Frank, bring two men along to bring back some food for these men and water for drinking and enough for coffee. It looks like we will be here for a while." He called one of his men to him. "Calixto, Señor Padget is el jefe until I return. Do what he tells you." He turned to Padget and said, "I must see to the defenses of the city. I will return before night fall."

Later, the men who went into the town with Toribio returned with food and water. The rebels started cooking fires to make coffee. Food was passed out and they all ate. Padget could see preparations for the upcoming battle being made in the town. Men were being placed upon the rooftops of the houses on the outskirts of the village. The sun started down and still Toribio had not returned.

"I wonder what's taking him so long," Ochoa said.

Two hours later when the light was nothing but a glow above the western hills the men rekindled the fires and heated coffee. Padget was holding a cup sipping it and looking down on the floodplain wondering why Toribio had not returned when he heard the sound of a horse from the direction of El Mulato. A Mexican Padget did not know rode into the light of the fire and dismounted.

"Hola, señor. El jefe asked me to tell you he is occupied for a little longer and to also ask you if you would you be good enough to stay until he can relieve you?"

"What's going on?" Ochoa said.

"It is a matter muy grave. Señor Gonzalez has returned to Presido. Francisco McComb went with him. He has turned over the command of the entire Army to Toribio. Toribio says to tell you he will be here as soon as he can. The federales are on the way here. They will march all night."

"I don't like it at all," Ochoa said. "If we make it through this, I think I'll just stick to hunting lions; it would be safer."

Padget swallowed the rest of his coffee and set the cup down on the ground. It was a bad time to be fighting. The Christmas season was when folks got together to celebrate and dream of the future, of pleasures of a home, a family, and good friends to sit and talk with in the evening, to share a glass of eggnog. It was all right, he decided the federales would not attack in the dark, because there was too much danger of things going wrong. He turned to

Calixto. "Come with me and we will check the men before turning in."

Thirty men were scattered across the hilltop. He went to the eastern end and crouched beside a short skinny rebel. "Anything?"

"Nada. Nothing." He had his sombrero upside down filled with cartridges.

Padget and Calixto moved on, crouching to talk with the men, offering them water, always telling them that there was nothing to worry about. The attack, if it came would be in the daylight. Nothing appeared on the hill side. There was little to see in the pale moonlight except the watch fires near El Mulato. Padget returned to where he had left his horse and lay down against his saddle.

Chapter Sixty-five

Ochoa was asleep and snoring lightly.

"Sir?" a Mexican sentry spoke nervously.

"I hear it, amigo." Padget heard the clink of trace chains and the thump of wheels, it was the sounds of artillery drawn behind horses. He heard the sound of cavalry, muffled by the soft sand of the flood plain.

The enemy had arrived and the second battle was about to begin.

Ochoa awoke and stood next to Padget. Calixto stood next to Ochoa. He inclined his head and said, "Can you hear it?" He spoke in Spanish.

Padget listened. Faint, but unmistakable he could hear the sound of picks and shovels thudding into the earth, then the ring of a crowbar against rock. "They're making an artillery battery," he replied in Spanish.

"In front of the village?"

"That's my guess," Padget said.

"They will be in range then," Calixto said.

"Long range," Padget said.

"We will see," Calixto said.

Not a man made a sound. They lay flat on the hill top letting their eyes adjust to the darkness. The moon was full, but slipped in and out between patches of cloud. An array of stars scattered throughout the night sky gave additional light, still they could not see the valley floor. They waited in the darkness until the first light from the sun just under the horizon showed the federales drawn up in formation in front of El Mulato. Beyond the Army a line of riders in blue uniforms, wearing sombreros, was strung out across the flood plain up river. They sat their horses, motionless, waiting. The time was by now mid morning and the air dusty.

"To cut off any retreat," Padget said to no one in particular.

"But would you look at that, only one cannon, and it's on our side," Calixto said.

The words were just out of his mouth when the cannon fired. The cannon ball could be seen in flight making a high arch and dropping into the village. The federales swabbed out the barrel and reloaded. A second round left the muzzle and hit inside the village.

"They are too good. We've got to put that gun out of action," Padget said. "Calixto, bring your best shots over to this end. Aim at the gunner and the officer there."

It took five minutes before the six riflemen were in place and during that time the cannon had fired three more times hitting the church in the center of town. Dust flew from the wall where the cannon ball hit, but remained standing.

"All right men, shoot those soldiers around the cannon. Calixto, try for the officer."

Six rifles went off in a ragged volley. Padget could see the dirt thrown up where the bullets hit the ground around the cannon. The men at the cannon didn't seem to notice they were being fired upon. The next volley was more precise and one of the crew of the cannon fell across the breech. The horse the officer was riding reared and started bucking. A bullet had creased his rump. Padget sat down and pulled the butt of his Winchester into his shoulder and took aim at the gunner. As the front sight centered on the man he squeezed the trigger. The gunner flexed his arm to pull the lanyard to fire the canon then fell forward over the breech and onto the ground.

Across the valley floor the federal cavalry were dismounted and firing their carbines towards the village. The range was long and the short barrels of the carbines not up to the distance. The rebels on the rooftops were firing back. Men started dropping in the enemy ranks. Then Padget heard the sound of the machine gun and looked over the valley floor trying to find it midst the soldiers. There on the far side of the valley through the dust raised by the Army he could see the yellow flicker of an automatic weapon as it raked the walls of the town with bullets. Men on the rooftops crouched down behind the façade, penned down by the intensity of the shooting. It was going to be a long shot. Padget sighted along the barrel and squeezed the trigger. He didn't see where his bullet stuck, but there was no visible reaction to his shot. The machine gun continued firing. He shot again with the same result.

He saw an officer pointing toward the hill he was on. Several soldiers turned his way and fired toward the rebels on the hill. The shots were short by a hundred yards. Again it was carbines the cavalry were using and the short barrels limited the distance of accurate fire. The officer issued an order and a troop of men mounted their horses and formed a skirmish line and moved toward the hill. At this point, only the six riflemen had been firing from the hill. The rest of the men were still holding their positions.

"Keep the men down Calixto. We will give them a little surprise," Padget said. He watched the officer give an order and the troop move into a trot starting up the slope toward the riflemen. The line of riders reached the slope of the hill and the officer gave another order and the line of horses broke into a canter. Half way up the hill the horses started running. The riders drew their carbines and began firing at the rebels on the hill. Answering fire from the rebels began to empty a few saddles. The charging troop was almost to the top of the rise, riding hard, vaulting boulders and shooting rapidly at the rebels.

Two of the rebel riflemen took a step backward. "Stand," Padget said. They stopped and fired at the approaching cavalry working the bolts of their Mausers rapidly, shooting again. Padget turned to Calixto. "Now," he said and Calixto waved his arm from rear to the front and the rest of the rebels who had remained concealed, stood up. The cavalry topped the hill, the horses lunging the last few feet because of the steepness. As they gained the level Padget shouted, "Now." Thirty rifles went off as one and the line disintegrated into a mass of falling, screaming men. The officer was the first to hit the ground and didn't move. What was left of the charge wheeled their horses and raced back down the hill. There wasn't enough left to regroup.

The rebels began cheering and waving their rifles, shouting vengase! Vengesae!

Padget raised the leaf on his Winchester and sat down looking once more for the machine gun. There. Holding the rifle hard into his shoulder he looked through the aperture and placed the front sight blade on the man sitting behind the gun. He squeezed the trigger and the man toppled sideways. The gun stopped firing. A soldier pushed him out of the way and started firing again. Padget was taking the slack in his trigger for the second shot when he heard a rifle go off next to him. The gunner fell just as Padget pulled the trigger. He turned and saw Ochoa lying prone on the hill, working the bolt of his Krag.

Padget saw an officer wave his saber and the

line of cavalry turned and galloped back up river and stopped out of range. The shooting stopped and the men on the rooftops began cheering. He could hear their mocking laughter as the federales retreated. "How's your ammunition holding out?" he asked Calixto.

"Bien. We've used only about twenty rounds here and those in the last volley about five. Only two men wounded."

The sun, now high in the sky, beat down with increasing intensity.

Chapter Sixty-six

Padget looked very carefully over the slope of the hill. There were three bodies on the hill just below him where they had fallen with the first volley. There were other bodies down slope he could not see. A dark brown horse was down to his left kicking with his right rear leg, the other was broken and he could not get up. Ochoa walked to the horse pulled his pistol and shot it behind the ear.

The federales were so proud of their machine gun that they had done a stupid thing and failed to secure their flanks. Now they would send out a large force to take the hills outside the town. They then would bring up the machine gun again and perhaps the field gun and things would get hot on the hill. Padget brought all the men to the north side of the hill. "Calixto," he said. "Have the men dig in over on this side. Two men to a hole spaced thirty feet apart. Here, here, and here across the hill. Have them eat as soon as they are done. We will be having company pretty soon." He sat down and pulled a cleaning thong from the butt of his rifle and ran a patch through the barrel.

Ochoa sat down beside him. "Mano, do you think they will attack again?"

Padget nodded his head. "Oh they'll attack all right, this time they won't make the same mistake; they'll send enough troops to get the job done."

"You know, Mano, this morning you reminded me of Bucky O'Neal the day he got his," Ochoa said.

"If we're going to get off this hill we are going to have to fight our way off," Padget said, embarrassed. He watched the troops below preparing for the attack. "And I'm not so damned sure we're going to make it off."

Padget, satisfied with the placing of the men, turned his attention to the plain below. "They're putting the guns in there." He pointed with his left hand to Ochoa and Calixto. The federales had put the field gun and the machine gun behind a low rock wall that ran east and west from an adobe house. He could not see what was in the shadows of the house. "Count the ammunition we have left. I'm afraid we used more than we could afford that last attack."

Ochoa handed Padget a folded piece of paper. "What's this?" Padget said.

"Deed to my place up in Colorado," Ochoa said. "If I don't make it off this hill I want you to have it — you and Pilar. Take Pilar, get married, go up there and raise a passel of kids."

"The last time I saw her she didn't want anymore to do with me and anyway you're going to be all right. Forget what I said about getting off this hill. I expect you and I will be hunting elk up in Colorado pretty soon." He held out the paper.

"No, Mano, hang on to that for me and if we go elk hunting you can give it back," Ochoa said.

Padget looked at Ochoa and saw a weariness he hadn't seen before. "Pardner, if that's what you want, okay." Padget stuffed the folded paper into his pocket and buttoned it. "You need a good fight, Dave," he said. "There's nothing like a good fight to raise a man's spirits. Two weeks from now we will split a bottle of tequila and be embarrassed this little talk ever took place."

The first howitzer shell cracked apart and both

men spun towards the explosion as the shards of broken shell casing spattered about them.

"Take cover!" Padget shouted.

Two men were down, one quiet and unmoving the other moaning and clutching his belly.

A second shell hit the hill bounced and went over the hilltop to land on the back slope where it exploded harmlessly. A third shell hit the forward slope buried itself in the ground and blew dirt and rocks over the defenders.

Padget watched the massing of what looked like a company of infantry. The officer, on a gray horse, waved his sword and the troops started walking toward the hill firing as they walked. "Hold your fire," Padget shouted. "Don't waste your ammunition."

The steepness of the hill kept the artillery from finding the range. They continued firing over the heads of the advancing infantry. Padget saw a troop of cavalry swing south to the point where the hill descended into the valley. The shells kept falling with decreasing accuracy. They were no longer spaced, but ragged in execution. Again and again the shells cracked and shook the hillside. The smoke from the explosions sometimes hid the attack from view.

Padget turned to Calixto. "Have the men take aim, but not fire until I shoot. Ochoa!" he continued. "You take the officer. When I fire, knock him out of his saddle."

The assault was coming and he had to leave his men exposed. This would be the second time they had to face cannon fire.

The advancing attack line reached the incline and was starting up the hill when the machine gun started. Padget could see the winking yellow flashes from its muzzle. The first shots were short and sprayed up dirt and rocks along the hillside in front of the rebel line.

"Cabrones." One of Toribio's young Mexicans lay clinching the stock of his Mauser. His knuckles were white.

"How are you called," Padget asked.

The young rebel, who looked about sixteen years old, blinked. "Pablo, señor."

"Where are you from?"

"Cuchillo Parado."

"Where's that?" Padget was watching the approaching line, but when the young man did not reply, looked at him. "Pues?" Well.

"South of Ojinaga, sir. About thirty kilometers."

"What does your father do?"

"He is dead. The guarda fiscales murdered him."

The machine gun had now found the range and bullets were filling the air around the defenders. One man down the line made a grunting sound and rolled on his side.

"Is there a cantina in Cuchillo Parado?"

"Si, Señor. La Mesa."

"One day you and I will drink some tequila in your cantina," Padget said. "And no one will believe the tales we will tell."

The boy grinned. "Si, señor."

"Is it a good cantina?"

"Yes. The best."

"And the tequila?"

"Very good, sir."

"Ojinaga tequila," Padget said with authority, "is made from the piss of goats."

The boy grinned as he was supposed to and Padget slapped him on the shoulder. "When the shooting starts hold hard," Padget said. "Understand?"

"Yes, sir."

"I'm depending on you." Padget stood up and straightened his jacket and walked down the line of defenders. A bullet passed his face. He watched the men crouching in their shallow scooped out holes. He must look calm in the face of this attack; he must let them know that the cannon and the machine gun, no matter how fierce, was not the end of the world. He remembered how as a young soldier in Cuba he had watched his sergeants and officers and how he had believed that if they could take the incoming fire, then so could he.

He stood in the middle of the line and stared down at the approaching line. He felt the cold grip of fear. His heart raced and thumped in his chest. There was a hollow feeling in his stomach. He told himself he would not move from this spot until he had counted to ten, and then decided a brave man would wait until sixty.

He knew the men would see and take heart from the fact he stood exposed on the hilltop. He noted that the machine gun had quit firing, perhaps from a stoppage. In thinking about the machine gun he lost count, and made himself start over again.

"Sir." It was the young boy he had spoken with. He was pointing to the left, downhill. Padget looked in that direction and saw the cavalry starting their charge up the left flank. He looked toward the flood plain over the advancing line of infantry.

THERE AIN'T NO MONEY IN IT

The guns were silent.

"Calixto! Get ready."

"Fire!" Padget yelled. He aimed at the officer on the gray horse holding the front sight on the middle of his chest and began to squeeze the trigger. Before he could fire the officer dropped his sword and fell forward over the front shoulder of his mount. The horse wheeled and ran across the infantry line knocking down two men in its effort.

Padget shifted his sights to the first soldier that he could see and pulled the trigger. The man stumbled, took another step and crumpled to the ground. He heard the concentrated firing from his men and the center of the infantry line wavered, then closed up and continued up hill. They were less than one hundred yards away.

"Fire!" Calixto yelled at the riflemen.

The rebels, knowing that survival depended on stopping the attack, fired round after round into the fast advancing rank. Padget was amazed at how much punishment the federale skirmish line could endure. Three of his riflemen on the north flank were pouring fire obliquely into the enemy.

In the front rank of the skirmish line, which was two deep, the officer would have put the raw recruits, boys conscripted from Ojinaga a few days ago and whose deaths would not damage the military. Behind them were the veterans, fifty or more seasoned troops who were shielded from the decimating fire of the riflemen on the hilltop and who would make the final assault on the rebel position. Now pushed by officers and sergeants, the survivors spread along the flank of the hill.

"Fire!" Padget reloaded his rifle and wasted a round into a man already falling.

"Fire!" A score of bullets tore into the advancing line, one spun a federale infantryman clear around, but the rest seemed to be soaked up by the surging, straining mass of men trying to reach the top. One man fell and was kicked aside by the man behind him. The air hissed and snapped with bullets. The recruits, who had not seen a rifle ten days ago, fired high over the heads of the defenders. One rebel rifleman, hit in the shoulder, went down, but continued firing from the ground.

"We've got them beat," Ochoa shouted. "Now kill the sons of bitches." Working the bolt of his Krag without taking the rifle down from his shoulder he poured five rounds into the now faltering ranks.

"Fire!" Padget yelled. Calixto had run out of ammunition and pulled his revolver and fired it at an officer who was trying to rally his men.

"Fire!" Bullets from the rifles of the defending force at point blank range poured downhill into the enemy.

Men's faces were black with powder and dirt. Their hands bled where they had reloaded, using stripper clips and working the bolts of their Mausers. Their teeth showed white in their powder marked faces as they opened their mouths to yell.

The federales inched back; wavered. The bullets cracked into them, smacking into flesh and still the bullets came.

"Fire!" yelled Padget and the federale line broke and ran. Chaos was rampant in the enemy ranks, the sergeants could not hold the conscripts and the retreat turned into a rout.

The cavalry pulled up short at the sight of the retreating infantry, wheeled and rode back down the hill leaving the infantry to their fate.

An infantry sergeant grabbed one retreating soldier and tore the rifle from his grasp. He turned and aimed uphill.

Padget threw up his rifle and centered his front sight on the center of the sergeant's chest, saw the flame of the muzzle blast and felt the slam of the bullet in his stomach. He tried to stay on his feet, but dropped his rifle clattering to the rock covered ground. The world was filling with pain. He heard a groan of pain and did not know it was his own. He was still trying to stay on his feet when his knees hit the gravel in front of him and his hands clutched at the warm fresh blood, bright red, and he was calling out and fell face forward on the hilltop. He curled up against the pain and the blood welled between his fingers. Then, the world went black, the pain stopped and he was still.

It was three o'clock in the afternoon, December 21, 1910.

Chapter Sixty-seven

The priest, spattered with blood, split the shirt across Padget's chest and saw the wound in his lower left abdomen. He shook his head and uttered a prayer. The blood welled up in the bullet hole and spilled down Padget's side onto the table. The priest leaned close to the muscled chest and noted that the breathing was shallow, almost inaudible, and then he picked up the wrist and felt for a pulse. For a moment he could not find it, and was about to give up, and then felt it. He shook his head, rolled the man on his side and saw there was no exit hole. He eased him down. There was not much he could do except stop the man from bleeding. He folded a rag and pushed it against the wound and directed the nun to bind it tight with strips torn from a blanket.

Ochoa looked at the priest. "What can I do?"

"There isn't much anyone can do for him. It is in God's hands."

"No! Calixto help me. I need a wagon and a team."

Calixto looked a question at Ochoa.

"I'm going to take him to Ruidosa. There's a doctor and a field hospital there."

"That's sixty miles," Calixto said.

"Sixty or six hundred; it doesn't matter, he needs help bad," Ochoa replied.

A wagon, hitched to a pair of tall bays was pulled to the church entrance. "Here, give me a hand," Ochoa said. They picked Padget up and placed him in the wagon and put blankets over him. Ochoa laid Wes' Winchester alongside him. "He'll need this for elk hunting," he said.

The pain was an unquenchable fire in Padget and sometimes he floated up through levels of pain and cried out. At other times he was deep in its searing grasp and his dreams spun and twisted inside him. The pain enveloped his entire existence and yet somehow seemed separate from him.

"Whoa! Hold on Pard we're nearly there. Just hang on." Ochoa whipped the horses into a faster pace and the wagon bumped over the trail bringing a moan from Padget's lips.

THERE AIN'T NO MONEY IN IT

Padget slept. He dreamed of his mother the day she died. She looked so frail under the coverlet. Coming out of the dream and into the pain, he remembered that she had been dead for years. He coughed and spat weakly, and the pain made him curl into a ball. He cried out again.

"Pardner. Please. Just for a little while. Hold on." Tears were streaming down Ochoa's face as he passed Las Viboras. "We've only got to go about ten miles."

He pulled the wagon into the ranch yard long after midnight, pushed the brake and wrapped the reins around it. He yelled, "Doc! Doc! Wake up!"

The sound of Ochoa's yelling broke through the fog and Padget tried to raise his head. "Where am I?" his voice a barely audible croak.

"We're here, Pard. Hang on just a little longer," Ochoa said, "Doc! Wake up."

A lantern was lit in the living room and the front door opened and Pilar stood holding the lantern over her head and peered out at them.

"Who's there? Dave, what are you doing here?" She asked.

"It's Wes, Pilar, and wounded bad. Where's the doc? Here, help me get him into the house."

"Wes, Oh, my God, Wes."

She ran down the steps to the wagon.

"Pilar, where is the doc?" Ochoa asked again.

"Doc is in town and won't be back until tomorrow," she said. "He had to go into Presidio." She held the lantern over Padget and the face she saw was pale and drawn. She moved the lantern down over his chest.

Padget sobbed in his pain and swore to himself he wouldn't die. He moved his hand down to shield the bandage. Pilar caught up his hand and pulled it to her face. She rolled the blood stained hand over and pressed her lips to his palm. "Oh, Wes. Oh, Wes." He tried to squeeze her hand, but didn't have the strength. Still holding his hand she shouted, "Pepe! Ramon! Bring a stretcher! Quickly!" She felt the bandage and the touch caused blood to well up through the soaked cloth.

The four of them got him out of the wagon and into the house and lay him on a table. Padget breathed in short, shallow gasps, and he swore again he would not give in to death. The pain covered his entire body and he tried to pull his legs up to his chest. Pilar held his legs down. "Get these clothes off him. Pepe saddle a horse and go to Presidio after Doc. Tell him he has to come now."

Ochoa said, "I'll go."

"No! You don't know where to find him. Pepe! Move!" The tears were rolling down her cheeks and she wiped them back with the back of her hand. "Ramon, bring the alcohol."

Blushing as they stripped Padget, Pilar swabbed the blood off his body with rubbing alcohol then covered him with a sheet and two blankets. She put a third blanket under him. "Ramon, start a fire." She looked at his face again. The eyes were red, the cheeks shrunken with an ashy pallor and his hair was soaked with sweat. She could not observe any breath, yet his fingers had not turned cold. She rubbed his forehead with a damp cloth. The eyes did not move. They stared blankly into space. "Wes, I love you. Don't leave me."

Padget's eyes moved, slowly, up to the face that peered down at him. "Pilar?" There was no strength in his voice.

The sun was just rising when Doctor Bush pushed open the door. "Is he alive?"

"Yes," she whispered. "But only barely. Hanging on by a thread, but alive."

Doc examined him and shook his head.

"Will he live?" Ochoa asked.

"No. The bullet is inside his abdomen. I can probe for a bullet in a man's chest if it hasn't collapsed a lung. I can set a broken arm or leg and suture open wounds, but a bullet lodged in the belly, I don't know of any doctor who could remove it. The pain will increase and the wound will abscess into blood and pus. And he will die," Bush said.

Pilar shook her head. "No! Doc he can't die. Please."

"There isn't anything I can do, Pilar. I know it's difficult to accept, but he isn't going to make it."

Padget was moved into Pilar's bedroom. She curtained off half of the room and lived with him. She was with him constantly, but the pain he endured was almost too much for her. She washed Padget and cleaned away the pus, re-dressed the wound each day and listened to the rumors that came back them from Mexico. Rumors that Orozco and Villa had been annihilated at Cerro Prieto; that the rebels had abandoned El Mulato; that the insurrection was finished.

A letter came from El Mulato, written by the priest there and dictated by Toribio Ortega and graced by the crosses and signatures of the twenty one survivors from the hill. The letter wished Padget to get better soon and said to come back to fight with them and that Señor Gonzalez had gone back to El Paso to provide more arms and ammunition. That Calixto said he was the bravest of all men and that the men who had been with him in the retreat from Venegas Rancho and on the hill, now called him Señor Gringo. Pilar read the letter to him over and over again, and sometimes when he was conscious he seemed very pleased.

Somehow he managed to hang on. Each morning Pilar expected to find him cold and stiff. She traveled to the little chapel at Ruidosa every day and prayed for his recovery. She made promises to God that if only he would spare her lover she would light a candle to Him everyday. Then she promised she would give up smoking and she did.

Doctor Bush shook his head and said that sometimes, with God's help, very rarely, a man would recover from such a wound. And indeed Padget seemed better. Then without warning he took a turn for the worse and caught a raging fever. The wound was still abscessed and the bandage changed twice every day. Pilar had to wipe the sweat from his forehead and listen to his ravings throughout the day and night. Doctor Bush had again given up hope and said the fever would kill him. He gave him a mixture of powdered quinine and black pepper, but the fever continued. Pilar was a wreck from worry and dread. Hope faded and it indeed seemed he would die.

There was an old Army remedy to bring down a fever Ochoa of and decided to use it. When Pilar was out he carried Padget outside, chipped the ice from the water trough and dropped him in. Padget yelled and jerked his legs to his chest and slid under, choking in the cold. Ochoa ran to him and wrapped him in a blanket and carried the wasted body back to his bed. Pilar returned and screamed that Ochoa had surely killed Padget, and Bush agreed with her that the treatment would be the end, but that night the fever went down. Pilar came back from the chapel and found him awake.

"Oh, Wes, Wes," she said, and took his hand in hers. "How are you feeling?"

"Awful." He looked it. His eyes were sunk in his skull and his face was almost gray, but he smiled weakly up at her.

Ochoa, now back in Pilar's good graces, took turns caring for him. They also took turns visiting the chapel twice a day to pray and light candles. Ochoa lit candles to Saint Michael, patron saint of warriors and prayed to him for Padget's recovery. Doctor Bush again, though cautious, said there was a slight chance of him recovering from the wound. Pilar and Ochoa prayed on.

Ochoa took Padget's rifle and revolver and cleaned them with a passion. He removed the cartridges from the cylinder and carefully wiped each one with an oily rag and replaced them. He swabbed out the barrel until it shone brightly when he held it up to the sun. He took the Winchester and sanded out the scratches and dents in the stock with a piece of sandstone then rubbed the wood with beeswax until it gleamed. He saddle soaped the holster and wiped it clean. Then he took them into the house. He pushed the door open and found Padget sitting up. There was a look of wonder on his face. He looked at Ochoa and smiled. "I'm better. I don't know how."

"Doctor Bush said it might happen."

"Bush said I would die." He saw the weapons in Ochoa's hands and asked, "What's that you have?"

"Just your Winchester and Colt; I figured you would be needing them pretty soon, if we're going elk hunting."

Padget felt a tear roll down his cheek and

brushed it away. "Thanks, Mano."

Pilar came into the room and flew across the floor and shamelessly kissed him full on the mouth. "Oh, Wes. Oh thank God. Oh...." she couldn't go on and started to cry.

She let him sit up in a chair the following week.

Chapter Sixty-eight

The week after he got out of bed he began exercising. He worked for hours in the courtyard strengthening his arms, and each day he walked further than the day before.

The sixth day he was able to walk all the way into Ruidosa and back and the only pain was a dull catching ache. He began to eat far beyond his normal intake, to regain his strength. He put on weight and on the twelfth day fired his Winchester, letting the sharp recoil thump into his shoulder. He forced his arms to hold the rifle steady and on his seventh shot hit the gourd that Ochoa had placed out one hundred yards from the house.

On the tenth day a group of riders showed up at the ranch, Texas Rangers patrolling the border to stop the smuggling of arms to the rebels. They watered their horses and continued westward. On the twelfth day Toribio, Calixto and three veterans of the El Mulato battle rode into the courtyard leading a tall dun.

They said they were still holding El Mulato and expected the federales to attack them again. They said there now were over seven hundred insurrectos, all armed with the new Mausers and when would Padget and Ochoa come join them again.

Toribio said forgive him that he forgot, Padget was not involved in the revolution. He laughed and said that he had to be on his way, maybe to find some other tejanos who, like Padget, also not involved in the revolution.

Padget shook hands with Toribio and said, "Some things have a way of changing, my friend."

As they rode out Pilar came to stand beside Padget. She put her arm around his waist. When she leaned against him he laid his arm across her shoulder and could feel the warmth of her body flowing through him as he pulled her close.

He turned in her embrace and kissed her upturned face. "It's everyone's fight."

"Tu eres mi Corazon," she said.

Addendum

TIME LINE FOR WES AND OCHOA

1909

October

2 - Wes Padget leaves Arizona for Texas

5 - Meets David Ochoa, an old friend on the trail

8 - Sell horses to Remount officer at Fort Bliss

11 - At the Rafter J – Meet Ira Bush and Harvey Phillips

12 - Inspect kill site, determine there are two jaguars

13 - Wes and Ochoa move to the Maccadoo Place

14 - Set out after stock killing jaguars

- 16 - Find cowboy killed by jaguars, storm wipes out tracks
- 17 - Wes and Dave split to cut for sign
- 20 - Shootout at Ojos Calientes
- 23 - 24th Preparation for hunting lions
- 27 - At Ojos Calientes the second time
- 28 - Visit Sherman ranch where jaguars killed a horse

November

- 1 - Walt attends stockman's meeting
- 25 - Thanks giving
- 26 - Posse to Mexico after rustlers
- 27 - Arrive in Talón
- 28 - Juana's 14th birthday rurales in Talón rape/ massacre
- 29 - Posse quits trail and starts back/rurales leave Talón
- 30 - Posse arrives Talón, Juana barely alive

December

- 1 - Wes arrive in Ojos just after midnight with Juana
- 9 - Wes finds turkey tracks in Wild Horse Canyon.
- 10 - Leave for hunt/ snow storm
- 13 - Wes and Dave leave for El Paso with horses

15 - Meet Army patrol
17 - Wes and Dave in El Paso
18 - Witness execution in Juarez/ Dinner with Bush
19 - Breakfast and proposition
20 - Wes and Pilar take a stroll after dinner
31 - Load riles and ammunition into wagons

1910

January
1 - Load guns at Alamore siding into wagons/ travel to Ojos
2 - Arrive Ojos Calientes with rifles, put guns in barn.
3 - Run guns to Villa's Camp/ Meet Frank McComb/
4 - Pilar packs up her stuff and goes to El Paso
5 - Pilar meets with Bush about a job.

April
Madero nominated President by the Anti-Reelectionist Party

May
8 - Pancho Villa kills the owner and son and loots ranch.
19 - Halley's Comet appears

June
Madero arrested in Monterrey for inciting rebellion.

July
12 - Wes and Ochoa sell Mexican horses to Army.

August
Madero petitions the Congressional Elections Committee to overturn the election. He continues to live in San Luis Potosi, under police watch.

September
Mexico appears prosperous, the budget is balanced, the currency is solidly on the gold standard, and the Treasury has a 62 million peso surplus in gold.

October
Congressional Elections Committee rules against Madero. He jumps bail, and flees to San Antonio Texas

November
28 - Juana's Birthday Party at Rafter J
29 - McComb Arrives at Rafter J/Madero crosses into Mexico

December

3 - Padget and Ochoa transport arms to Mexico.

15 - Skirmish at Venegas Rancho

21 - Battle of El Mulato